CW00864348

IMPOSTER

RAY FLOYD

This book is dedicated to the memory of my brother Mark

PROLOGUE

Bubba Franklin was dog-tired as he neared the end of his epic journey. He'd left Seattle four days earlier and was less than an hour from his final destination in Richmond, Virginia. The semitrailer behind his rig was packed with computer hardware and software destined for a newly built government office complex.

The head dispatcher at the computer company had promised him a fifteen percent bonus if he could deliver the goods within ninety-six hours, and he fully intended to collect. Bubba was grossly overweight, and the cabin of his Peterbilt reeked of smoke and stale sweat. As many long-haul truck drivers did, Bubba used cocaine to keep himself alert whenever he felt fatigue setting in.

He was presently on a two-lane surface road in a rural area of Virginia, and he checked that there was no slow-moving traffic ahead of him before bending his head down to snort some white powder. He flung his head back as he felt the sharp burn of the cocaine in his nose and the jolt as it hit his brain.

It was only then that he noticed the stop sign on the side of the road that was partially obscured by an overhanging tree branch. He cursed loudly as he blew through the intersection at roughly fifty miles an hour.

———

Dillon Hunt, aka Michael Harper, was in high spirits. He was speeding northwards on route sixty to his home in Fredericksburg, Virginia, where his charming and very pregnant wife Vanessa waited patiently for him.

He hadn't seen her for over three months, but such was the burden to be shouldered in his line of work. Michael Harper was a field agent with the FBI and was currently working undercover on an assignment in South Carolina.

He had taken on the persona of Dillon Hunt in order to infiltrate a paramilitary militia group whose extremist views had them hell-bent on ridding the United States of every Muslim.

Upon accepting the mission he'd had but one condition; he wanted to be present for the birth of their first child. His handler for the operation, Diedra Wolfe, had promised him that it wouldn't be a problem.

With Vanessa's due date fast approaching, Diedra had made good on her promise. Dillon Hunt had recently received permission from the militia leadership to leave the compound to be with his deathly ill mother in her last days.

Diedra had promptly made arrangements for an older, female FBI agent to impersonate Dillon's 'dying mother' at Mercy Hospital in Fredericksburg, should the militia group feel the need to verify his story. It was the same hospital where Vanessa was scheduled to give birth to their baby boy.

He was singing stridently along to 'Radar Love' on the radio when he abruptly discerned the sign of approaching danger in his peripheral vision. The colossal tractor-trailer was upon him so rapidly he didn't even have time to react.

CHAPTER ONE

Daniel Harper stared incredulously at the judge as he read out the sentence; fifteen years. For what? For scamming a few horny men out of a trifling amount of money.

He opened his mouth to protest, but the judge pre-empted him by banging his gavel and staring gravely at him. "Only thirty years old and already your third fraud conviction, Mister Harper. It's obvious that there is little chance of you being rehabilitated, so I've decided to give you the maximum penalty under law. Perhaps a lengthy stay in prison will get you back on the straight and narrow."

Daniel hung his head in disbelief as the stern judge continued, "As for your co-accused, Miss Cox, I sentence you to three years in the state penitentiary." Lisa Cox was standing next to Daniel and flashed the judge a grateful smile. She was wearing a snug-fitting black dress that showed all her curves as well as ample cleavage. "It is obvious that Mister Harper was the mastermind behind this little scam and took advantage of Miss Cox's affections for him," the judge concluded.

Daniel smiled inwardly; *if only you knew the truth, you lecherous old bastard*. Lisa was a master manipulator who used her considerable beauty and charm on just about every man she met.

She would target lonely-looking married men attending conventions in Las Vegas, telling them that her husband would only be arriving the following day and that she was quite drunk and feeling very horny. Once she had the man naked in her hotel room, Daniel, 'the husband,' would charge through the door and demand to know what was going on.

She would feign horror at his unexpected arrival and say that the man had made her drunk and was taking advantage of her. Daniel would riffle through the man's pockets and remove his cell phone. "I think that your wife deserves to know about the scumbag she married."

As the victim begged and pleaded, Daniel would finally agree not to make the call, but only if he was paid the sum of five thousand dollars in compensation for his pain and suffering. The plan had worked perfectly until Lisa targeted the wrong man. He was only wearing his wedding ring in memory of his long-dead wife and had reported the scam to the Las Vegas police. They had set up a sting operation that resulted in the open-and-shut case that had recently concluded.

———

"What do you mean he's dead?" Diedra demanded. "I spoke to him just a couple of hours ago. What the hell happened?"

"Just an unfortunate traffic accident from the looks of things," the voice on the other end of the line said. "Doesn't appear as if AAM had anything to do with it." AAM was the acronym for Americans Against Muslims, the militia group that FBI agent Michael Harper had infiltrated.

"Dammit, I'm really going to miss Mike, he was one of our best," Diedra said sadly. "Needless to say, I also get to tell his pregnant wife that he'll never be coming home."

"Don't worry about that, I'll do it."

"No, I was his immediate superior," Diedra countered. "It's my responsibility."

"Actually, I need you on the next plane to Las Vegas."

"Vegas! What the hell's in Vegas?" Diedra asked.

"Not what, but who. Believe it or not, we've managed to track down Michael's identical twin, Daniel. He's just received a lengthy prison sentence, thanks to my intervention. I'm sure that he'll be more than willing to do anything to get out of it."

CHAPTER TWO

D iedra stared down at the twinkling lights of Las Vegas as the
FBI Learjet came in to land at McCarran Airport. She was
feeling equal amounts of sadness at the sudden loss of her colleague
and disbelief at her boss's outrageous plan.

FBI Deputy Director Walter Shaw was the man who'd sent her
on what she considered a fool's errand. The audacious plan that
he'd concocted called on Michael Harper's twin brother to replace
him as Dillon Hunt and continue the infiltration of AAM.

There were several reasons why she thought that the idea was
insane, the main one being that Mike had been a highly trained FBI
undercover operative, while Daniel was nothing more than a
habitual criminal. Also, what were the chances that a cowardly jailbird would risk his life in exchange for a reduced sentence? *Just about
zero*, she mused.

On the positive side, Mike had infiltrated the AAM only six
weeks ago and no one there knew him really well yet. The main
reason that Director Shaw was unwilling to give up on the operation
was the alarming intel that Mike had managed to gather before his
untimely demise. Apparently the militia group were planning
several deadly terror attacks against Muslims living in America.

From the information that they'd received, the attacks would be well planned and would take place sometime within the next couple of months.

That didn't give the FBI enough time to insert a new operative to stop the attacks. The new president had been very alarmed when briefed on the situation by the FBI director. His anti-Muslim stance was well known and he feared that his opponents and detractors would use the attacks to condemn his policies.

Diedra sighed and concluded that that was the only reason for what amounted to a hail Mary pass. Her bosses didn't want to be the ones to tell the ill-tempered president that they had failed in their mission.

After the sleek jet landed she was met by the Special-Agent-in-Charge, or SAC, of the Las Vegas field office. Eddy Lane was a lanky, jovial man whom she'd met previously. "What brings you to my neck of the desert?" he asked with a grin.

"Afraid that it's need-to-know, Eddy," she replied. "What have you been told so far?"

"Walter Shaw called and told me to arrange an interview for you with a prisoner by the name of Daniel Harper, that's about it. I was ordered to meet your plane and escort you to the jail, ensuring nothing stood in your way."

Diedra glanced at her watch and noted that it was just after nine in the evening, local time. "You mean that I'll get to see him straight away?"

"You bet," he replied. "This comes all the way from the very top."

CHAPTER THREE

Daniel Harper looked up in dismay as the attractive woman wearing a severe skirt-suit entered the interrogation room. He'd been around the block a few times and knew a federal agent when he saw one. Not to mention that he'd also been unceremoniously bundled from his cell at this time of night. He'd already been waiting for almost an hour in the stark, windowless room and none of the guards had answered his many questions as they'd hand-cuffed his hands to the metal bar set into the table in front of him.

For her part Diedra tried her utmost to contain her astonishment as she took in the features of the man seated before her. He was indeed an exact replica of her recently deceased friend and colleague. Sure, his hair was longer and he wasn't quite as buff as Mike had been, but otherwise he was the spitting image.

Quickly recovering her composure, she took a seat opposite the man and introduced herself, "I'm Supervisory Special Agent Diedra Wolf with the FBI, and you are?"

The man smiled. "As I'm sure you're well aware, I'm the esteemed Daniel Harper, jailbird extraordinaire."

Diedra was somewhat taken aback by the man's ability to make light of the situation, considering he'd just received a lengthy jail sentence. The dimples that appeared when he smiled reminded her so much of Mike, she felt a tightness in her chest. She motioned for her escort to leave, removed a folder from her briefcase and placed it on the table.

Daniel glanced at it with interest. "What could the feds possibility want with me? As far as I know I haven't broken any federal laws."

Diedra's voice cracked a little. "I'm here about your brother, Michael Harper."

Daniel's eyes narrowed. "What about Mikey, is he okay?"

As far as Diedra could remember, Mike had only mentioned to her once that he had a twin brother and clearly didn't want to talk any further about it. Whatever had transpired between them had obviously hurt him deeply, so she hadn't pressed the issue. Now she took a deep breath. "I'm sorry to tell you that your brother Michael is dead."

Diedra noticed him flinch, but otherwise he showed no visible reaction. He sat there stone-faced for a moment before asking in an even tone, "How did it happen?"

Diedra answered quickly, "Car accident, he didn't suffer at all."

Daniel just nodded. "I haven't seen or heard from Mikey in four years, since he finished law school. Last I heard he'd joined the FBI."

Diedra confirmed this. "He and I worked together and were also close friends. I share your pain at his loss."

"Is, I mean was, he married?" Daniel asked. "I remember he was dating this girl in college. I think her name was Vanessa or something."

"Yes, they were married a few years back. Mike was on his way home to witness the birth of his first child when it happened. Sadly, his wife was so broken by the news that she immediately went into labor. She's currently in hospital in Virginia, where she just gave birth to their child."

Daniel whispered something that she didn't grasp. She leaned in close and asked him to repeat what he'd said. "Boy or girl?" he asked.

"It's a boy."

Diedra was totally unprepared for what happened next. The tough man began quivering as tears poured down his cheeks.

CHAPTER FOUR

I t took Diedra forever to calm down the distressed prisoner. She had the guard come in and remove Daniel's handcuffs while ordering him to bring two cups of coffee. After he'd sipped half his coffee he finally looked ready to continue. Looking somewhat embarrassed he eventually said, "Sorry about that."

"I understand, losing a loved one is never easy."

"It's not just that; knowing that I also have a nephew who I'll never see suddenly overwhelmed me. I was a major disappointment to Mikey, and I thought I'd come to terms with that." He gave a weak smile. "I guess I was mistaken."

"I don't understand, how do twin brothers end up as polar opposites, one an FBI agent and the other a career criminal?"

Daniel looked her in the eyes. "It's a long story, how much time do you have?"

Diedra glanced at her watch. "Actually, I've got all night. Why don't you go ahead and tell me your story, after which I'll let you know the real reason I'm here."

Daniel took a deep breath. "I guess it all started when we were both six years old. Up to that point we were so identical in every way that even our mom and dad had trouble telling us apart. Our mother had taken us to a local park where we were playing on the swings. Mikey was two swings over from me when he fell off and started crying. I immediately jumped off my swing and went to help him. Unfortunately the kid next to me connected his swing with my head, one of those heavy, old-fashioned wooden ones." Daniel paused a second before continuing. "Apparently I was knocked unconscious and was blue in the face, as I'd stopped breathing. Luckily for me, one of the women at the park was a nurse who performed CPR to bring me back. I ended up in hospital for several days with a severe concussion and persistent headaches. The doctors ultimately assured my parents that there was no permanent damage and sent me home. It was only a few weeks later that my parents began to notice my unusual behavior."

Daniel paused to take a sip of coffee, and Diedra couldn't help asking, "What was it?"

"Mikey and I had always been smart kids, but suddenly I was able to recall recent events with absolute precision, including dates and times. I was also able to recite things I'd read or shows I'd watched word for word. My parents had me tested by a prominent neurosurgeon who came to the startling conclusion that the knock to my head had resulted in an eidetic memory."

"I've heard of that," Diedra interrupted, "that's like a photo-graphic memory, right?"

"It's sometimes called that, yes," Daniel replied. "However, photographic memory refers only to visual stimuli, such as reading a book and remembering its exact contents afterwards. Eidetic memory refers to exact recall across all five senses. It usually only occurs in young children, but specialists have determined that the blow to my head made it a permanent feature of my brain."

"So you've still got it? That must be amazing."

Daniel shook his head sadly. "A blessing and a curse."

"How so?"

"Be patient, I'm getting to that part. At first it was awesome. I cruised through school and the first two years of college with almost perfect scores. Mikey also did very well, but he had to study hard to keep up with me." Daniel gave cynical laugh. "If I'd been in his shoes I probably would have been jealous, but he was always the first to congratulate me on my successes. Our father was a senior vice-president with a large marketing firm in San Francisco and both Mikey and I attended nearby Stanford University. Both of us received football scholarships, so attending an expensive Ivy League school wasn't a problem."

"I know that Mike studied law; what did you study?" Diedra asked.

"I was studying for an MBA, really easy for a person with a perfect memory. Just had to pay attention in class and I could visualize every lecture to the smallest detail. We were both great athletes; by our junior year I was the starting quarterback and Mikey was a wide receiver."

"Sounds like a fairy-tale upbringing, what the hell went wrong?"

"A weekend trip to our cabin in the mountains," Daniel replied. "Mom and Dad were in the front of the car, Mikey and I in the back. We came up behind one of those huge lumber trucks when my dad suddenly cursed and slammed on the brakes. A massive log had come loose and was bouncing towards our car. It smashed into the front of the roof of the car, killing both our parents instantly. The car flipped on its side and eventually skidded to a halt, my head a few inches from the asphalt."

Diedra's hand flew to her mouth. "My God, that's terrible," she said. "Were you and Mike badly injured?"

"Just a few cuts and bruises," he replied, "although Mikey's airbag didn't deploy and he was knocked unconscious."

"And you?"

"To this day I wish that I had been. I was trapped in the damn car for over an hour before being freed by rescue workers. I can still remember every little aspect of that hour of hell, the ticking sound coming from the hot engine, the smell of my parents' blood seeping from their crushed bodies. Now you know why I said having an eidetic memory is a curse."

"Let's take a break for a while and I'll get us some more coffee," Diedra said softly. "We can continue later."

CHAPTER FIVE

"Are you sure that you're okay to continue?" Diedra asked.

"I'll be fine," Daniel replied. "As I mentioned earlier, our family was well off, and both my mother and father had substantial life insurance policies as well as a policy that paid off the mortgages on both the cabin and house, which were both eventually sold. All the money was paid into a trust account, and Mikey and I have been receiving a five thousand dollar a month allowance from the trust. We were to receive equal shares of the capital in the trust on our thirty-first birthdays, which is September third this year."

"How much are we talking?" Diedra asked.

"One of Dad's accountant friends is the head trustee, and he made some solid investments. Last I heard it was a little over two and a half million dollars each."

"As Mike wasn't married when your parents died, I suppose you'll get it all now?"

Daniel slammed a hand on the table. "I don't want it all, I just want my brother back. Anyway, I'll make sure that Mikey's wife and kid get his half."

"That's very generous of you."

"The least that I can do. Besides, I'm facing fifteen years in prison, so it won't really help me much."

"We'll discuss that later," Diedra said cryptically. "Did you both return to college after the accident?"

"Yes, we rented a two-bedroom apartment close to the university and tried to continue with our courses. Mikey threw himself full tilt into his studies and achieved amazing results. I think it was in memory of our deceased parents."

"And you?"

"Exactly the opposite. I kept experiencing with amazing clarity that hour I was trapped in the wrecked car. I thought that I was losing my mind."

"Did you ever tell your brother or see a shrink, or something?"

Daniel laughed harshly. "There was no need as I discovered the perfect solution to the problem."

"And that was?"

"Booze, drugs and loose women. It didn't take long for me to be kicked off the football team and a full expulsion from the university followed soon after."

"What did Mike have to say about that?"

"Oh, he tried to help, but I was angry and just pushed him away. You see, he never knew that I'd remained conscious after the crash. I pretended that like him I had no memory of the accident whatsoever."

"Why would you do that?"

"To protect him, of course. If neither one of us remembered anything, then there was nothing to talk about."

"Makes sense, I guess. What happened next?"

"One day Mikey and I had a huge argument. I moved out of the condo and into a small studio in a bad part of 'Frisco."

"Why? With five thousand dollars a month you could have afforded something much nicer."

"Needed the money for the booze and drugs, which were much easier to acquire in my seedy neighborhood. Ultimately my habit got so bad that I needed more money. I started ripping off depart-ment stores and eventually got caught. Mikey came to my rescue and hired a fancy attorney to defend me. I ended up doing only three months in prison."

"You don't look like an addict now," Diedra observed. "Did that set you straight?"

"Not exactly." Daniel laughed. "My cell mate in prison was in awe of my total recall. He said that I was a fool and that with my memory I should have gone to Vegas and made a fortune counting cards."

"Let me guess, as soon as you got out you came to Vegas?"

"You bet your sweet ass I did. It was so damn easy, and within a month or so I was flush with cash, over five hundred thousand easily."

"Back to the drugs then?"

"Oh no, blackjack was my new drug of choice. Besides, you need a clear head to count cards, so I didn't even drink anymore."

"So what went wrong?"

"I knew that card-counting wasn't illegal per se but was frowned upon by the casinos and could get you blacklisted. I spread out my gambling amongst the larger casinos and never visited the same casino twice in one week. I didn't realize that Vegas was such a small, close-knit community with strong mob ties even to this day."

As a federal agent, Diedra felt the need to intervene. "That's just a rumor, it hasn't really been proven."

"Oh, believe me, it's true. I've got the scars to prove it."

"They beat you up?"

"That's an understatement; they almost killed me. One night, three hoods were waiting for me outside my apartment. They hustled me inside and demanded to know where I kept my ill-gotten gains. Being stubborn, I only disclosed the truth after a thorough beating. Once they had the money they beat me some more and left me bleeding on the kitchen floor."

"That's terrible."

"It definitely wasn't pleasant, but at least I got to meet Lisa."

"Who's Lisa?"

"She was my neighbor, and currently my girlfriend and co-accused. Once the gangsters left she came to my aid and took me to hospital, probably saved my life."

"Tell me more about her."

Daniel looked at his empty cup. "How about another coffee before I continue?"

Diedra rose. "You've got it. I could use one too."

CHAPTER SIX

After a short break Daniel continued his story. "As I mentioned earlier, Lisa was staying in the apartment next to mine the night I was badly beaten. She heard the commotion and waited until the men had left before peeking through the half-open front door. She saw me lying on the floor and came to check if I was still alive."

"Why didn't she call the police when she heard what was happening?" Diedra asked.

"Lisa didn't have the greatest relationship with the local cops to put it mildly," Daniel replied. "I'll never forget that first image of her; she was cleaning my bloody face with a wet cloth when I opened my eyes. My first thought was that I'd died and that she was an angel sent to deliver me to heaven. Her beauty took my breath away, not to mention her stunningly perfect body."

Diedra shook her head in disbelief. "You noticed her body even though you were half dead."

"She was wearing nothing but a flimsy negligée thing," Daniel said in his defense. "Besides, I'm a guy. As long as we still have a pulse we're going to check out a really hot chick."

"Men," Diedra said with wide eyes.

"That's us in a nutshell." He laughed. "I promptly realized that she wasn't an angel 'cause I was in so much pain. Besides, I didn't really think that heaven would be my final destination at that stage of my life."

"So she took you to hospital. What happened after that?"

"She came to visit every day until I was released about ten days later. She drove me home and helped me straighten up my apartment. I asked if I could take her out to dinner as a thank you and she just laughed at the idea. My face was still swollen and my two black eyes had taken on a yellowish tinge."

"Not your ideal first date."

"Exactly. Anyway I also had no money as they'd even taken the cash from my wallet, and the next payment from the trust wasn't due for a couple of weeks. Instead she invited me over to her place for dinner, which consisted of pizza and plenty of beer. We both had way too much to drink and ended up in the sack."

Diedra just rolled her eyes. "What a surprise."

"Actually, it was one of the greatest experiences of my life. It wasn't just sex; for the first time in my life I actually made love to a woman. She was so tender and not just because of my injuries. I was vulnerable because of the mixture of pain meds and alcohol, so we both shared our stories of how we'd ended up in Vegas. She cried when I told her about the accident and its effect on me."

"I'm sorry, I didn't mean to make light of it. So what was Lisa's story?"

Daniel stared pointedly at the recorder on the table. "This has to be strictly off the record."

Diedra reached over and turned off the device. "Okay, go ahead."

"Unfortunately, it's a tale as old as time. Both her parents died when she was only four years old, and she ended up in the foster care system. She was a wild child and too difficult to handle for the first few families. By the age of thirteen she'd calmed down a bit and ended up with yet another foster family. At first everything was great, she started paying attention in school and her grades rapidly improved. Then, shortly after her fifteenth birthday, she began to blossom into the beautiful, curvaceous woman she is today."

"Let me guess," Diedra interrupted. "Foster dad thought he had all rights to her body."

"At first, yes. Then he decided he could make some money on the side by selling her wares to all his buddies. Foster-daddy warned her about telling anyone about their extra-curricular activities. No one would believe her and she'd just end up back at the orphanage."

"The son-of-a-bitch!" Diedra said angrily.

"Indeed," Daniel nodded, "however he finally got what he deserved. After about a year of the abuse, Lisa finally had enough. Foster-daddy crept into her room one night and ordered her to kneel in front of him. She meekly complied, but instead of receiving the pleasure he expected, she produced a razor-sharp carving knife and sliced off his dick."

"Way to go." Diedra almost clapped her hands in delight before regaining her composure. "I mean, that's assault with a deadly weapon. Taking the law into your own hands is never a good idea," she said without conviction. "What happened to her foster dad?"

"She didn't stick around to find out. Believe it or not, the asshole had actually shared the proceeds from his buddies with her as if he were her pimp. She'd saved up all the money, plus as much as she could steal without getting caught. She had over a thousand dollars to her name and headed for the nearest bus station. She bought a ticket on the next bus out of town, which happened to be destined for Las Vegas."

"So she doesn't even know if the asshole survived?"

"Doesn't know, doesn't care," Daniel confirmed. "Now you know why I asked you to turn off the recorder. If you pursue this, I won't know what you're talking about."

"Don't worry, we've got much bigger fish to fry, but I'll get to that later. Please continue."

"Once here, she quickly learnt how to use her street smarts to separate horny men from their money. She started small, pickpocketing, etcetera, but soon graduated to full-on scams. Her favorite was to lure men to a busy motel. Once the man was naked, she ordered him to hand over his wallet, watch and all jewelry. She'd show them her underage ID and tell them she'd scream for help if they didn't comply. Most did, begging for her not to take their wedding rings."

"It's so sad that she ended up as a prostitute."

"Oh no, you misunderstand. She swore to me that she's never been paid for sex since she left her foster home."

"And you believe her?"

"I do! We became a fantastic team, coming up with elaborate scams. We're even renting a beautiful condo on the west side."

"So you really do care for her?"

"More than that, I totally love her. She's about the only person on this planet that I can relate to."

"Wow, I didn't realize that your relationship was so tight. I was given to believe that you were just a couple of opportunists."

"Well, now you know the whole story. Speaking of which, I think it's time you come clean about what you want from me."

CHAPTER SEVEN

Diedra leaned forward and asked, "How much do you know about your brother's FBI career?"

"Nothing at all. Mikey eventually got tired of bailing me out of trouble. It was shortly before he graduated, and we never spoke again."

"He was a brilliant and dedicated agent, top of his class at Quantico. He was promoted to senior field agent within four years of joining the FBI, the youngest to ever do so."

"As I mentioned earlier he was totally driven after the death of our parents, so I'm not really surprised."

"His specialty became undercover work. He helped take down a major drug-smuggling operation in Florida as well as an organized crime operation in Chicago. He was busy working his third under-cover op until his tragic accident."

"I'm very proud of his accomplishments, but I still don't see what this has to do with me?"

Leaning back, Diedra gave a wry smile. "We want you to take his place on this latest mission."

After almost falling off his chair in shock, Daniel finally managed to speak. "Have you lost your mind? I don't work for you guys, I'm a criminal not a fed."

"Mike was supposed to be visiting his sick mother. We can pretend that she died and he had to stay on for the funeral. That should buy us enough time to get you up to speed."

"Up to speed. Up to speed on what? Who was he investigating?"

"I'm not really supposed to disclose that information until you've agreed to cooperate, but I suppose I can bend the rules a little."

"How nice of you," Daniel spat sarcastically.

Diedra ignored him. "Mike had recently infiltrated a militia group in South Carolina that's opposed to Muslims living in the United States. He was roughly six weeks into the assignment."

"Let me guess, these are some really nasty characters with lots of guns and bombs and things. Why not just get another undercover agent to do the job?"

"Firstly yes, they are well armed, and most of the top leadership appear to be ex-military. Secondly, Mike just learned that the group was planning a large attack against the Muslim community in the near future. We simply don't have enough time to insert another agent in time to stop the attacks."

"Suppose I did happen to agree to your harebrained scheme, what's in it for me?"

"My boss has already spoken to the attorney general's office. In exchange for your cooperation, they have agreed to reduce your sentence from fifteen to five years. You could be out in three."

"Hang on a second!" Daniel shouted. "You guys are the reason I received such a lengthy sentence, am I right?"

Diedra simply shrugged without denying the accusation. "The FBI has a really close relationship with the Justice Department."

"Son-of-a bitch, you guys really are something."

"We do what we have to in order to defeat the bad guys. So, what's your answer?"

"My first instinct is to tell you to shove your deal where the sun don't shine. On the other hand, I certainly don't want to be stuck in jail for the next fifteen years."

"You could be out in ten with good behavior."

"Still way too long. I need a cigarette and a few minutes to think."

"Oh great, you're a smoker. You'll have to quit that habit."

"Whatever, please just get me a cigarette."

"You can't smoke in here. I'll get the guard to watch you outside."

"Just do it."

———

Diedra noted Daniel's inscrutable expression upon his return. "So, come to a decision yet?" she asked casually.

"I have indeed; don't think you're going to like it, though."

The FBI agent appeared crestfallen. "You won't do it?"

"Oh, I'll do it, however my conditions are not quite the same as yours."

Diedra perked up a little. "What do you want?"

"Complete absolution, my latest conviction goes away in its entirety."

"My bosses won't like that, but I'll give it a try."

"I'm not done yet. The same goes for Lisa, and we get released immediately. Also, both our past criminal records are wiped clean as well."

"Are you crazy? They'll never agree to that."

"Let's look at this rationally," Daniel said calmly. "You guys are expecting a criminal to take the place of a highly trained federal agent, putting his life in mortal danger. I really don't think that I'm the crazy one here."

"I suppose you're right. I'll give them a call, but I honestly don't think that they'll go for it."

"Like you said earlier, the FBI and Justice Department have a close relationship. If they want me bad enough, they'll make it happen."

CHAPTER EIGHT

After a short phone call Diedra returned to the interrogation room with mixed feelings. She was surprised at how quickly Director Shaw had agreed to Daniel's demands. Now she had the unenviable task of running a raw recruit in a highly sensitive and dangerous undercover operation. The director had also hinted that her entire career hung on a successful outcome to the op.

Daniel took one look at the agent's face and his own lit up. "They agreed, didn't they?"

"They did," she replied. "Though I wouldn't get too excited just yet. We have a lot to cover and very little time. One small mistake could mean the end."

"The end of the op or the end of me?"

"Both."

"That's just great, so what happens now?"

"You'll go back to your cell. The paperwork for both your releases should be completed by noon tomorrow. Once that happens you and I will fly to Virginia and I'll start briefing you on the AAM."

"What's an AAM?"

"Americans Against Muslims, the militia group you'll be infil-trating."

"Is that the best they could come up with? Not very creative, are they?"

"They may not be creative, but they are still a major threat to national security. Please don't underestimate them."

"I promise that I'll be a good boy and pay attention during my training, on one condition."

"What now?" Diedra asked in exasperation.

"I want to spend at least a couple of hours at our condo with Lisa. Let's face it, it may be the last time I get to see her."

"I suppose that's only fair. I'll give you exactly two hours together. You're allowed to tell her that you're helping out the FBI with a case, but no details. Agreed?"

"Agreed. See, you're not as tough as you make out to be."

"You ain't seen nothing yet. Wait until your training starts!"

CHAPTER NINE

Daniel flopped onto the ground and sucked in deep breaths. He'd just completed the obstacle course at the FBI's training facility in Quantico, Virginia.

Diedra stood above him, stopwatch in hand. "That was pitiful!" she barked. "I've seen old ladies do it faster."

"Give me a break." He gasped. "It's only my first time, next time will be much faster."

"It better be. Remember, Mike was in tip-top shape. You have to look exactly like him when you return to the compound. Speaking of which, you have an appointment right now to get your hair cut and your teeth whitened."

"I need a smoke."

"I told you, no smoking. Are you using the patches I gave you?"

"I am," he said, lifting his shirt to show her. He then pointed to a scar where a broken rib had pierced his skin. "What about my scars, how are we going to get rid of them?"

"Fortunately, no one at the compound ever saw Mike without his clothes on. All your scars and that stupid tattoo won't be noticeable unless you get naked."

"You never know," he grinned, "are there any women at this compound?"

"Actually there are quite a few. However, I thought that you were so in love with Lisa?"

"I am, but what if I need to use my considerable charms to elicit information from one of the hotties?"

Diedra smothered a smile. "Give me a break." She was actually quite impressed with Daniel so far. She'd given him volumes of information about the AAM on the flight from Vegas and was amazed that he seemed to remember every little detail. *This just might work,* she thought.

———

Later that afternoon Daniel entered a small briefing room to find Diedra and a nerdy-looking man poring over a file. He was just returning from his grooming session and Diedra nodded approvingly. "Much better. This is agent Milford Olson, he'll be going over all of Mike's debriefing transcripts with you."

"Hi, I'm Daniel Harper," he said pleasantly, sticking out his hand.

Agent Olson ignored the outstretched hand and snarled, "That's the sort of thing that's going to get you killed! You are no longer Daniel Harper; from here on out you will only answer to the name Dillon Hunt, got it?"

"Geez, sorry. Dillon Hunt, I like it."

"Please forgive Agent Olson, he and Mike were good friends and he doesn't really give this mission much chance of success." Diedra gave the geeky agent a sharp look.

"Well that just fills me with all sorts of confidence," Dillon Hunt said.

"I'll leave you two for now," Diedra said. "I'll see you later for basic firearms training."

"No rest for the weary," Dillon commented as she left.

"SSA Wolfe can be a real ballbuster at times," the diminutive agent said. "Just wait until she gets you on the mat for your unarmed combat training."

"Can't wait. Okay, what's first?"

"I need you to read and thoroughly memorize the following transcripts. They describe your brother's interaction and conversations with other members of the AAM. Here is a stack of photos as well. Where specific names are mentioned, I want you to find the corresponding photo and memorize the face as well."

Dillon looked at the large pile and grinned. "Sure, no problem."

"Yeah right," Agent Olson said skeptically. "I'll be working over there on that computer, call me if you have any questions."

Dillon studied the material for just over three hours before calling the agent over. "What's your question?" he asked.

"No question, I'm done."

"Like hell you are!" Olson said brusquely. "This is not a joke, now get back to it."

Dillon indicated the pile on the desk and said, "Ask me anything you want."

"Okay, I'll play your little game," he said, grabbing the stack of photos. "I want the person's name and any conversation with Mike." He proceeded to show all the images, somewhere in the region of fifty or so.

Once Olson was done, he appeared flabbergasted. "How the hell did you just do that?"

Dillon laughed. "Eidetic memory. I guess Diedra didn't tell you?"

"No, she didn't. You just did in three hours what I figured you couldn't do in three weeks. Your chances of survival just rose from ten to twenty percent."

CHAPTER TEN

Two weeks later Diedra declared herself satisfied. Not only had Dillon Hunt, aka Daniel Harper, impressed her with his ability to remember all the pertinent information, but his progress in other areas was also outstanding. She only had to show him once how to strip and reassemble a firearm and within ten minutes he was just as proficient as she was.

In the beginning she had kicked his ass in unarmed combat training, but he quickly learned to read her moves and expect what was coming. He would block her blows and respond offensively as she'd taught him, leaving her flat on her back on the mat.

His fitness had also improved dramatically, and he completed the obstacle course in almost half the time of his first attempt. His breathing was still a little ragged as his lungs sought to repair the damage of eight years of smoking.

She'd ensured that he was seen often around the hospital where his 'sick' mother was. After ten days the unfortunate woman 'passed away' and Dillon was to attend Margaret Hunt's funeral the following day.

Diedra handed Dillon the burner phone that the AAM had issued his brother and said, "This will be your first contact with them, try not to sound nervous. Remember you're burying your beloved mother tomorrow, so try to sound bereaved."

He took a big breath and pressed the call button. "Dillon, thanks for calling," a deep voice said. "How's your Mom?"

His voice choking, Dillon said, "Hi, Carl. I'm afraid that she passed away." Carl Boyd was a senior member of the AAM who'd asked Dillon to stay in contact with him.

"I'm so sorry to hear that," the voice said. "Are you still coming back here?"

"Of course. The funeral's tomorrow and I have few things to sort out. I should be back there in about three or four days," Dillon said.

"No hurry, you're going through a rough time. Just let me know when you'll be arriving so I can alert the guards."

"Will do." Dillon ended the call.

Diedra clapped her hands. "Perfect. You should have been an actor."

"Mikey and I were quite the thespians in our youth. We both took drama and acted in many school plays together."

"Just as well." Agent Wolfe grimaced. "You're about to play the biggest role of your life."

———

Diedra went to great lengths to ensure that the so-called funeral appeared legitimate. She enlisted the aid of a local acting school, who were more than happy to let their students play authentic roles as family and friends of the 'deceased.' Also present were a handful of FBI informants who were each paid two hundred dollars to act as bereaved mourners. There were about thirty-five or so people gathered around the gravesite as the oblivious priest gave the final 'ashes to ashes' speech.

None of people gathered were members of the FBI for a reason. Diedra fully expected the AAM to send someone to check out the funeral. Mike had mentioned on many occasions that the group was ultra-paranoid, especially about new recruits such as himself. It had been three weeks before he was even shown where the compound was.

During that time the AAM had diligently researched his deep-cover persona, Dillon Hunt. The FBI team had gone to great lengths to create Dillon Hunt's background, all the way back to pre-school. His older brother had apparently perished in the north tower on September 11, giving him great reason to hate Muslims.

Diedra spoke into her tactical mic from her position on a rooftop overlooking the cemetery. "Check out that grey sedan parked alongside the road on the west side."

A few seconds later one of the agents closer to the vehicle responded, "Two white males, one with binoculars and the other taking photos of the mourners. I've sent images of them back to HQ for facial recognition analyses."

Diedra was pleased with herself for predicting the AAM's moves. Just one member of the FBI present at the funeral would have blown their whole operation sky-high, probably resulting in Daniel's death.

They observed the suspect vehicle for another ten minutes before it eventually drove off. The agent who'd spoken to her earlier contacted her again. "Confirmed, the occupants of the car were Carl Boyd and Rusty Hicks, both members of the AAM."

"Roger that," she responded, feeling both elated and worried. She was happy to have passed this test but worried about what lay in store for the new Dillon Hunt once he arrived at the compound. She'd had total faith in her partner Mike Harper's abilities, but his brother was a different story. She wasn't sure how he'd react once he started feeling the enormous pressure of being undercover with his very life perpetually in danger.

CHAPTER ELEVEN

Diedra and Dillon lay concealed behind a bushy outcrop as they observed the AAM compound through high-powered binoculars. He'd studied the high-resolution satellite reconnaissance photos, but she wanted him to get a feel of the place before he entered it the following day.

The compound occupied roughly five acres that had been cleared in the middle of thick South Carolina forest. A narrow dirt road was the only way in and connected to the main tar road about two miles to the south.

"We've checked ownership of the entire property, which encompasses almost two hundred acres," Diedra said. "The deed is held by a shell company registered in the Cayman Islands."

"So we know nothing," Dillon said.

"I never said that. The FBI has resources you'd never believe. After some digging we found two directors listed for the company, Jerry Barnes and Sandra Woods."

Dillon looked quizzically at the FBI agent. "I don't remember those names from the AAM list."

"At this point we're assuming that they are the founders of the

AAM and the top leadership. Mike never got to meet them so we can't really confirm that. You see how the camp is split almost down the middle by that high wooden fence?"

"Yup, see it."

"Well, Mike never got to enter the inner sanctum. As you can see, there are numerous buildings that are covered by camo netting, most of which are also obscured from our vision by thick stands of trees and bushes. We presume that's where the leadership and senior members live."

"Mike and the other newer recruits sleep in that large barracks-style building on the south side of the fence. They're utilized mostly for guard duty and other menial tasks, such as cooking, laundry, etcetera. Carl Boyd, the guy you spoke to on the phone and who spied on the funeral, was Mike's immediate superior in the organization. He also appeared to be in charge of security and organized the guard rosters."

"Does he also sleep in the barracks?" Dillon asked.

Diedra shook her head. "No, he's obviously quite senior in rank. At night he disappears back into the northern section."

Dillon changed topics suddenly. "Is this where the FBI does most of its spying from?" They were on a slightly elevated ridge about a mile from the compound.

"Yes, but like I mentioned earlier, we also make use of satellites and drones."

"Aren't you concerned that they'll discover your little observation post?"

"Not really, we're on BLM land here, separated from their property by an electrified fence."

Dillon took one last look through his binoculars. "Looks like my first order of business will be to get myself invited into the so called inner sanctum, am I correct?"

Diedra hesitated a moment. "I'd like to tell you to take it slowly, but according to Mike's intel, the attacks are going to happen quite soon. Do whatever you have to without compromising your safety and identity."

———

Diedra was quiet on the drive back to the FBI's temporary base for the mission, located on the outskirts of the small town of Union, South Carolina. The town had a population of around ten thousand and was roughly twelve miles southeast of the AAM compound.

The agency had leased a large colonial-style mansion that was currently home to the six-member team, which included the nerdy Milford Olson. An FBI Hostage Rescue Team (HRT) was on standby in Virginia and could be on site within a matter of hours.

"Penny for your thoughts," Dillon said, breaking her reverie.

"I'm just concerned for your safety," she said. "This is the first time I've had to put a civilian in such a dangerous position."

"I'm sure your superiors aren't quite as worried. To them I'm just a jailbird and thus totally expendable."

"To be honest, that was my initial reaction as well. However, I've got to know you in the last few weeks and you remind me so much of Mike. Your walk, mannerisms and speech are almost identical to his. This whole thing is actually quite surreal."

"Chill out," Dillon said. "You've known Mikey for years and can hardly tell us apart. Besides, I've just 'buried' my mother so they won't be suspicious of any slight personality change. I'm not going to do anything stupid to endanger this operation, or myself for that matter."

"I'm glad to hear that. I really don't need another Harper brother's death on my conscience."

"Why would Mikey's death be on your conscience? Is there something you're not telling me?"

"No, nothing like that. His death truly was an accident. It's just that he wasn't keen to take on this mission because of the impending birth of his first child. I really wanted him to work this, so I promised to get him home in time. If I hadn't done that, he'd still be alive."

"It's ridiculous to blame yourself. I honestly believe that when your time is up, that's it. Nothing you said or did could have changed that."

Diedra shrugged. "Perhaps you're correct. Although, if that's the case, I sincerely pray that your time isn't nearly up."

CHAPTER TWELVE

U pon their return to the temporary base Diedra finally received the news she'd been waiting for. Milford was on hand to greet them as they exited the nondescript SUV. It had dark-tinted windows to prevent anyone from seeing the occupants.

"We finally managed to ID the two leaders," he said excitedly.

She cracked a wry smile. "Excellent work, who are they?"

"Follow me and I'll show you."

"I thought that we knew that already," Dillon said. He searched his computer-like brain. "Jerry Barnes and Sandra Woods, right?"

"We recently discovered that those are just aliases," Diedra replied as they entered the large dining area, converted into the war-room. Computers, communication devices and other equipment he didn't recognize cluttered every available square foot of the huge room.

Milford waved them over to a large monitor where the faces of a man and woman were prominently displayed. "Meet Jason Price and Kaitlyn Forbes, founders and co-leaders of the AAM. We eventually got facial recognition hits on the photos from the compound."

"I thought that they never showed themselves outdoors; how did you manage to get photos of them?" Dillon asked.

"Mini drone," Diedra replied with a grin. "More specifically, a beetle mini drone."

Dillon was amazed. "I thought that was just the stuff of movies."

Milford jumped in. "The FBI doesn't screw around. We have the most advanced surveillance technology known to man." He picked up a small hummingbird and handed it to Dillon. "This little bird flies exactly like the real one. It takes video, photos and records sound as well."

Dillon inspected the incredibly life-like replica in his hand. "If you have this equipment why would you need someone on the inside?"

"Unfortunately you have to be within a hundred yards of the compound to operate these mini-drones," Diedra replied. "We took a big risk a couple of days ago, but to do it long-term is out of the question. HUMINT is still the most reliable way to gather information. Anyway, enough of the surveillance lecture. Milford, tell us more about these two."

Agent Olson pointed to the man first. "Jason Price, age forty-one. Former Navy SEAL captain and younger brother of Ensign Wayne Price. Ensign Price was killed aboard the USS Cole when it was attacked in 2000 by Al-Qaeda suicide bombers."

"I'm starting to see a pattern here," Dillon commented. "All the members of the AAM seem to have lost loved ones to Islamic terrorist attacks."

Diedra turned to him. "Most, but not all. Although they do try to recruit family of terror-attack victims, their social media pages and website also encourage anyone who is anti-Muslim to join them."

Milford appeared put out by the interruption. "The woman's name is Kaitlyn Forbes, age fifty."

"Looks at least ten years younger," Diedra commented. "What's her story?"

"Her husband died on September 11 in the south tower. He was the founding partner of a large investment company and a very wealthy man. At the time of his death his estimated net-worth was well over four hundred million dollars."

"I assume that she inherited the bulk of his fortune?" Diedra asked.

"Indeed she did," Milford answered.

"So now we know who's bankrolling the entire AAM operation," Dillon said.

"There's no doubt that her initial contribution paid for the land and the basic compound," Diedra said. "However, they've become more self-sufficient lately. The AAM is suspected of being behind several bank robberies and armored-car heists that have occurred over the past two years."

Dillon interrupted. "Let me guess, not enough proof to get a search warrant."

"The robberies were carried out with military precision by men wearing masks and full combat gear," Diedra said. "To answer your question, almost no evidence to work with."

"Well, Jason Price is a former Navy SEAL," Dillon said, "and I'm sure that many of the senior members are also ex-military."

"Precisely, just remember that when you're strutting around the compound. These people won't hesitate to kill a traitor," Diedra warned. She pointed at the monitor and asked Agent Olson, "What else do we know about these two?"

"They both apparently ceased to exist around four years ago," he answered.

"About the same time the shell company was established in the Caymans," Diedra said.

"Quite correct," Milford confirmed. "Records show that the widow Forbes sold everything and transferred her fortune to a bank in the Bahamas. She flew to the Caribbean a few days later and hasn't been seen or heard from since. Jason Price received an honorable discharge from the navy about five years ago. He was working as a consultant for a large multi-national security firm when he also vanished from the radar."

"I wonder how the two of them met," Diedra mused.

"Probably at a support group or something," Milford offered.

"Since nine-eleven there are quite a few of those around the country."

"Could be," Diedra acknowledged. She turned to Dillon. "Time for you to eat something and get some rest. Tomorrow is the big day."

CHAPTER THIRTEEN

D illon Hunt tried to slow his beating heart as he turned onto the dirt track to the compound. The reality of what he was doing had hit him as he'd left the safety of the FBI base. He was driving the exact same type of rental sedan that his brother had used when he lost his life; even the license tags matched.

He followed the winding dirt road until he came to the entrance of the compound. Two guards were on duty and he instantly recognized them from the pile of photos he'd studied.

"Hi, Steve," he said as one lifted the boom and the other approached his vehicle.

"Hey, Dillon, Carl warned us that you'd be arriving today. Man, I'm really sorry to hear about your mother."

"Thanks, I guess she's in a better place now."

"Damn straight, this world has turned into a real shithole!" the guard exclaimed. Dillon remembered that Steve's mother and father had been aboard the doomed plane that had crashed into the pentagon.

"You know the drill," Steve said, and Dillon exited the vehicle. He raised his arms as the guard ran a wand over his body. His brother had described in his notes how everyone who entered the compound was subjected to a search for surveillance devices. He then placed his phone in a container as their use while on the property was strictly prohibited.

The other guard greeted Dillon before inspecting his vehicle. After a few minutes they were both satisfied and indicated that he may enter. Dillon drove through the entrance, appreciating how Daniel must have felt when he entered the lion's den.

He parked his car, grabbed his backpack from the passenger seat and walked towards the guard barracks. His legs felt like rubber, and it took all his willpower not to turn around and get the hell out of there.

He took a deep breath and entered through the open door. He was met by a chorus of greetings from the six men inside the building, all of whom expressed their sympathy at his loss. His quick mind rapidly identified the occupants and he greeted each of them by name.

Dillon noticed a number of empty bunks. "Where's everyone?"

"Cooking and laundry duty," one of the men answered. "We got the day off since we're on guard duty tonight."

"Of course, suppose it'll take me a day or two to get back into the schedule."

Just then a loud voice behind him called out, "Dillon, good to see you again."

He turned and instantly recognized Carl Boyd. The man was six and a half feet tall and built like a brick outhouse. His warm, friendly face belied the fact that he was a seriously dangerous character. Dillon knew from his files that Boyd was a former army ranger who'd served several tours in the Middle East.

Dillon strode forward and went to shake his hand. The big man ignored the proffered hand and enveloped him in a massive bear-hug. "How you doing?"

"Not so great, you know how it is."

"Sure do, just take it easy for a day or two. I'll leave you off the rosters for a while."

"That's not necessary, I like to pull my own weight."

"You definitely aren't a slacker, that's one of the things I like about you. I'll come with you tomorrow to return your rental and we'll stop for a couple of drinks on the way back. I'll put you on the next day's guard list, how's that sound?"

"Thanks, Carl, I appreciate it."

"All right, get unpacked, dinner is in thirty minutes."

———

Diedra let out a big sigh of relief as Dillon and six men left the barracks and headed for the mess hall. She and another agent were watching the compound from their observation post on the nearby ridge. "Looks like they bought it," she said to the man lying next to her.

"So far so good," the agent said. "Just hope he doesn't do anything foolish and get himself killed."

"He should be okay. I just hope that he remembers to check the time during the surprise inspections."

During one of his first debriefs, Mike Harper had informed them that Carl Boyd and some of the senior members conducted random inspections of the newer recruits. They examined their belongings and checked them for spying devices.

During his training the FBI had removed one of Dillon's teeth and replaced the molar with an implant. It contained a tiny GPS device that emitted a signal for only two seconds at exactly fifteen minutes past every odd hour, and his watch was synchronized to the transmitter. The chances of him being checked at precisely that time were incredibly remote, but he could always delay for a few seconds should that happen. "What should I do?" he'd asked Diedra.

"I don't know, pretend to stumble or sneeze or something," she'd told him. "You're a bright boy, I'm sure that you'll come up with something. You only need to buy a couple of seconds."

"Did Mikey have one of these?" he'd asked.

"No, we never thought it crucial in the beginning. All that changed, and we were going to fit him with one while he was in Virginia," she'd told him.

"What changed that made it necessary?"

"The news of the impending attacks on Muslim targets. Initially the mission was only to gather information on the compound and raid it once we had enough evidence of illegal weapons and such. The game rapidly got a lot more deadly and so we decided that we needed to track his location."

Dillon had laughed uneasily. "And I'm the lucky fool who gets to complete this deadly game."

CHAPTER FOURTEEN

L ater that night Dillon lay on his army-style bed, but sleep evaded him. The enormity of what he was attempting had finally hit home, and he was beginning to think that maybe prison would have been the wiser alternative.

He'd casually strolled around the southern part of the compound after dinner to get a better feel of the place. The entire base was surrounded by a sturdy fence topped with coils of razor wire. The vegetation on the outside of the fence had been cleared leaving a fifty-yard gap that the roving guards patrolled at night. He also knew from his brother's notes that a net of infrared motion detectors was activated after dark.

During his walk the gate in wooden fence separating the two sections had briefly opened to allow a vehicle to leave. He'd caught a glimpse of several log cabins as well as a large barn-like structure. The car was a late-model BMW X5 with heavily tinted windows, and he'd wondered if the two elusive leaders were the occupants.

Besides feeling like a condemned prisoner, he was also missing Lisa. His thoughts drifted back to the last couple of hours that they'd spent together in Vegas.

At first she couldn't believe their luck at being released and having their criminal records expunged. However, after hearing that it was conditional on his helping out the FBI, she quickly changed her tune. "Don't give me that crap that you're just helping on a case," she'd said. "They wouldn't have done all this unless what you're doing is extremely dangerous."

He'd tried to placate her and they'd argued for over an hour before he'd given in and told her some of the details of the operation. "You're replacing your brother as an undercover FBI agent," she'd squealed. "Are you out of your friggin' mind?"

"It's either that or fifteen years in prison. Don't worry, I've got this. A few months from now it'll be over. We'll take my inheritance and move to the Caribbean. Maybe buy a nice boat and start a dive-charter business." She'd started crying and he'd held her for a while before they'd made love for what he hoped wasn't the last time.

He flipped onto his side and tried to get comfortable on the thin foam mattress, covering his head with a pillow in an effort to drown out the snores of the men around him.

———

Meanwhile Diedra was wide awake and sleep was the last thing on her mind. She and four of the team members were in the war room reviewing the day's events. "Looks like our boy might even make this work," Milford Olson commented.

"Don't count your chickens," Diedra said. "I wouldn't be surprised if he makes a run for it after a day or two."

"He's a lot tougher than you're giving him credit for. I'll be the first to admit that I initially thought that the whole idea was crazy. After spending some time with Daniel I started to pick up some of the traits that Mike had, courage and tenacity being the two that might get him through this."

"Just got another ping," Rusty Hicks interrupted. The ATF agent was monitoring the surveillance equipment, which included Dillon's GPS tracker.

Diedra checked her watch. "Right on time. At least we know the damn thing's working." Before anyone could comment, her cell phone began ringing. She answered and was surprised to hear Deputy Director Shaw on the line. "You're up late, sir."

"Just returned from Washington," he said curtly. "I was briefing the president on our progress."

"As I mentioned earlier, the insertion was successful."

"The president doesn't care about the details, he just wants results." Shaw sounded tired, and Diedra almost felt sorry for him. "Speaking of which, he's decided that Homeland Security will also be involved in this operation," Shaw said bitterly.

"What the hell! The FBI and ATF clearly have jurisdiction."

"Apparently Deputy Director Roger Wells over at Homeland got a whiff that a terror attack on American soil was imminent," Shaw said. "The president agreed with him that they need to be a part of this, so that's that. Two agents from Homeland Security will be joining your team tomorrow."

"As long as they stay out of my way and don't screw up this operation."

"Just play nice," Shaw said resignedly. "You know what a pain in the ass Wells can be."

CHAPTER FIFTEEN

The following day Dillon followed Carl Boyd to Union County Airport located on the southwest edge of town. It accommodated the only car-rental agency in the small town, and his brother had rented his ill-fated vehicle from there.

Diedra had already sorted out the accident with the company, and the insurance company had paid out for the destroyed sedan. The car that Dillon was returning belonged to the FBI, and they'd pick it up after he and Carl left.

Driving back through the town, Carl asked Dillon if he was hungry. He checked his watch before replying, "I could go for a burger at Ruby Tuesday's."

The big man smiled indulgently. "I'm sure that's not the only reason you want to go there."

Dillon pretended to be embarrassed. "I haven't seen her for a while, she's probably already moved on."

The 'she' he was referring to was Arleen Cooper, dayshift barlady at Ruby Tuesday's and his brother's FBI contact. She'd managed to get a job at the bar many of the AAM members frequented just before his brother's insertion into the militia group.

They'd quickly pretended to strike-up a romantic relationship, and he normally spent Friday nights at her place 'doing the nasty,' as his fellow AAM members called it. Arleen had rented a small apartment above the bar, and it was there that his brother would do his weekly de-briefs.

Dillon had been introduced to her at the temporary base, and she'd quickly gone over the fake relationship details with him. "Mike always called me honey, and for God's sake no pawing or kissing me in public. Your brother wasn't into public displays of affection."

He'd leered at her. "I'll try to keep my hands off you, but I'm not promising anything; you're quite a good-looking gal."

Arleen had blushed. "Just remember I'm a highly trained agent. I'll kick your ass if you try anything." At five-foot-two the diminutive agent looked anything but lethal. She had short auburn hair cut in a retro-style bob and a very pretty freckled face.

She ran to greet him as they entered the bar, giving him a big hug. "Why didn't you tell me you were back, I really missed you."

"I missed you too, honey," Dillon said, trying not to sound too awkward. "I just wasn't sure that we'd still be an item."

"That's nice. Do you think because I work in a bar that I'm some sort of a slut or something?"

"No, nothing like that," he said quickly. "It's just that we haven't been together very long, and all the other guys were always hitting on you."

She turned to Carl and smiled. "Well, luckily I had someone to protect my virtue in your absence. Carl kept everyone in their place, and no one's going to argue with him."

"Was only a pleasure, ma'am," he said in his Southern drawl.

"Thanks for that, Carl," Dillon said.

"No problem, now let's get a couple of beers and after that I'll head out. You two obviously have some catching up to do, so I'll come back and fetch you tomorrow morning."

"But it's Monday, we're only allowed to stay out on Fridays."

Carl winked. "Don't argue, just enjoy it. You've been through a lot. Tomorrow night you're back on guard duty."

After Carl left Dillon had a burger and a few more beers as he waited for Arleen to finish her shift at five. Being a Monday afternoon the bar was fairly quiet, and they chatted as he sat at the deserted bar counter. "This Carl really seems like a nice guy," Dillon commented.

"He is, a real Southern gentleman. It was Carl who recommended that Mike join the AAM, and even though he was Mike's superior they quickly became friends."

"I don't know all the details; how did that happen exactly?"

Arleen laughed and Dillon couldn't help but notice how her pert little nose crinkled as she did so. "Oh, we put on quite the show," she answered.

She checked that none of the patrons were within earshot and leaned forward conspiratorially. "I'd only been working here a couple of days when Diedra came up with a plan. One of the networks was airing a piece about the rise in Islamic terror attacks around the globe. It was scheduled for a Friday night and we knew that the bar would be full of AAM members. The first thing I had to do was ensure that I was working that night so I could control the TV."

"I thought that you only worked the dayshift."

"I quickly took care of that problem. After my shift on Thursday afternoon I spiked poor Chantelle's green tea concoction before I left. She always brought it to work in a sports bottle and kept it in a fridge in the back. Needless to say she was in no condition to come in on Friday and the manager asked me to work a double shift. Around six that evening your brother came staggering in and took a seat at the bar close to the TV. He ordered about six double bourbon on the rocks over the next two hours."

"What?" Dillon said in surprise. "Mikey hardly ever drank, he would have been flat on his back by then."

Arleen grinned. "It's amazing how much strong iced tea looks like bourbon."

"I get it," Dillon said with a chuckle. "He was stone-cold sober."

"Well, the drink that I served him after the program started at eight was real. He made sure to spill some on his shirt, and he reeked of alcohol. About fifteen minutes into the show he started ranting and raving about Muslims and terrorists and threw his glass at the TV, narrowly missing the screen. The bouncer rushed over and was about to kick his ass when Carl appeared out of nowhere. He warned the bouncer to back off and led Mike to a quiet booth at the back."

"I would have given anything to see that."

"It was quite hilarious," Arleen admitted. "Anyway, Mike gave Carl the cover-story about his brother dying in the Trade Center on nine-eleven and how much he hated Muslims. Needless to say Carl was delighted to hear this and eventually gave your brother a ride back to the cheap motel where he was staying. He returned the following day to see if Mike was okay and told him a little about the AAM."

"No mention of the attack on American Muslims, I'm sure."

"Oh no, he just mentioned that America would be a much safer place if all Muslims were forced to leave. Mike agreed emphatically and asked if he could join the group. Carl laughed and said that it wasn't that easy. He took down Dillon Hunt's details and said that he first had to run a full background check."

"I bet that you guys were nervous while waiting for the results."

"Not really, our people had done an excellent job of building his cover. It's amazing what you can do as a government agency with unrestricted access."

"I know that firsthand," Dillon said dryly.

Arleen giggled. "Oh yes, the fifteen-year sentence."

"I'm glad you find it so amusing."

"Sorry about that." She pointed to her chest. "By the way, what do you think of them?"

Dillon blushed at being caught out. "If you're going to wear a loose top, no bra and lean over like that, you better expect that every guy's going to look at your boobs."

"Just yanking your chain. It befits my role as a flirtatious bar-lady and I do really well with tips."

"I'm sure you do, and to answer your question, they are small but firm and really quite exquisite."

It was Arleen's turn to blush and she mumbled, "Thank you."

"So now what?" Dillon asked.

"Now I start my cash-up, after that we go up to my apartment so you can rock my world, lover-boy."

Not knowing whether she was joking or not, Dillon just laughed.

CHAPTER SIXTEEN

A rleen unlocked the door and Dillon followed her into the tiny apartment. She turned to him. "It's not much but the owner of the bar also owns the entire building, so the rent for bar staff is really cheap."

"Is he also a member of the AAM?" Dillon asked.

"Not as far as we know, but he's definitely sympathetic to their cause." Arleen walked ahead and gave him a quick tour of her home. The small living room was neatly furnished with a two-seater couch, two easy chairs and a coffee table. A small flat-screen TV perched atop a low entertainment center, and the room flowed into a kitchenette containing a tiny dinette table and two chairs. Two doors to the right of the living room led to the bathroom and only bedroom.

"Only one queen-size bed," Dillon commented. "Where did my brother sleep? The couch is way too small."

"In the bed with me, of course." Arleen noted his shocked look and gave one of her patented laughs. "Don't even go there, we were both professional government agents. Nothing ever happened, and besides, he was totally dedicated to his wife."

Dillon grinned. "So I get to sleep with you too."

"Sleep is the operative word, Mister, try anything funny and your sweet ass will be on the floor before you know what happened."

Dillon held up both hands. "Hey, I can't be held responsible for what I do in my sleep. I'm just happy that you noticed that I have a sweet ass."

Exasperated, she countered, "That's not what I meant. Come over here and let's get to work." She took a seat at the small dinette table and opened a laptop.

Dillon moved a chair next to hers and sat down, careful to ensure that their knees weren't touching. She entered a long password before looking at him. "You'll need to memorize this code in case something happens to me."

He glanced at her and noticed that she wasn't joking. He cleared his throat. "Go ahead."

She recited a random twenty-figure code containing a jumble of letters, numbers and symbols.

"Got it."

"Sure you do, don't be a wiseass. I'll write it down and you can study it later. I find it easier to break it up into segments."

Dillon just smiled and repeated the complicated code verbatim.

Arleen was impressed. "Oh yes, I forgot that you're some sort of boy-genius or something."

"Not a genius per se, I just remember the exact details of everything that's happened so far in my life."

She looked fascinated. "That must be so cool."

"You'd think so," he said cryptically. "Alright, what's next?"

Arleen showed him how to turn on the video function. "Give your report as much detail as possible. Who and what you saw, who you spoke to and what was said. Pay special attention to any weapons or anything that seemed out of the ordinary. If you need to draw any diagrams, here's a pen and pad."

Arleen went to the fridge, grabbed a couple of beers and handed him one. "It's thirsty work." She took hers over to the small couch where she sat cross-legged and observed him.

At first Dillon was a little self-conscious, but after a few minutes he got into the swing of it. Next thing he knew it was almost an hour later and he was done.

Arleen came over and touched him lightly on his back. "Now that was really impressive. I thought that Mike was good at giving reports, but you remembered every single conversation word for word."

"Just like watching a movie playing in your head," he said with a hint of sadness. "So, what happens now?"

"Your report goes onto a thumb drive, which I'll drop into a P.O. box tomorrow when I go to collect my mail at the local Post Office. One of the team will collect it later for analysis. Now, this is the part where I normally give you Diedra's instructions for the coming week. Remember this normally happens on a Friday night, but you've only been there a couple of days so just keep doing what you're doing. If you do get the opportunity to stand out from the rest, take it immediately. Volunteer for any-and-everything; we need to get you into that secure section as soon as possible."

Dillon saluted smartly. "Will do, ma'am. So what now, bedtime?"

"Now you take me out for dinner. Don't think you're getting me into bed on an empty stomach."

CHAPTER SEVENTEEN

Although Arleen possessed a car, they decided to walk the three blocks to a small Italian place on the corner of Thompson and Rice. "They have the best pizza," she said enthusiastically.

It was a cold early spring night and Dillon zipped up his windbreaker before saying, "I'm more of a pasta guy myself."

She took his hand. "Can't really go wrong with pasta at an Italian restaurant either."

"What's with the hand-holding? I thought my brother wasn't into PDA's."

"He wasn't, but we always held hands in public to keep up appearances; don't read too much into it."

They reached Sergio's and the warmth hit him as he held the door open for her. It was past nine on a Monday night and the place was almost empty. Only two of the dozen or so tables were occupied, both by couples. The bistro had a relaxed ambience and tables were covered with red-checkered tablecloths in true Italian style.

The hostess greeted both of them by name and led them to a table by the window. She left after taking their drink orders and Dillon said, "I take it you and Mikey used to come here often?"

"Every Friday night without fail. Like you, your brother loved his pasta."

"Our mother was half-Italian," Dillon said wistfully. "She really knew how to cook."

Arleen leaned over and took his hand. "Mike told me what happened to your parents. I'm so sorry."

"It was a long time ago," he said dismissively.

"Still, it must have been awful."

"I'd rather not talk about it if you don't mind."

The waitress returned with their drinks, and Dillon was thankful for the interruption. She took their food order, and after she left he tried to lighten the mood by saying, "So I presume that you like to sleep in the buff?"

Arleen grinned. "Nice try, mister, panties and a long Pink Floyd t-shirt that belonged to your brother. He also kept some other clothes there, including a set of long flannel pajamas which you'll be sleeping in."

"Yeah right, he always slept in his boxers, just like me."

"You got me, boxers are fine, just remember what I said about ending up on the floor."

———

It was past eleven by the time they returned to the apartment. "You go first," Arleen said, indicating the bathroom. "I put out fresh towels and there's a new toothbrush for you as well."

"So thoughtful," Dillon said. "I'll domesticate you yet."

She kicked him playfully in the ass as he walked past. "Many have tried, and all have failed."

Ten minutes later he exited the bathroom and asked, "Which side of the bed?"

"You sleep on the right side. My side has a lamp. I need to read a little every night before I fall asleep."

"I'll probably need to get one of those sleeping masks then."

Arleen walked to the nightstand, opened a drawer and produced a red and black mask. "You and your brother really are identical," she said, handing it to him before heading for the bathroom.

She returned twenty minutes later, wearing the t-shirt as promised. He noted that the length had been exaggerated as it barely covered her red panties, which he got a glimpse of as she climbed on the bed.

"What're you staring at?" she asked.

"Nothing, I just remember that shirt of Mikey's is all. He's had it since our college days."

"Sorry, I didn't mean to sound bitchy." She leaned over and kissed him gently on the cheek. "See you in the morning."

CHAPTER EIGHTEEN

D illon accompanied Arleen the following morning as she went down to the bar to begin her shift. Carl was scheduled to pick him up around eleven, which gave him just enough time for a hearty breakfast of bacon and eggs.

As he ate he reflected on the previous evening's events. He really enjoyed Arleen's company although their flirtations had come to nothing and he'd fallen into a deep sleep within minutes. *I need to be careful, she's really cute and there's definitely some sort of spark between us*, he thought. *The last thing I need is another relationship to cloud my judgement; just remember how hot Lisa is.*

He was on his second cup of coffee when Carl entered the bar. "Time to go," he said, "we need to stop off at the market to pick up supplies for the base."

Dillon gave Arleen a goodbye hug and she kissed him softly on the cheek. "See you on Friday, and please be careful," she whispered.

Carl drove the large pickup to a nearby market, where the supplies were quickly loaded into the back. The order had been called in ahead of time, and Carl signed for it after a careful check that everything was there.

He noticed the look on Dillon's face. "We have an account here which is settled at the end of every month."

Dillon saw an opening. "It must cost a fortune, how does the AAM afford it?"

"We have some wealthy sponsors," Carl replied. "Also, we occasionally pull a mission to augment those funds."

"I'd love to go on one of those missions," Dillon said enthusiastically. "Guard duty and working in the kitchen doesn't really do it for me." He recalled from the notes he'd read that no mention of any 'missions' had been made before.

"Just remember that you're still on probation," Carl said firmly. "Probies don't get to do stuff like that."

Dillon didn't want to push it. "I get the picture, just wish that this damned probation was over already."

Carl gave him an understanding look. "Don't worry, buddy, not too much longer."

What the hell does that mean? Dillon thought. *Apparently we're running out of time. If this mission isn't a success, my ass will be right back in prison.*

———

Later that night Dillon was cursing his probation yet again. It was bitterly cold as he patrolled the outside perimeter of the camp. He was paired with Cindy, one of ten women currently on probation with him. He recalled his brother's prior conversations with the butch-looking woman from Alabama, since they'd been paired together previously and had spoken at length. Apparently no one in her family had been killed or maimed by Muslim terrorists. She was just a devout racist who firmly believed that the United States belonged to white people only.

He quickly tired of her racist tirades and tried to tune her out, wondering how his brother had put up with her. They came to the section where the elite members lived and he noticed that the fence was covered with canvas, making it impossible to see inside. *If I didn't have this motor-mouth with me, I could make a small hole and have a peek inside*, he thought.

Spotlights were situated every fifty yards or so atop the fence posts. They illuminated the cleared area between the base and the forest. His gloved hands cradled the AK-47 that he'd been issued, while his annoying partner had hers slung over her shoulder. *The stupid bitch would be dead before she could even point the damn thing.* He smiled to himself.

Knowing that on guard duty Dillon would be issued with an AK, it was one of the weapons he'd been trained on at Quantico. They were legally available in the U.S., but only in the single-shot version. A quick but illegal adaption soon restored them to full automatic, such as the ones they were carrying.

During his abbreviated training Dillon had asked Diedra why they didn't just raid the compound and arrest the leaders for the possession of illegal weapons. She'd just laughed. "What, they'd probably receive a couple of months' probation and that's it. We need to arrest them with explosives or bombs in their possession to make this operation worthwhile. Then, facing a lengthy prison sentence, one of them will probably turn and we'll have the rest for conspiracy to commit murder."

CHAPTER NINETEEN

Friday couldn't come quickly enough for Dillon. Three consecutive nights of guard duty in the freezing cold had left him tired and irritable. His only saving grace was that he hadn't been paired with the annoying Cindy after that first night.

A couple of large trucks took the probies into town to blow off some steam. Carl and several of his men took over guard duty on Friday nights. *Gives them a great chance to search through our belongings,* Dillon mused. He had endured two random electronic wand checks already, neither of which was close to his GPS chip's transmission time.

Most of the men and a few women disembarked in the parking lot of Ruby Tuesday's, where they would be picked up at midnight. The rest either went to the movies or one of the restaurants in town.

Dillon realized just how fortunate he was to spend the night with Arleen in a soft, comfortable bed. His brother had really chosen the right person in Carl to befriend.

Arleen had already finished her shift and beckoned for Dillon to join her at a booth near the back. He did so and she rose to hug him. "I got us a booth 'cause it gets quite hectic and rowdy at the bar counter on Friday nights. By the way, I'm impressed to see that you're still alive and well."

He gave a tired smile. "Man, am I glad to see you."

"Missed me already?" she asked teasingly.

He blushed. "I just meant that it's nice to be away from the camp and to sleep in a comfortable bed tonight."

"I'm just messing with you. We'll have a couple of drinks and then head upstairs to do your report."

Dillon glanced around. "The waitresses are all busy. I'll go to the bar and get them. What are you having?"

"Just a light beer. I suggest that you have the same. Mike always drank Coors Light."

"I know that!" he retorted. Arleen looked hurt and he quickly apologized. "I'm sorry, I didn't mean to snap. I'm just really tired."

She took his hand and said softly, "I understand, you're under constant strain pretending to be someone you not. Welcome to the not so glamorous world of undercover work."

"Don't forget the three nights of freezing guard duty either."

"Poor guy, why don't we shine off the drinks? We can go upstairs and you can take a nap before you do your report."

"No, I'll be fine. I can't think of anything more relaxing than having a drink with a pretty girl."

———

Diedra was far from impressed. The two Homeland Security agents had just arrived at the mansion and were already trying to take over. Alec Burns was the senior of the two and treated his colleague, Amanda Baker, as if she were his slave. She even had to make two trips to their vehicle to collect his things.

"What do you mean it's classified?" Burns barked. "I have all the necessary clearances!"

"The FBI doesn't just hand out the identities of their undercover operatives," Diedra said in exasperation. "All you need to know is that we have someone on the inside. There's absolutely no reason for you to know their identity."

"I'll call my director if you don't give me his name right now!" Burns said nastily.

"His or her name." Diedra smiled. "I never said that it's a guy. While you're at it you can call the president too if you like. Unless Director Shaw tells me otherwise, you're out of the loop on this."

"We'll just see about that!" He grabbed his cell phone and stormed from the room.

Diedra glanced at Amanda, who just shrugged. "Agent Burns can be a little intense at times."

Milford Olson laughed. "A little intense, I thought that he was going to have a stroke or something."

Alec Burns returned to the war-room about five minutes later in a much calmer mood. "Director Wells informed me that you are in charge here and what you say goes. Agent Baker and I are just here to observe and report back to him. I apologize."

Diedra stifled a grin. "Apology accepted." *Homeland probably doesn't want to take the heat if this op goes south*, she thought.

CHAPTER TWENTY

Dillon once again verbalized his report while Arleen sat on the couch and observed. She still marveled at his ability to recall everything with such amazing clarity.

After watching for a while her attention began to wander. She found herself thinking about what it would be like to make love to him. She'd had a huge crush on his brother Mike that she'd never revealed to anyone. Of course she'd never acted on it because of Mike's marital status.

Are you out of your mind, woman? she admonished herself. *They may look identical, but this isn't Mike. He's just a petty criminal, and besides, he's got someone back in Vegas waiting for him.*

Dillon caught her staring at him. "Why the intense look? You're sorta freaking me out."

Flustered, she stammered, "Sorry, it just blows my mind that you have such perfect recall, that's all."

"I'm not some sort of freak, if that's what you're suggesting?"

She recovered nicely. "Not at all. I'm just in awe. I wish that I had your ability."

"Be careful what you wish for, it just might come true."

"That's the second time that you've dismissed your gift as if it's a curse. What aren't you telling me?"

"Maybe I'll tell you one day," he replied. "Right now I could use another drink. I've got to get this finished and get some sleep."

Arleen stood and retrieved a couple of beers from the fridge. "We don't have to go out to eat tonight. I'll go down to the bar and pick up a couple of take-out burgers."

"Thanks, I appreciate that. I wouldn't be very good company tonight anyway."

"No problem, what's your pleasure?"

He winked. "Wouldn't you love to know?"

"Still haven't lost your sense of humor, I see," she said dryly. "I meant what sort of burger do you want?"

"I know, just teasing. Make mine a bacon cheeseburger with plenty of fries, I'm starving."

Arleen grabbed her purse. "See you in half an hour."

Dillon continued recording his report and finished up about twenty minutes later. Arleen still hadn't returned, and he used the opportunity to snoop through her apartment. He found nothing of interest except for a 9mm automatic pistol in the top drawer of her bedside table.

He lay down on the bed and was almost asleep when he heard Arleen's voice. "Wake up, sunshine, dinner is served."

They sat at the dinette table and Dillon quickly devoured his burger and fries. "That's it, I'm going to brush my teeth and hit the sack."

"Go ahead, I need to edit and download your report," Arleen said. "I'll join you later."

CHAPTER TWENTY-ONE

Carl once again picked Dillon up from the bar the following morning. They were on their way back to the compound when Carl made a joke about him getting lucky twice in one week.

Dillon laughed loudly and the big man glanced over at him. "I must say, you seem a lot more relaxed since you've returned. Not quite so intense."

Dillon thought quickly. "I guess that my mother's passing had quite a profound effect on me. You only get one life, which you have to live to the fullest."

"Very true," Carl agreed. "Remember what you said the other day about wanting to go on one of our missions? Do you still feel the same way?"

Dillon felt his heartbeat accelerate. "Of course," he replied quickly.

"What if it wasn't exactly legal?" Carl asked.

"No problem, if it advances our cause, I'm in."

"How good a driver are you?"

Dillon had spent several afternoons in Quantico at the FBI's advanced driving course. "Pretty good," he answered.

RAY FLOYD

Carl pulled the big SUV over to the shoulder. "I trust you, but I need to see for myself."

They swapped seats and Dillon immediately put the powerful vehicle through its paces. There was almost no traffic on the small back road, and he performed several J-turns, handbrake turns and a few other aggressive driving maneuvers.

Carl was impressed. "More than pretty good I'd say. Where'd you learn to drive like that?"

"Spent quite a few years working corporate security, which included driving around high-profile targets," he answered, knowing that Dillon Hunt's backstopped résumé would confirm that. It also gave credence to his knowledge and ability with various weapons.

Dillon was still driving when they entered the camp and was surprised when Carl pressed a remote that opened the wooden gate and motioned for him to pass through to the secure northern compound.

Noting the look on his face, Carl laughed. "Congratulations, your probation is finally over. You're now one of us."

———

Diedra and Agent Olson were watching the AAM compound from the overlook when Carl and Dillon returned. "He did it!" she exclaimed as Dillon and Carl exited the SUV.

"I told you that he had it in him," Milford exclaimed.

"Yeah right, in the beginning you wanted nothing to do with him."

"But I changed my tune pretty damned fast. Can't wait to tell the others about this."

Diedra hesitated a little. "There's no need for Burns and Baker to know about this right now."

"Still pissed that Homeland crashed our party?" Olson laughed. "Okay, I'll keep it on the down-low."

"I'd just rather get some concrete, actionable intelligence before claiming any success," Diedra said.

CHAPTER TWENTY-TWO

arl gave Dillon a quick inspection of his new digs. It was in total contrast to his previous accommodations as no expense seemed to have been spared. Where the southern section was just dirt, a parking area and several utilitarian buildings, the elite section was covered with lush grass, trees and numerous log cabins.

Carl led him to one of the cabins. "Welcome home. You'll be sharing this with three other guys. There are four bedrooms and two bathrooms, so you'll have your own bedroom and a shared bathroom."

The tour continued and Dillon took in the well-furnished living room and neat kitchen area. "All meals are taken in the communal dining hall," Carl mentioned, "but you're welcome to keep your drinks and snacks in here." He opened the sliding-glass door off the living room that led to a large deck with four lounge chairs. "What do you think?" he asked.

"Definitely a step up from the army-style living I've gotten used to," Dillon answered.

"We take care of our own," Carl said proudly. "Come, let me show you the rest." Dillon followed him around the remainder of the enclosure. He pointed out a large barn-like building off the parking area. "That's where our weapons and specialist vehicles are kept, it's very secure and only a few of us have keys. That's the dining hall." He indicated a large log structure adjacent to the barn.

Dillon gave it a cursory glance, wondering what Carl meant by 'specialist vehicles.' *Definitely need to get a look inside there*, he thought. "How many people in this section?" he asked, hoping he didn't sound too inquisitive.

"With you, eight of the ten smaller cabins are now fully occupied, so that's thirty-two. Including myself, there are six senior leaders. We share those three larger cabins at the back." He pointed. "The co-founders of AAM, Jerry and Sandra, share that really large cabin next to us. So, that gives you forty people in total."

"Impressive," Dillon said. "When do I get to meet everyone?"

"No time like the present. Jerry and Sandra are busy conducting a lecture in the dining hall."

Dillon followed the big man. "I wondered where everyone was."

———

Dillon quickly took in the scene as Carl ushered him through the rear door of the large hall. There were four large wooden tables towards the back with two smaller ones near the front. Two buffet-style serving areas against the walls flanked the seating area, and a small stage and podium occupied the front of the building.

They quietly slipped into two empty chairs at the rear-most table, and Carl leaned over and whispered, "The guy speaking is Jerry Barnes, and the woman seated next to him on the stage is Sandra Woods. As I mentioned earlier, they are the co-founders of AAM."

Except that isn't their real names, Dillon thought. *I wonder if Carl knows that?*

"The five guys seated at the front table are the other senior leaders," Carl continued. "I usually sit with them."

"What about the four young people at the other table?" Dillon whispered back.

"That's Jerry and Sandra's table," Carl replied. "The teenagers arrived while you were away. They all stay in one cabin, and none of us are allowed to interact with them in any way."

"Isn't that a bit strange?"

"All that Jerry would say is that they are pivotal for our first strike against the Muslim community."

Dillon let it go at that, knowing that he had to find out quickly what the so-called first strike entailed. He concentrated on what Jerry Barnes was saying to his enraptured audience.

"The following is a quote from the Quran, verse five point thirty-three; *'The punishment of those who wage war against Allah and His messenger and strive to make mischief in the land is only this, that they should be murdered or crucified or their hands and their feet should be cut off on opposite sides or they should be imprisoned.'*" He finished reading and looked sternly at his audience. "Note the word 'murdered' in that passage."

Dillon glanced at Carl, who seemed captivated by his leader's words. He was about to comment but thought better of it.

"The next quote from the Quran is verse eight point twelve," Jerry Barnes continued. "Just as frightening as the previous one; *'when your Lord inspired the angels... I will cast terror into the hearts of those who disbelieve. Therefore strike off their heads and strike off every fingertip of them.'* And last but not least, verse seventeen point sixteen; *'And when We wish to destroy a town, We send Our commandment to the people of it who lead easy lives, but they transgress therein; thus the word proves true against it, so We destroy it with utter destruction.'* If any of you had any doubts about what we're facing, just remember, the Muslims have been instructed by their God to murder and maim anyone who does not believe in Islam. In fact, there are more than one hundred mentions in the Quran where non-believers of Islam should be killed."

A murmur went up throughout the room and Carl turned to Dillon and whispered, "Heavy stuff, hey?"

"Is it really true?" Dillon whispered back. "I can't imagine that any religion would promote the wholesale slaughter of anyone that didn't believe."

"You bet your ass it is. That's the reason why we have to take the battle to them, especially here in America."

Dillon turned his attention back to the stage, where Jerry Barnes had taken his seat and Sandra Woods rose to speak. She was an attractive older woman who spoke in a strong voice. "Make no mistake, we are battling for our very existence. Our enemy will not rest until every non-Muslim is dead or in prison. Like most of you, I have personally felt the tragedy of their jihad against us. That Halloween attack in New York a few years back where a Muslim man killed eight people on a bike path is just the beginning for innocent people living in the USA. As you all know, similar attacks have already taken place throughout Europe. The coward apparently followed the Islamic State's advice on social media on how to carry out vehicular attacks. As law-abiding Americans, none of us will be safe until all followers of Islam have been purged from our homeland. I also want you all to think about this; every suicide-bomber and murderer is guaranteed seventy-two virgins awaiting him in Paradise. What does that say about a religion where men are doing nothing but screwing young virgins, while the poor young girls in the afterlife do nothing but wait their turn to be defiled by a murderer?"

Sandra Woods took her seat to rapturous applause as Jerry Barnes once again spoke into the microphone, "I see that our latest member has arrived. Carl, please bring Mister Hunt up to the front."

Dillon was mortified as Carl ushered him up to the stage. "I was thinking more of one-on-one introductions," he whispered to him.

Carl just smiled. "Nonsense, you're a full member of AAM now, embrace it."

Jerry Barnes shook Dillon's hand. "Pleased to finally meet you, Mister Hunt, I've heard good things about you."

Dillon managed a weak smile. "Thank you."

Barnes turned to the microphone and introduced Dillon, giving a full account of his brother's death on nine-eleven. "I have no doubt that Dillon will be a tremendous asset in our reverse-jihad."

The large crowd whistled and applauded while Dillon grinned stupidly and waved at his new compatriots.

CHAPTER TWENTY-THREE

arl led Dillon through the hall and introduced him to all but the four teenagers seated at the founders table. "I don't expect you to remember all their names," he said, "but after a while you'll get to know them."

Already done, Dillon thought. *Although I'd better be careful and pretend not to remember all of them.* "Quite a few military-looking guys," he commented.

"You got that right," Carl said. "We're fighting a war here on our own soil, so there won't be any pussyfooting around. Speaking of which, when was the last time you fired a weapon?"

"It's been a while, not since I left the security company a couple of years ago."

"No problem, we have a shooting range close by. I'll take you over tomorrow and get you up to speed."

"Sounds good, so what now?" Dillon asked.

"Go and grab your stuff from the barracks and get yourself situated. It's almost time for lunch, after which you and I will attend a briefing on the upcoming mission that I mentioned earlier."

Dillon collected his meager belongings, accepting congratulations from his former probie cohorts on becoming a full-time member of the organization. He knew that there was only space for eight more people in the elite northern section but decided to keep that to himself.

During lunch he chatted to the other people seated at his table as Carl had re-joined the other senior leaders at the front. He pretended not to remember most of their names and innocently asked questions that would give him more information about them. As he'd mentioned to Carl, most were tough-looking ex-military men, with a few equally tough-looking women as well.

Most had lost friends, family or comrades-at-arms to Al-Qaeda, ISIS, the Taliban or other radical Islamic groups. The general consensus seemed to be an end-game where Islam was totally eradicated in the United States. After what he'd heard, Dillon couldn't exactly say that he disagreed with them.

As he finished a meal of far-superior quality to what was served in the southern section, Carl came up and asked if he was ready.

"Ready as I'll ever be," he replied, following Carl to his senior-leader cabin where the briefing was to be held.

There were seven men and one woman already seated in the large living room, and Carl quickly made the introductions. "You've already met everyone, but this time you need to remember everything I tell you."

"No problem," Dillon said confidently.

"These five guys are Mike, Jimmy, Alec, Kurt and Dave. Together with me, they'll be the main operational force. Darren here is a driver and Steve is a tech expert. This beautiful young lady is Alicia, hacker extraordinaire."

The pretty young girl gave a big smile. "Carl, baby, you say the sweetest things." She was small and elven-like with short dark hair, her face and body adorned with several piercings and tattoos.

"Dillon here will be the other driver," Carl said.

The men all nodded while Alicia jumped up and gave him a peck on the cheek. "Welcome to the team, hope you're not as fuddy-duddy as the rest of them."

Carl grinned. "We prefer to call it serious. Dillon will drive the operational vehicle and Darren the support vehicle."

"Hey, unfair," Darren exclaimed. "I'm more senior, why does he get to drive the getaway vehicle?"

Dillon turned to Carl in surprise. "Getaway vehicle?"

"Oh, didn't I tell you? We're going to rob a bank," Carl said innocuously.

CHAPTER TWENTY-FOUR

"Rob a bank!" Dillon exclaimed.

Carl held up a hand, turned to Steve and asked, "Is the room secure?"

The tech expert replied, "Swept it myself." He indicated a complicated-looking device perched on the coffee table. "White-noise jammer in case somebody has a parabolic mike aimed at us."

"One can never be too careful," Carl said. He turned to Dillon. "You don't have a problem with this, do you?"

"Are you kidding, wouldn't miss it for the world," he replied enthusiastically. "I've been dying for some action."

"Well, hopefully nobody will die," Carl said wryly. "Speaking of which, we only use non-lethal weapons. Unlike our fucked-up enemy, we don't kill innocent civilians."

"Good to hear," Dillon said. "So where's this bank we're going to hit?"

"Good question. You know the old adage, 'don't shit where you eat'? Well, we're going a couple of states over so they don't suspect us."

Alicia clapped her hands. "Goody, I've never been to Florida."

Carl smiled at her. "Sorry to burst your bubble, Ally, but wrong direction. We're going to hit the Southern Trust Savings & Loan in Montgomery, Alabama, five days from now."

Alicia pouted. "Alabama, could you have found a more boring place?"

Carl's look became serious. "We're robbing a bank, not going on vacation. I'm going to need you to hack into the branch at Union and South and take control of all their systems."

Alicia grinned. "A walk in the park. If I can hack NASA and the NSA, I can pretty much get in anywhere."

"Which is why we love you so much," Carl said. "Two of our guys have been watching the bank from an apartment building across the street for the last few weeks."

"I wondered where Frank and Ed had disappeared to," Steve said.

"Now you know," Carl said. He brought up a Google Earth image on a large monitor, pointing to a narrow alleyway behind the bank. "Darren, you'll park the support vehicle there. You guys will also be responsible for ensuring that nobody escapes through the rear door."

"What if someone triggers a silent alarm?" Dillon asked.

Carl glanced at him. "Good question. Steve and Alicia will be in the support vehicle with all the necessary technical equipment. Alicia will hack into the bank's security system and disable it, along with all the building's landlines."

"What about cell phones?" Alicia asked.

"Steve will use a military-grade jammer to block all signals," Carl answered. "Ed and Frank report that there are two armed guards in the bank at all times, one by the front door and one by the employee-access gate. They're both on the older side, probably retired cops. Alec and Kurt will pretend to be bank customers and neutralize them with tranquilizer guns ten seconds before we enter."

"Is ten seconds enough?" Jimmy asked.

"The darts contain a fast-acting drug used to sedate elephants and rhinos. As long as neither of them has heart problems, they should be okay."

"What's my role?" Dillon asked.

"You'll drop Jimmy, Mike, Dave and myself right in front of the bank then continue on, pull a U-turn and park on the other side of the street, about fifty yards from the building. You'll pick us up again once we exit the bank."

Dillon frowned. "Why not just stay in front of the bank?"

"There's no parking on that side of the street, and besides, it'll be too obvious. You'll be performing two U-turns, so make sure there are no cops around. Frank and Ed will be observing from their vantage point and will let you know if they see any law-enforcement personnel."

"Speaking of which, what if the cops do arrive at the scene? Jimmy asked.

"Ed will call in a bomb threat to the Capitol Building five minutes before we enter the bank. It's on the other side of town and should keep the local cops busy for a while," Carl replied.

"What's our escape route?" Dillon asked.

"You'll continue west on Union, then take the on-ramp here onto the I65 north. After it crosses the Alabama River you take Route 152 east to this warehouse just north of the Montgomery Zoo. Frank and Ed report that it's empty and will confirm that again before we arrive. Darren will be following behind us in the support van with an EMP cannon mounted in the rear. If any cops do try to follow us, Steve will disable their vehicles with a burst from the cannon. Once we're in the warehouse, we'll change the license plates and color of our vehicles. Then we're back on Route 152 until we are out of Alabama. Any questions?"

"Won't it just be easier to ditch the vehicles?" Dillon asked. "Repainting them could take a while."

Carl laughed. "Who said anything about repainting them?"

Dillon looked confused. "You just did."

"No, I said we'd change the color of the vehicles. They are both covered with electroluminescent paint that changes color at the flick of a switch. Our SUV will go from white to red and the support van from white to dark grey simply by changing the electrical current."

"First jammers and EMP cannons, now this," Dillon exclaimed. "You guys sure have some impressive shit."

Carl grinned. "You ain't seen nothing yet."

CHAPTER TWENTY-FIVE

The following day Arleen pretended to be surprised by Dillon's arrival at the bar on a Saturday night. Diedra had called her earlier on her burner phone to give her the news that he'd made it into the secure section of the compound. They both knew that it was standard procedure for new members to celebrate at the bar.

"What are you doing here?" Arleen asked. "Can't get enough of me?"

"Can't blame me, babes, you know that you light my fire," Dillon replied.

The dozen or so AAM members that accompanied him laughed and whistled, and she could tell that they'd already had more than a few drinks.

Dillon whispered in Arleen's ear as he hugged her, "Got something really important to tell you."

"I hope that you'll be able to stay over at my place tonight," she said, loud enough for Carl to hear.

Dillon looked at the big man with a pleading expression and Carl said, "What the hell, it's your party. Besides, after tonight we'll all be confined to base for the next week."

"Thanks, Carl," Dillon said enthusiastically.

Arleen wondered what the news was and why Dillon wouldn't be allowed to leave the compound. She knew that full members of the AAM were free to come and go in the evenings when not on duty. She sat patiently through all the toasts and congratulations trying to drink as little as possible. Dillon on the other hand drank so much she worried that he might pass out. It was almost midnight as she helped him up the stairs to her apartment. He leaned heavily on her and she struggled to get the keys out of her purse.

After she'd closed the door she turned to him and said fiercely, "You can't be getting drunk like this, you'll blow your damn cover!"

"Gotcha!" he said, suddenly standing upright. "Told you I was a good actor."

Arleen was amazed. "You're not really drunk? You drank enough to floor an elephant."

"You seem to forget that, unlike my brother, I used to be an alcoholic as well as a drug addict. It takes way more than that to make me drunk."

"You must be so proud," Arleen said dryly.

Dillon ignored the comment. "I assume that Diedra told you about my promotion?"

"She did. I was also acting when I seemed surprised to see you."

"Good work, but what you don't know is that these guys want me to help them rob a bank next week."

"What! Oh my God, that's brilliant news."

"I know, we just have to arrest them during the robbery and our job here is done. I'm really starting to miss my dull, civilian life."

Arleen powered up the computer. "Get all the robbery details on the record ASAP."

Dillon nodded. "Perhaps a cup of black coffee before I begin. I may not be shit-faced, but I do have quite a buzz going."

———

Arleen listened intently as Dillon gave a detailed summary of the upcoming bank robbery in Alabama. She gave a gasp when he mentioned the electromagnetic-pulse cannon and another when he revealed the use of color-changing paint. "That stuff is still in the developmental stage at top-secret military sites," she commented once he'd finished.

Dillon gave her a serious look. "They must really have friends in high places. I wouldn't underestimate them."

"Believe me, we don't. I need to get this info to Diedra right now. I'll call her and tell her I'm sending it via encrypted email. She'll want to give you detailed instructions before you leave in the morning."

"Go ahead. While you do that, I'm going to bed. The next few days are probably going to be quite hectic."

"All right, I'll try not to wake you when I come to bed."

"Unless you're feeling horny. In that case I won't mind."

Arleen grinned at him. "Dream on, Mister. And by the way, good job. Your brother would be proud of you."

———

It felt like he'd just fallen asleep when Dillon felt Arleen shaking his shoulder, telling him to wake up. "Aah, so you are feeling horny," he said sleepily.

Arleen held up her phone. "Shush, you idiot, Diedra's on the line, she wants to speak to you."

Dillon sat upright and grabbed the phone. "What's up?"

Diedra got right to the point. "Were Jerry Barnes and Sandra Woods present at any time during the planning of the robbery?" she asked.

"I would have put that in my report if they were," he said testily.

"Relax, I just needed to make sure. So, as far as you know, the only people involved in the upcoming robbery are the ten at the briefing and the two already in Montgomery?"

"Correct, but I'm sure that all the top leadership know about it as well."

"Hearsay!" Diedra shouted.

Dillon was confused. "What?" he asked.

"That's what any decent defense attorney would say," Diedra

replied. "We won't be able to arrest anyone else at the AAM without concrete proof that they had any knowledge of your robbery group's actions."

"So, what are you saying?" Dillon asked.

"We need to let the bank robbery in Montgomery go ahead without any interference," Diedra replied.

"You've got to be joking?"

"I don't joke about things like this," she said calmly.

"What if someone gets killed or something? Surely the FBI will be held responsible."

"You said that they're only using non-lethal weapons. Anyway, nobody needs to know that we had prior knowledge of the robbery details."

"I can't believe this! I thought that my time here was almost up."

"Sorry to burst your bubble. The good news is that once you've taken part in this little exercise of theirs, they're more likely to let you in on the upcoming attack on the Muslims."

"Good news indeed," Dillon said sarcastically. "What if I get killed or hurt in Alabama?"

"You're a big boy, I'm sure that you can take care of yourself. Now, I need you to do a report on all the people you met in the secure compound. We need to run background checks and profiles on all of them."

"Right now!" Dillon exclaimed, looking at his watch. "It's almost three in the morning."

"Then you'd better get started. Who knows when you'll be allowed out of the AAM compound again?"

CHAPTER TWENTY-SIX

Dillon finally finished his summary around five-thirty on Sunday morning. Arleen had the day off and had agreed to drop him off at the compound around midday. "Back to bed," she said to him. "You can still get about five hours sleep."

"Don't have to tell me twice," he said, exhaustion showing through in his voice.

Arleen waited until he was asleep before contacting Diedra on her burner phone. "What's up?" the senior agent asked.

"I'm worried about Dillon. I don't think it's a good idea for him to take part in the upcoming bank robbery," Arleen answered.

"I understand your concern," Diedra said. "We've just got to put our faith in him and hope that he doesn't crack under the pressure."

"I could always give him something that'll ensure he's too ill to participate in the robbery," Arleen persisted.

"Believe me, that idea already crossed my mind. Deputy Director Shaw and I discussed the situation at great length last night. We eventually concluded that Dillon has to become a reliable and trusted member of the inner circle as soon as possible, and his participation in the bank robbery is paramount to that happening."

"I understand," Arleen said reluctantly, "but for the record, I think that we're pushing him way too fast."

"Duly noted, I just hope for all our sakes that you're wrong."

———

There was no rest for Dillon when he returned to the AAM compound. "Hope you had a good time last night." Carl winked. "Now it's back to work. We're going over the details again and again until everyone knows their role backwards."

They were in the living room of Carl's cabin, and several of the robbery team present groaned, while Alicia pleaded, "Please, Carl, give us a break."

"Tell me that when you're in prison or lying in a morgue!" he barked. "We'll stop when I'm satisfied."

Dillon had never seen this harsh side of Carl and kept his mouth shut, paying attention as they went over the contingencies. "What are our options if the local police do arrive?" Carl asked the group.

"Neutralize with non-lethal weapons and evade capture," one of the men answered.

"Correct!" Carl snapped. "Under no circumstances are innocent people to be harmed or killed by our operation. Do I make myself clear?" He glared at everyone present, and one by one they assented.

"So we should just surrender if escape becomes impossible?" Steve asked.

"That is correct," Carl answered. "Remember, we have friends in high places who'll make sure you don't spend forever in jail."

"Good to know," Dillon said. "When does this show get on the road?"

"We leave here early on Wednesday morning, staying overnight at a motel close to the Alabama border. We want our footprint in Alabama to be as small as possible. We'll leave the motel just before sunrise and be in position for the op at around ten-thirty."

Dillon noted the various military references, reinforcing his knowledge that Carl was a former special-forces operative. "When do I get to see my vehicle?" he asked.

"I think we're done here for now," Carl replied. "You and Darren follow me and we'll go check out your rides."

The two men dutifully followed their leader to the barn-like structure. Carl produced a ring containing several keys and unlocked the heavy padlock that secured the large door. "Very few people get the privilege of entering this building," he said over his shoulder, "you two keep what you see in here to yourselves. Understand?"

"Understood!" the two men said in unison. They helped Carl roll the heavy door open and he entered and flipped a switch. The cavernous interior was suddenly bathed in bright light and they both gasped.

Dillon was the first to speak. "Is that what I think it is?"

"If you're asking if it's a tank, then you would be correct." Carl grinned. "Well, actually a two man mini-version with a ninety-millimeter cannon mounted on top."

Dillon's eyes swept the interior, taking in as much as possible. "Very impressive, quite the arsenal," he said, pointing to a caged-off area toward the rear off the structure.

Carl led Darren and Dillon over and said proudly, "Got everything from handguns and automatic rifles to machine guns and RPG-7s."

"I thought we only use non-lethal weapons?" Dillon asked. "All this stuff looks pretty lethal to me."

"You bet your ass it is!" Carl replied. "Make no mistake, when the war against Islam starts, and it will soon, we'll be ready."

Dillon wanted to ask for more details, but Darren interrupted by asking, "Is one of those mine?" He pointed towards four white panel vans parked against the rear wall.

"No, they'll be used for something else," Carl said quickly.

Wonder what the hell that'll be, Dillon mused. The four vehicles all had raised suspensions to accommodate extra-large tires, as well as rugged-looking bull-bars on the front.

Carl led them to two white vehicles parked near the front. "These are your babies. Dillon, behold, the Jeep Grand Cherokee Trackhawk. It has a seven-hundred horsepower Hellcat engine, does zero to sixty in three and a half seconds and a top speed of one hundred and eighty miles per hour."

"I love it," Dillon said enthusiastically, noting the dark-tinted windows.

"Yeah, rub it in." Darren was less enthusiastic as he took in the plain-looking Ram ProMaster van parked alongside.

"Looks aren't everything," Carl quipped. "This baby has a two hundred and eighty horsepower V-6 engine, not to mention this." He led them to the rear of the vehicle and opened the double doors.

"What the hell is that?" Darren asked.

Carl smiled. "That's the electromagnetic-pulse-cannon I mentioned earlier. It'll stop any vehicle following you dead in its tracks. Well, anything built after nineteen-seventy with a microprocessor," he added.

Darren took in the contraption and seemed unconvinced. "Looks like something out of a Star Wars movie."

"Believe me, it works just fine," Carl said.

"So, these vehicles also change color at the push of a button?" Dillon asked, doubt showing through in his voice.

"Let me show you," Carl said. He remove a key from the bunch and opened the driver's door to the Jeep. He inserted the key into the ignition and powered up the beast. "Works off the battery so the ignition needs to be on," he explained. He showed them a dial built into the glove box. "Stand back and watch."

The two men watched in amazement as Carl twisted the dial and the vehicle's paint color swiftly changed from white to red. "I thought that you were just yanking our chains," Darren said. "It's like some sort of magic trick."

"Not magic, just technology." Carl climbed out the impressive-looking SUV. "Darren, your van does the same, except it'll turn a dark grey."

Equally astounded, Dillon asked, "When can we take them for a spin?"

"You need to get used to them, so I guess tonight will be fine. Just remember to stay on the back roads," Carl answered.

CHAPTER TWENTY-SEVEN

A lec Burns eyed Diedra with suspicion. "You're sure that there's nothing going on?" He and Agent Baker had just entered the war-room at the mansion, causing all conversation between the ATF and FBI members present to come to a screeching halt.

"Of course," she answered sweetly. "You'll be the first to know if we get any new intel from our undercover operative." In actuality, they had been arguing about what role to take during the upcoming robbery.

Some reasoned that it made more sense to warn the local federal authorities, who could then advise the local police not to intervene during the robbery. "There's no way that the local cops are going to sit idly by while a major bank in their town gets robbed," Diedra had argued. "Nobody but us must ever know that we had prior knowledge, especially the two new arrivals."

"This isn't exactly by the book," one of the ATF guys had protested.

"Desperate times call for desperate measures," Diedra had argued. "Remember that our ultimate goal here is to prevent a major terror attack on US soil. I'll take full responsibility for this decision."

———

Dillon felt relatively calm and relaxed as he lay in bed on Sunday night. The big SUV had handled like a dream, and his confidence was growing that the robbery would be successful. The main reason for his sense of well-being, however, was the fact that he'd gotten to speak to Lisa before leaving the bar earlier in the day.

Arleen would have been furious had she known, but she was speaking to the bar manager and he'd excused himself to use the restroom. He'd earlier noticed a pay-phone near the restroom entrance, which he surreptitiously used to contact his girlfriend in Las Vegas.

Lisa was ecstatic to hear from him and immediately asked when he was coming home. He'd lied and said that it wouldn't be much longer and promised not to get himself injured or killed.

When she'd pressed him for details on what he was doing or where he was, he'd told her that he loved her and hung up. Just hearing her voice had buoyed his spirits, and he felt ready for whatever lay ahead.

———

Arleen wasn't sure what she was feeling as she lay in bed in her small apartment, although conflicted would probably be the correct term. Dillon Hunt, aka Daniel Harper, had managed to get under her skin in a very short period of time. He had a great sense of humor and was always laughing and joking, unlike his more serious and driven brother, Michael.

She had tried to stifle her feelings for him in the past weeks, but the danger of his participation the upcoming robbery had brought her concern for him to the fore. It wasn't so much the physical danger, although if he cracked under the pressure and broke his cover, he was surely a dead man.

She had worked many undercover assignments and knew that even many of the best-trained agents eventually succumbed to the stress of a dual life. She tried to allay her fears by remembering how upbeat he'd seemed on the drive out to the compound.

Her lips still tingled from the hard kiss on the mouth she'd given him before he'd climbed out of the car. He'd seemed surprised, but he'd probably figured she was just playing her role since the guards at the gate were watching.

She eventually gave up on falling asleep, turning on the bedside lamp and reaching for her book. It made her think about how ridiculous he looked wearing the black and red sleeping mask, and she let out an involuntary giggle.

CHAPTER TWENTY-EIGHT

H*ere we go*, Dillon thought, bringing the SUV to a quick halt in front of the bank. Carl and the remaining three members of his team exited and strode towards the door without glancing left or right, as if they had important business inside. Alec and Kurt had just reported on the tactical frequency that the two guards had been neutralized.

No one seemed to notice anything untoward as he eased the Jeep forward, performing a quick U-turn further down the street and easing into a parking spot about sixty yards from the bank.

He heard one of the lookouts, Frank or Ed, say in his earpiece, "All clear, no cops around."

There had been all sorts of commotion on the drive to the bank as police cars rolled code-three towards the Capitol Building that had just received a bomb threat.

Darren had parked his van earlier in the alleyway behind the bank, where Alicia had quickly neutralized the bank's entire security system.

Dillon kept his vehicle running to take advantage of the powerful air-con, still feeling sweat dripping under the heavy tactical vest that Carl had insisted they all wear.

After what seemed like an eternity, he heard Carl's voice in his earpiece, "Ready for exfil, all clear?"

After a short pause, one of the lookouts replied, "Clear in the front."

"Back is also clear." Darren's voice crackled in his earpiece. Alec and Kurt would exit through the rear door and into the van.

Dillon shifted into drive and was about to press the accelerator when several things happened at once – Carl exited the front door carrying two large bags, his face still covered by the latex mask he'd slipped down when entering the bank. A passing tan-colored sedan suddenly screeched to a stop directly in front of the bank, and its lone occupant jumped out and pointed a pistol at Carl.

Dammit, probably an off-duty cop. Dillon thought. He heard one of the lookouts shout, "Front exit compromised, everyone exit through the rear!"

The cop was shouting something at Carl, the body of his car protecting him from a frontal attack. Without thinking Dillon pushed hard on the gas pedal and flew towards the unsuspecting cop. The dismayed man turned as the huge SUV barreled down on him, trying desperately to adjust his aim at the driver. The front of the SUV narrowly missed him and Dillon opened his door, hearing a thud as it connected with the unfortunate man, who bounced off the side of his vehicle and crumpled into a heap.

Dillon brought the Jeep to a halt and shouted at Carl to jump in. The large man moved quickly, yanking open the driver-side rear door and tossing in the bags. He clambered in, slammed the door and shouted, "Drive!"

Not needing to be told twice, Dillon floored it, making a left turn on two wheels. Another left brought him into the alley behind the bank, where he slammed to a stop behind the van. The other four members of Carl's team were waiting anxiously and quickly piled in. "Where are the bags?" Carl barked.

"We put them in the van!" one of the men shouted. "What the hell happened?"

"No time for that now." Carl turned to Dillon. "Get us the fuck outta here, exit plan B!"

Dillon nudged the Jeep past the van and Darren followed him at high speed down the alley. When Dillon reached the main road he braked and slowly made a right turn, trying not to draw attention. The van followed and Carl tapped Dillon on the shoulder. "Do you remember the route?"

"Of course, left at the next intersection then right onto the I-65 and over the river," Dillon calmly replied.

"That's it. And thanks for the quick thinking back there, that guy had me dead to rights."

"No problem, just hope I didn't hurt him too bad."

"I doubt it, you weren't going that fast." Carl turned and quickly explained what had transpired to the rest of the group.

They all congratulated Dillon, a couple of them patting him on the shoulder. "It was nothing," he said nonchalantly as he eased the SUV onto the I-65 north. He glanced in his rear-view mirror to make sure that the van was still following before exhaling slowly. "Looks like we made it."

His words were barely cold when the wailing sound of multiple sirens started up behind them.

CHAPTER TWENTY-NINE

Dillon felt an icy chill down his spine. "What the hell!" he cursed. "Where'd they come from?"

Carl turned and peered through the rear window. "Looks like a couple of highway patrol vehicles." He shouted into his mic for Darren to bring his van alongside the Jeep. "We've got to keep them behind us!"

As the van edged next to the SUV Steve's eager voice sounded in their earpieces, "Want me to zap them?"

"Do it!" Carl replied. "About a three-second burst."

Dillon checked his mirror again. The pursuing vehicles were about thirty yards behind them, traveling alongside each other at high speed. Suddenly both cars came to a screeching halt and Steve shouted in elation, "Sonofabitch, it worked, both cop cars are disabled!"

"Great job, Carl said.

Instead of acknowledging his leader's congratulations, Steve shouted, "Uh oh!"

"Now what?" Carl asked.

"Got a police chopper closing in fast," Steve replied. "What now?"

They were on the bridge crossing the Alabama River, and their off-ramp to R-152 would be coming up soon. Carl quickly instructed both drivers to slow down and let the helicopter catch up.

"Are you crazy?" Dillon shouted. "We need to go faster, not slower!"

"We'll never outrun a chopper," Carl said calmly. "Steve, wait 'til he's within two hundred yards and hit him with the EMP."

"Are you sure?" Steve said. "Won't they crash?"

"That's why I want both of you to slow right down," Carl replied. "At slow speed and low altitude they'll probably survive."

Dillon and Darren both brought their vehicles down to around thirty miles per hour, and a few seconds later Steve shouted, "He's in range!"

"Zap him!" Carl shouted.

"He's going down!" Steve shouted excitedly, then, "Oh shit!"

Dillon's rear view mirror was suddenly filled by the image of the stricken helicopter as it slammed into the tarmac and skidded towards them at high speed. "Floor it!" he shouted to Darren, as he did the same.

The powerful SUV's engine roared and it bucked forward, leaving the slower van behind. Carl turned and watched in horror as the swirling blades of the chopper came ever closer to the van behind them. Suddenly the left-hand skid of the chopper buckled and collapsed, bringing it quickly to a halt. The swirling rotor blades made contact with the road, snapping off and flying in several directions. One narrowly missed the van, and Carl fervently prayed that no bystanders in the vicinity had been hit by the airborne missiles.

"Damn, that was close!" Darren shouted. "Off-ramp's coming up. Dillon, you take it first and I'll follow."

"Roger that!" Dillon shouted, getting into the swing of things. Adrenaline was rapidly coursing through his veins, and he'd never felt more alive.

"The warehouse will be coming up on our right in about four miles," Carl said as they turned east onto the R-152. "Both of you keep within the speed limit and don't do anything stupid to attract attention."

———

"The shit's hitting the fan in Montgomery." Milford Olson looked up from his computer screen where he'd been monitoring law enforcement communications from the town.

"What do you mean?" Diedra asked.

"The getaway obviously didn't go quite as smoothly as planned," he answered.

"Please tell me that Dillon's okay and that no one's dead."

"The fugitives appear to have vanished into thin air. However an off-duty cop was injured and three occupants of a crashed police chopper have bruises and minor injuries."

"How bad is the cop?" Diedra inquired.

Olson squinted at the screen. "A couple of broken ribs and a major concussion, but sounds like he'll be okay."

Diedra exhaled. "Thank God for that." It was one thing to cover up the robbery, but if anyone was killed it would probably mean the end of her career and possibly even jail time. "Anything else?"

"A highway patrol cop has whiplash from being rear-ended. Apparently two of their chase cars just suddenly stopped running."

"I guess that their EMP device really does work then. Probably how they brought down the chopper as well," Diedra said grimly.

"These guys are decidedly more dangerous than just some dumb-assed militia group," Olson said. "They have technology and weapons that aren't even supposed to exist yet."

Diedra fixed her subordinate with an icy stare. "That's what concerns me. They obviously have high-ranking support from both the government and military sectors."

"Let's face it, a Muslim-free America is probably on the wish-list of most truly patriotic Americans," Olson said.

"Can't say that I don't agree with them," she grudgingly admitted. "Just don't like their methods. Terrorism remains terrorism when non-combatants are murdered."

"Amen to that," Olson said. "What time are Tweedle-Dee and Tweedle-Dumb returning?" The demeaning nicknames had recently been bestowed upon the two intrusive Homeland Security agents.

Diedra checked her watch. "We've still got plenty of time; erase or hide any mention of the robbery in Alabama. Burns would love to get his grubby little paws on something juicy like that." The annoying agent had been bugging her to take a look at the AAM compound. With Dillon out of the compound, it had been the perfect day for the two of them to accompany the surveillance team. It also gave Diedra and her team the freedom to monitor the events occurring in Alabama.

Olson smiled. "Sooner or later we're going to have to give them something definitive."

Diedra chuckled. "Yeah, but I envision it being later, not sooner."

CHAPTER THIRTY

Dillon watched as Carl and Steve deftly replaced the license tags on the two getaway vehicles. Off came the fake Mississippi tags and on went fake Georgia tags. *Clever misdirection,* Dillon thought. *They'll be expecting us to head west instead of east.*

The SUV and van had already undergone their amazing color transformations inside the abandoned warehouse. "Okay, has everything been transferred to the van?" Carl asked.

"All done," Darren replied. "Your vehicle is clean."

The plan was to put all the incriminating items, such as tactical vests and money bags, in the van. The Jeep with its seven occupants would proceed on the I-85 north past Atlanta and into South Carolina. The van would follow a couple of miles behind, giving them plenty of warning should the lead vehicle encounter any roadblocks.

"Remember, obey the traffic rules at all times," Carl said to Darren. "All it takes is one illegal lane change and the three of you are busted."

Steve and Alicia would accompany Darren in the van, and the pretty little computer wizard said, "Don't worry, I'll smack him upside his head if he does anything stupid."

"You know I like it rough, baby." Darren smirked.

"In your dreams." Alicia laughed.

"Enough, you two," Carl growled. "Alright, everyone to their vehicles, let's get this show on the road."

———

Arleen was in a buoyant mood as she served a customer at the bar. She'd just received a text from Diedra on her burner that everything was okay and that Dillon's tracker indicated that he was currently traveling through Georgia.

Should be back later tonight, she thought. *I wonder if he'll come to the bar tomorrow?*

Her thoughts were interrupted as a stunning-looking brunette entered and sidled up to the bar. "What'll it be?" Arleen asked her pleasantly.

"Light beer please," the woman answered.

Arleen handed her the drink. "Haven't seen you here before, just passing through?"

"New to town," she answered. "In fact, maybe you can help me. I'm looking for somebody." She fumbled in her purse and extracted a photo. "Have you seen this guy around?"

Arleen took the photo, looked at it and just about had a coronary. The photo showed the beautiful woman wrapped in the arms of none other than Daniel Harper, aka Dillon Hunt.

CHAPTER THIRTY-ONE

D illon and the Jeep's other occupants waited on the roadside a few miles from the compound and Darren pulled the van in behind them a few minutes later. Carl jumped out the SUV and stretched his legs. "Good job, everyone," he said.

The van's three occupants exited the vehicle and Carl, Alec and Kurt took their places. They would drive it to an undisclosed location where the money from the robbery would be counted and stashed away. "No point in having any evidence on AAM property," Carl had mentioned earlier. "And the fewer people who know where it's located, the better."

While Darren, Steve and Alicia climbed into the SUV, the van executed a U-turn and sped off. Dillon pulled to a stop a little later at the entrance to the compound. The two guards approached and ordered everyone to exit the vehicle. Dillon noticed that they were both from the secure section and not probies. "How come you guys are pulling guard duty?" he asked. "It's not Friday."

"The probies were all sent packing yesterday," the guard replied grimly.

"What the hell for?" Alicia asked. "Now we have to do all the cooking, cleaning and guard duty."

"The head honchos got word yesterday that an undercover federal agent had infiltrated our organization," he replied. "Since the probies hadn't all been properly vetted yet, they figured that it'd be safer just to get rid of everyone."

"Man, that sucks," Darren said.

"Security's also been tightened," the guard said. "Sorry, but I've got to check all of you with the wand. You also need to empty your pockets and your carry bags."

Dillon glanced at his watch, relieved to see that it was nowhere near transmission time. *How the hell did they figure out that they'd been infiltrated?* he wondered. *I need to get this info to Diedra as soon as possible.*

———

"Are you comfortable?" Arleen asked.

"As comfortable as can be expected," Lisa Cox answered dryly, lifting her duct-taped wrists. She was seated on the small couch in Arleen's apartment.

Arleen held her pistol loosely and regarded Daniel Harper's girlfriend. "What the hell were you thinking?" she asked the beautiful woman. After she'd gotten over her initial shock of seeing the photo in the bar, Arleen had reacted casually. She'd told the woman that she had seen the man in the photo and in fact knew where he lived, and that she would take her to him after she'd finished her shift.

Arleen got Lisa up to her apartment by saying that she needed to fetch her car keys. Opening the bedside drawer, she'd produced the gun instead of the keys.

Ignoring the question, Lisa said, "I take it that you're FBI, working with Daniel?"

"Damn straight, are you trying to get him killed?" Arleen hissed.

"I missed him and wanted to see him," Lisa said defiantly. "Just wanted to make sure that he's okay."

"Well, thanks to your little stunt, you could well have blown his cover. How many other people have you shown that photo to?"

"You're the only one, I promise," Lisa answered contritely. "I really wasn't trying to put him in any danger."

Arleen tried to check her temper. "How long have you been in town and where are you staying?"

"I only arrived this morning on the Greyhound. I checked into a cheap motel on the outskirts of town."

"Here's what's going to happen," Arleen barked. "We're going for a drive to the motel where you're going to collect your things and check out. Two agents will meet us there and take you to meet my boss. If I were you I'd lose the attitude; she's not nearly as nice a person as I am. You'll be very lucky not to end up back in prison."

CHAPTER THIRTY-TWO

The following morning after breakfast Carl convened a meeting of the robbery participants in his cabin. "First, the good news," he said. "We counted the money and it came to a little over two and a half million dollars. That will go a long way to helping our cause."

After the applause and whistles died down Darren asked, "How did you get the bank manager to open the safe so easily?"

"Quite simple really," Carl replied. "We knew that the manager and his assistant were having an affair, so I held a gun to her head and threatened to blow her brains out if he didn't cooperate."

"Very clever," Dillon said. "I suppose the gun wasn't even real?"

Carl grinned. "Oh, it was real alright. I was the only one carrying a lethal weapon, since I couldn't trust you lot not to disobey orders."

Dillon was shocked. "Would you have shot that off-duty cop if I hadn't intervened?"

"Put it this way," Carl replied. "I wouldn't have killed him, that's for sure. Probably would have put a round in his right shoulder, causing him to drop his weapon."

"Not the easiest of shots," Dillon said doubtfully.

Alec laughed loudly. "I served with Carl in the SEALs; he could shoot the balls off a gnat from a hundred yards. Believe me, he would have made the shot."

"Thanks for the endorsement, Alec," Carl said. "Now for the not so good news. As you all know by now, we recently received news that the FBI has a mole inside our organization. Since all of us on this side of the fence had been thoroughly vetted, the leadership thought it expedient to release all the probies. That's not to say that it isn't possible that the spy is still among us. For that reason security has been tightened and random checks will be carried out on all personnel, me and the other leaders included."

"What about all the chores?" Alicia asked.

"Glad you asked." Carl grinned at her. "I know how you love peeling potatoes and chopping onions."

"The kitchen is my worst nightmare," Alicia moaned. "Please, I'll do as much guard duty as possible instead."

"The duty rosters for the next month have already been placed on the notice board in the dining hall," Carl said. "You guys are welcome to switch shifts or chores, as long as the duty officer is informed before the shift starts."

"I like to consider myself a budding chef," Dave said to Alicia. "You can have all my guard duties and I'll do your kitchen shifts."

"Done," Alicia said, leaping over and giving Dave a kiss on the cheek.

"One more thing," Carl said. He reached into a backpack and began tossing a stack of bills to everyone present. "Ten thousand dollars each in recognition of a job well done."

Every member of the inner sanctum already received a two thousand dollar a month stipend to buy toiletries and such. "Oh boy, now I can get a PS4," Steve said.

"Such a child," Alicia ribbed him. "I'm going into town tonight to get shit-faced. Who's with me?"

There was a general consensus from everyone and Carl cautioned, "Enjoy it; most of you start your shifts tomorrow."

As they all filed out, Carl grasped Dillon by the shoulder. "Wait a second."

Now what? Dillon thought. *Please tell me I'm not a suspect.*

Once they were alone Carl turned to Dillon. "I just wanted to thank you again for saving my ass back there. The truth is, I had both my hands full with the money bags and the cop probably would have shot me long before I reached my gun."

Dillon waved him off. "It was nothing."

"Oh, yes it was!" Carl persisted. "That cop could have shot and killed you. I'll never forget this. If there's ever anything you need, just let me know."

"Now that you mention it, how about lending me your car so I can stay overnight at Arleen's?" Dillon asked.

Carl enveloped Dillon in a giant bear hug. "You got it, buddy. At least I know one thing for sure, you're not an FBI spy."

"How's that?" Dillon asked.

"No federal agent would have taken out a cop like that and risked his own life to save me," Carl said emphatically.

———

In the war-room at the FBI's temporary base, Diedra's attitude toward Lisa was not quite as friendly. "I should just throw your dumb ass back in prison!" she shouted.

Lisa was close to tears. "I'm sorry," she choked out.

"Sorry just doesn't cut it. This isn't some sort of game. People's lives are at risk!"

"I didn't realize that he was working undercover," Lisa said. "He just said that he was helping you guys with a case."

Diedra was exasperated. "He wasn't supposed to tell you anything at all. I should throw him back in prison as well!"

"Please don't!" Lisa wailed. "What if I promise to be on the next bus out of town?"

Diedra was about to reply when Agent Burns entered the room. "Who's she?" the annoying agent asked.

"Nobody you need to know," Diedra said brusquely. "Just one of my CI's who stepped out of line, it has nothing to do with our operation."

"Okay then," Burns said, although his expression showed that he didn't really believe her.

CHAPTER THIRTY-THREE

Dillon's mood was upbeat as he entered the bar just after five in the afternoon. Diedra would surely be upset that the AAM knew about the FBI's undercover operation but pleased that he wasn't a suspect because of his actions during the robbery.

Arleen had just finished her shift and came over to greet him. "I'm glad that you're here, I thought that we'd go and catch a movie tonight."

She seemed a little tense, but he dismissed that as a result of the robbery in Montgomery. They had a quick drink before leaving the bar. As they climbed into Arleen's car, she turned to him. "We're not really going to the movies. Diedra wants to see you straight away."

"Is it about the off-duty cop?" Dillon asked. "I didn't hit him that hard. Anyway, I heard that he wasn't too badly injured."

"You'll find out when we get there," Arleen replied cryptically, remaining silent during the rest of the journey. She kept checking her mirrors to see if they were being followed, and once she was satisfied, she pulled the car into the drive leading to the mansion.

Arleen parked her car around back and led him to the pool house that was separate from the main building.

As they entered, Diedra and Agent Olson rose to greet him.

"Glad to see that you're still in one piece," Diedra said, although she didn't sound particularly happy.

"What's going on?" Dillon asked. "You guys are all acting really weird."

"Maybe you should ask her!" Diedra barked as Milford Olson let Lisa into the room.

"What the hell?" Dillon stammered. "What are you doing here?"

"Good question," Diedra said as the couple embraced.

"I'm so sorry," Lisa replied. "I missed you and just wanted to make sure that you were okay."

"How the heck did you manage to find me?" Dillon asked.

Lisa's face took on a smug look. "Remember that computer dude that cloned the room keys for us that one time? I gave him the number you called me from and he traced it to the bar here in Union."

"Dammit, woman, you were just supposed to wait for me. What were you thinking?" Dillon asked.

"Excellent question!" Diedra shouted. "What the hell were YOU thinking when you called her?"

Dillon's face reddened. "Sorry, I just wanted her to know that I was okay and not to worry."

Diedra exploded. "Well, that sure turned out all right; your dumb-ass girlfriend was showing your photo all over town!"

"I'm not a dumb-ass!" Lisa retorted angrily, swiveled and pointed at Arleen. "That woman there was the only one who saw the photo."

"So you say," Diedra responded irately.

"Okay, enough!" Dillon interjected. "What's done is done. I have important information regarding our operation."

"Spoken like a true federal agent," Lisa said proudly.

Diedra addressed Olson, "Take her back to the house, we'll do the debrief here. I don't want those two idiots from Homeland to see Dillon."

"Who the hell is Dillon?" Lisa asked.

"I am," Dillon replied. "Dillon Hunt is my alias."

"Whoa! Again, too much information," Diedra said quickly.

Lisa grinned. "I like it, sounds manly."

Dillon grinned back. "Thanks." He turned to Diedra. "I think that Lisa should stay and get caught up on what we're doing, I may need her help."

"Are you out of your frigging mind?" Diedra exploded once again. "One civilian on this op is already giving me grey hair, I sure as shit don't need another one!"

"Just listen to what I have to say first," Dillon said calmly. "If you don't agree, you can ship her out first thing tomorrow."

"I always wanted to be a spy," Lisa said happily.

"We're not spies, we're government agents," Arleen said in a condescending tone.

Exasperated, Diedra gave in. "Okay, she can stay for now. What's the big news?"

Dillon paused before dropping the bombshell. "The AAM know that they've been infiltrated by the FBI."

The lead agent's face paled. "What the hell? You've got to be joking."

Dillon's expression turned serious. "I wish that I was. They don't know who it is yet, but they're taking extreme precautions. They got rid of all the un-vetted people and are doing random checks and searches on all the remaining members, even the leadership."

Olson interjected, "A few days back we observed all the people from the southern section leaving and wondered what the heck was going on."

Diedra fixed Dillon with an icy stare. "Any idea how they found out?"

"All I know is that they have someone on the inside who leaked the info," Dillon replied.

"I trust everyone on the team," Diedra responded emphatically, "as well as those at FBI and ATF headquarters. We would never have gotten this far if any of them was an informant."

"What about the two new kids on the block?" Arleen suggested.

Dillon looked confused. "What's she talking about?"

"Homeland Security recently found out about the impending attack and sent a couple of agents to join us," Diedra responded.

Dillon looked angry. "Nice of you to tell me."

"You didn't need to know," Diedra said.

"Would you have told my brother?" Dillon asked.

Diedra hesitated. "I see your point; from now on we won't keep anything from you."

"Much appreciated," Dillon said sarcastically. "Now tell me about these new guys, do they know my identity?"

"Actually, it's one guy and one woman, Agents Alec Burns and Amanda Baker. And no, they don't know your identity yet," Diedra replied.

"It must be one of them," Olson said. "Everyone else involved in the op knows Dillon's identity."

"Remember how hard Burns pushed when he first arrived?" Diedra asked. "I think that it's about time that we had a little chat with him."

"What about her?" Arleen asked, pointing at Lisa, who'd followed the proceedings open-mouthed.

"Yeah, what the hell do you need her for?" Diedra asked Dillon.

Dillon quickly described the large shed that contained all the vehicles and weapons. "I need to get hold of a key so that I can investigate further. It might contain clues as to where the attack will be taking place."

"And what does Lisa have to do with that?" Diedra asked.

"She just happens to be the best pick-pocket I've ever known," Dillon replied.

"You must be so proud," Diedra responded dryly. "Whose pocket is she going to pick?"

"Carl always carries his bunch of keys around with him. If I can get him to the bar, Lisa could strike up a conversation with him and do her thing," Dillon replied.

"What if he doesn't respond and just ignores her?" Arleen asked.

Lisa spoke firmly, "Please, I know what I'm doing. No man on earth will ignore me, especially when I'm wearing a really low-cut dress."

"Unless he's gay," Olson commented.

Diedra finally cracked a small smile. "Okay, you three stay here and work out the details. Agent Olson and I are going to have a little chat with Burns."

CHAPTER THIRTY-FOUR

"I don't know what you're talking about," Homeland Security Agent Alec Burns protested.

"Is it true that your father was badly injured in the attack on the Pentagon on nine-eleven?" Diedra pressed. She and Agent Olson were grilling the hapless agent in the mansion's well-appointed and private study.

"Of course, I've never kept that a secret," Burns replied. "He lost a leg and was totally blinded."

Diedra persisted. "One would think that you'd be totally sympathetic to AAM's cause."

"Look, I hate radical Islam as much as the next man," he affirmed, "but facilitating a terrorist attack on American soil, I draw the line at that. I took an oath to protect this country from all enemies, foreign and domestic."

"So, you never contacted the AAM leaders to inform them that the FBI had infiltrated their ranks?" Olson shouted.

Burns appeared shocked by the allegation. "Are you crazy? Of course not. I don't even know the identity of your undercover agent."

"But you tried pretty hard to find out," Diedra said. "Even phoned your deputy director if I remember correctly."

"Of course I did, he's the one who ordered me to find out the agent's identity as quickly as possible," Burns retorted. "When I told him that you wouldn't budge, he ordered me to back off and find out some other way."

"Why would he be so interested?" Diedra asked.

Burns glared at her. "You'll have to ask him yourself. He informed Agent Baker and myself that we were going on a top-secret mission and not to contact anyone at the agency besides him. I was just obeying orders."

"Sounds pretty fishy to me. So no one else at Homeland knows about our infiltration of the AAM?" Olson asked.

"Not as far as I know," Burns answered. "Surely you're not suggesting that the deputy director is involved with this militia group?"

Diedra ignored the question. "What about Agent Baker, what's her story?"

Burns laughed. "Forget it, she only recently graduated and joined the agency. This is her first assignment. Besides, she's dating a Muslim dude who works the Middle East desk at Homeland."

"Be a good cover," Olson commented.

"Look, why don't you just give the two of us a lie-detector test?" Burns asked. "You'll see that I'm telling the truth."

"That's an excellent idea," Diedra said. "Agent Olson, please set it up. In the meantime, I want both your cell phones and you'll be confined to your quarters."

Burns looked her in the eyes. "If that's what it takes, you'll see that we're both totally innocent."

Diedra returned his stare with a grim expression. "You realize that if both of you are cleared, it means that Deputy Director Roger Wells of Homeland Security is probably our mole?"

———

Back at the pool house Lisa asked Arleen, "So what's your role in this little scam?"

"It's a major federal investigation, not a little scam," Arleen replied pointedly. "I'm Dillon's contact at the bar, pretending to be his girlfriend."

"Oh, that's nice!" Lisa said heatedly. "Have you tried to screw him yet?"

Arleen tried to keep her voice even. "Actually, I'm way too professional for that. We both keep to our sides of the bed."

"What!" Lisa choked. "You sleep in the same bed together?"

Dillon overheard the question as he returned from the bathroom in the pool house and answered, "Yes, we do. Don't worry, babes, I've only got eyes for you."

"You'd better. Besides, she's not your type," Lisa said. "You prefer your women more feminine."

Arleen pretended to ignore the implied insult and asked Dillon, "Okay, so what did you have in mind?"

"First, I need to get Carl to the bar," he replied. "That might take a few days. Just tell everyone that Lisa is an old friend who's in town to visit for a few days. That means that the two of you will have to be nice to each other, think you can manage that?"

Lisa pouted. "I can if she can."

Arleen glared at her. "Like I said, I'm a professional. Just remember that Dillon's life is on the line here, so don't screw up."

"Mmm, Dillon, I really do like that name. Maybe you should consider a permanent change, babes." Lisa laughed.

"Back to the plan, please," Arleen said. "What's next?"

"Once Carl's at the bar you'll text Lisa to come down, if she isn't already there."

Lisa appeared horrified. "What do you mean come down? I'm staying at her place?"

"Of course, where else would an old friend stay?" Arleen replied, finally enjoying herself.

"But there's only the one bed," Lisa said.

"That's right, honey," Arleen said sweetly.

"Just keep your hands to yourself, I don't swing that way," Lisa said.

Arleen gave Dillon a sly wink. "Don't worry, you're not my type."

Dillon continued, "Once Lisa enters the bar, you'll introduce her to Carl and me as an old friend visiting you. After a short while I'll leave the two of them alone. Lisa, you sweet-talk him, ask him to buy you a drink or something."

Lisa laughed. "Please, babes, remember who you're talking to, I got this."

"I know you do." Dillon grinned. "Just don't overdo it. Carl is a real Southern gentleman."

"My favorite type," Lisa said. "What do I do once I've got the keys?"

"Excuse yourself and head to the ladies' room. There you'll make a quick imprint of the key, return to the bar and get the keys back into his pocket."

"Describe the key to me," Lisa ordered, suddenly all business.

Dillon grabbed a pen and pad from the table and quickly drew a rough sketch. "There's six keys on the ring. None of the others look like this one, it's an old-fashioned padlock key."

"Got it," Lisa said confidently. "What do I use for the impression?"

"Arleen, can you organize a small tin filled with baker's clay or something?" Dillon asked.

The agent appeared slighted by her small part in the plan. "I'm sure that it's something I can handle."

"Good, once you FBI guys have the impression, get the key made for me as soon as possible."

"Aye aye, Captain," Arleen said sarcastically. "That just leaves one question."

Dillon raised an eyebrow. "What's that?"

Arleen stifled a laugh. "Which one of you is sleeping in the bed with me tonight?"

CHAPTER THIRTY-FIVE

As it turned out, neither Lisa nor Dillon got to share Arleen's bed. Lisa slept in the bedroom of the pool house, while Arleen, Olson and Diedra listened intently as Dillon recorded the events that occurred in Montgomery.

"What made you do it?" Diedra asked, referring to Dillon's actions when the off-duty cop drew his weapon on Carl.

"Several thoughts went through my head at once," Dillon answered. "First and foremost was the fact that Carl seemed to be my greatest ally at the compound. Secondly, if I got busted as well, there goes the whole operation. That would mean that Lisa and I were headed back in prison."

"Weren't you worried about getting shot?" Arleen asked.

"To be honest, the thought did cross my mind for a split second, but then instinct took over and I just floored the gas pedal."

"On the downside, you could have killed that cop," Olson said severely.

Dillon grimaced. "That was never my intention. I swerved just before I hit him, knowing the door would do far less damage."

"And you were correct," Diedra said, "he's due to be released from hospital in the morning."

"Good to hear, now where was I?" Dillon went back to recording the next sequence of events. It was just after four-thirty in the morning by the time he finished.

"Alright, you three had better get back to Arleen's apartment before the town starts waking up." Diedra said. "Are we all set on the key thing?" she asked.

"We are," Arleen answered. "When do you think you'll get Carl to the bar?" she asked Dillon.

"Won't be tonight," he answered. "I'm on guard duty. I'll try for tomorrow or the day after."

"What if he doesn't bite?" Olson asked.

Dillon laughed. "Believe me, after saving his ass in Alabama, I'm his favorite person right now. He'll be there, I guarantee it."

———

Carl was checking on the guards as Dillon brought the car to a stop at the entrance boom, just after six in the morning. He'd taken a shower and changed his clothes at Arleen's but still felt tired from pulling an all-nighter.

"You're back early," Carl commented as the guards searched the vehicle.

"Arleen has an old friend staying with her for a few days," Dillon said. "Hardly got any sleep with the two of them catching up, you know how women are."

"I do indeed." Carl laughed. "You really look beat, better get some rest before your duty tonight."

"Is it okay if I give breakfast a miss?" Dillon asked.

"Sure, no problem. I'll let the others know," Carl said. All meals were normally compulsory for those not on duty.

"How about you and I grab a couple of beers tomorrow afternoon?" Dillon asked.

"Don't know, things are quite hectic here right now," Carl said.

"Come on, the least you can do is buy a drink for the guy who saved your ass."

Carl smiled. "Alright, since you put it like that, I'd be happy to."

CHAPTER THIRTY-SIX

Dillon and Carl entered the bar just before four the following afternoon. They took a seat at the bar and Dillon leaned over and gave Arleen a kiss on the cheek. After she served their beers, Dillon watched out the corner of his eye as Arleen sent a quick text on her phone.

Lisa entered the bar right on cue about five minutes later. She looked stunning in a little black dress that showed plenty of cleavage. "Well, aren't you a big fella?" Lisa said, taking the empty barstool next to Carl.

"Excuse me," Carl said, flustered at receiving attention from such a beautiful woman.

Arleen laughed as she came over. "Carl, I'd like you to meet my friend Lisa. She's staying with me for a few days."

"Oh!" he said, sounding relieved. "Pleased to meet you, ma'am."

"Pleasure's all mine," Lisa said coyly, holding out her hand for Carl to kiss.

After he did so, Lisa said to him, "Such a gentleman, a Texan too by the sound of your accent?"

"That's correct, ma'am," he replied, "born and raised in Fort Worth."

"A Dallas Cowboys fan then?" she inquired.

Carl smiled. "Of course, America's team."

"Pity that they aren't doing so well lately," Dillon said. "Worst thing Jerry Jones ever did was getting rid of Jimmy Johnson as head coach. Especially after winning him two Super Bowls."

"Couldn't agree more," Lisa said. "I actually tried out to be a Cowboys cheerleader, but didn't quite make the cut."

"Their loss," Carl said, trying to keep his eyes from straying to her ample breasts.

"Well, aren't you just so sweet," Lisa said. She put her hand on his arm and stood on tiptoes to give him a kiss on the cheek.

He appeared flushed and stammered, "Can I buy you a drink?"

"I would love that," Lisa said, giving him a seductive smile. "A dirty martini with two olives, but first I need to powder my nose and fix my makeup. Where's the little girls' room?"

Carl couldn't see any sign of a blemish on her perfect face but pointed out the ladies' restroom anyway. "I'll be right back," Lisa said. He tried not to watch her tight ass wriggling as she walked away but failed miserably.

"Isn't she something else?" Dillon asked, returning from where he'd been talking to Arleen.

Avoiding the question, Carl asked, "How does Arleen know her?"

"High school friends, grew up in the same small town in Iowa," Dillon replied. "You know what they say about corn-fed girls."

Carl had no idea but nodded anyway. He waved for Arleen to come over. "Two more beers and a dirty martini with two olives."

"Don't let my friend take advantage of your generosity," Arleen said sternly.

"She's not," Carl said quickly. "I offered."

Just then Lisa returned and asked, "What's going on?"

"I don't want you asking my customers for drinks," Arleen said.

"I didn't!" Lisa said defensively. "Come, Carl, let's go sit at a table, Arly can be such a cow sometimes." She put her arm around him and led him to a booth at the back, calling over her shoulder, "Please bring our drinks over, bar-lady," in a bitchy voice.

Carl gave Dillon a bewildered glance, but he just shrugged as if to say, 'you're on your own, buddy.'

Arleen whispered to Dillon after delivering the drinks, "When do you think she'll do it?"

"Already done," Dillon said confidently.

"What? I didn't see anything."

"I could hardly tell either, and I was looking for it. I told you she was good," Dillon said proudly.

———

"Well?" Alec Burns asked.

"You and Agent Baker both passed," Diedra replied.

The Homeland Security agent looked smug until Milford Olson said, "There are many ways to evade a lie-detector test."

"I'm the best in the business. If I say they passed, then they passed," Jeanna Moore said indignantly. The FBI consultant had flown in from Virginia that morning to administer the test.

"I'll take your word for it, thank you for your time," Diedra said, trying to defuse the situation. "Agent Olson, please have one of the ATF agents drive Miss Moore to the airport."

After they left, Agent Burns asked, "So what now?"

"We have to assume that Deputy Director Wells leaked the information," Diedra replied.

"That's impossible," Burns argued. "He has the highest possible security clearance."

"All the more worrisome," Diedra said. "Think about it, how much easier would his job be without any Muslims living in America?"

"I suppose so," the agent said grudgingly.

"Will he be arrested?" Amanda Baker asked.

Diedra just laughed. "We have no proof at this point, just suppositions. We'll try to get presidential approval for surveillance on him."

"Or we could use the situation to our advantage," the pretty young agent said.

"Agent Baker, this is really out of your league," Burns said belligerently.

"Quiet, Burns!" Diedra barked. "Let's hear what she has to say."

"What if we used Director Wells to relay disinformation to the AAM?" Baker asked.

"I like it." Diedra laughed. "Agent Burns could name one of the other AAM members as the FBI undercover agent. If he gets expelled then we'll not only have evidence on Wells, but our man will be safe as well."

"So it is a man?" Burns said triumphantly.

"I suppose that you guys deserve to know the truth after every-thing I've put you through," Diedra said. She gave them the abridged version of how Daniel Harper became Dillon Hunt.

"Wow, that's ballsy," Burns said in admiration once she'd finished. "Using an ex-con to take the place of a dead FBI agent."

"Won't they just kill the person that we throw under the bus?" Baker asked, concern showing through in her voice.

"It's a chance we'll have to take," Diedra replied. "However, I severely doubt it. Killing a supposed federal agent will bring way too much heat down on them. They'll be trying to stay under the radar with the upcoming attack that they're planning."

CHAPTER THIRTY-SEVEN

Diedra and her team, which now included the two cleared Homeland Security agents, spent hours combing through the files of the rest of the AAM members. The scapegoat had to be someone who was a likely candidate.

Eventually Agent Burns said, "I think that we've found our man."

"Who is it?" Diedra asked.

Burns handed her a file. "Vincent Post, aka Quinton Small. After some serious digging it appears that Mister Post only came into existence about twelve years ago at the age of twenty-eight. It seems that he assumed the identity of a baby that died of complications a few months after being born in nineteen seventy-eight."

Diedra quickly read the file. "So, Quinton Small served a six-year sentence for sexual assault on a minor. He was a registered sex offender until he just disappeared from the radar a year after being released."

"Precisely," Burns said. "I seriously doubt that he's told anyone at the AAM what his real name is. A group like that wouldn't take kindly to a child-molester."

"No doubt," Diedra confirmed. "They probably only checked

back about ten years, during which time he served as a firefighter in New York and a productive member of society, using the name Vincent Post. Probably told the AAM that he lost many comrades when the Twin Towers collapsed."

"Perfect," Agent Olson said. "Just the mere fact that he's using an assumed name will be enough for the AAM leadership to believe he's the mole."

Burns jumped in, "And on the upside, who really cares if they do kill a child-molester."

"Now, Agent Burns, we need to do our best to make sure that doesn't happen," Diedra said, but she didn't sound very convincing.

Burns shrugged. "If you say so. Should I make the call to Director Wells?"

"Let's wait a day or two," Diedra replied. "I want Dillon to be in the loop when this goes down. I promised not to keep anything from him in the future."

"Who cares, he's just a jailbird," Burns said dismissively.

"We care!" Agent Olson said severely. "He's risking his life for this mission, something I don't see you doing."

"Now boys, play nice," Diedra said. "I also want him to have the key before we do this. Maybe during all the commotion he can sneak a look inside that barn."

———

Dillon was on guard duty again, although with summer in full swing it wasn't cold, so he didn't mind too much. He was manning the boom-gate and was paired with an un-talkative former soldier. This gave him time to reflect on the unexpected appearance of Lisa.

They hadn't managed to spend any time alone together, but he hoped that would change tomorrow night when he spent the night at Arleen's apartment. *Not that Arleen's just going to just hand over her bed so we can do the wild-thing*, Dillon mused. Was it his imagination, or did Arleen seem jealous? She definitely appeared put out by Lisa's arrival on the scene.

His reverie was interrupted by the arrival of a large truck. Its brakes squealed as it came to an abrupt halt in front of the boom. The other guard didn't seem surprised by the late-night appearance of such a large vehicle and said, "I've got this." He approached the driver, but Dillon couldn't make out the muted conversation.

The guard indicated for Dillon to open the boom and the truck roared through, heading towards the large barn. *Strange that he didn't search the truck or the driver,* Dillon thought.

"What was that all about?" Dillon asked when the guard returned.

"Nothing you need to know about!" he said curtly.

Now you've made me really curious, Dillon thought. *Hope I get that key tomorrow night.*

CHAPTER THIRTY-EIGHT

Dillon's arrival at the bar the following afternoon was greeted enthusiastically by Arleen, who gave him a warm kiss on the mouth. Was it just his imagination, or had she glanced quickly at Lisa straight afterwards?

Carl had accompanied Dillon once again and he headed straight over to where Lisa was seated at the bar. "Well, if it isn't my favorite Cowboy," she gushed, rising to give him a kiss on the cheek.

Dillon felt a twinge of jealousy but figured he deserved it after Arleen's greeting. She went back behind the bar and served their drinks before saying, "Why don't the four of us go out to dinner when I get off shift? It'll be fun, like a double date."

"Oh, that sounds great," Lisa said enthusiastically.

What the hell, Dillon thought. He knew that the two women were playing some sort of game, but he couldn't quite figure it out. "Carl has to get back after a couple of drinks," he said quickly. "He's on duty tonight."

Carl grinned broadly. "That's not a problem, I'll just call one of the guys and have him cover for me."

Great, Dillon thought, *there goes any chance of me having alone time with Lisa.* "Awesome!" he said, although his tone and expression definitely didn't convey much enthusiasm.

Arleen gave Dillon a winning smile. "It's set then. Lisa, darling, why don't you go upstairs and put on something more appropriate. I'll do the same when I finish up here."

"Of course, bestie," Lisa said sweetly. She downed the remainder of her martini and said, "I'll see you boys in a few."

"I'll make the call while we wait," Carl said, heading toward the restrooms.

Once they were alone, Dillon whispered angrily at Arleen, "What the hell are you up to?"

"Whatever do you mean?" she asked innocently.

"The key thing's been done already. There's no need for Lisa and Carl to keep hanging out."

"Oh, that." She laughed. "I just figured that Lisa is probably jealous of our pretend relationship. Now she gets to have one too."

Dillon frowned. "Well, I don't like it. What if she lets something slip?"

"As you said earlier, she's the best. I'm sure that she can handle this."

He sat fuming until Carl returned a few minutes later. "No problem, everything's arranged."

Dillon managed a fake smile. "Great."

They sat nursing their beers until Lisa reappeared in all her glory. She'd gone all out with her outfit and make-up and looked absolutely stunning. Every male head in the establishment swiveled to watch her as she sashayed up to the bar.

"Wow, that's some outfit," Arleen commented. "We're only going to a local restaurant, not the Governor's Ball."

"Oh, this old thing." Lisa leaned forward to give Carl an eyeful of her ample cleavage.

"Well, I think that you look magnificent," Carl said. "What do you think Dillon?"

Dillon shrugged. "Okay I guess, although now I feel underdressed for the occasion."

"As always, you look just fine, babes," Arleen cooed. "Shift's over, now it's my turn to go and throw something on. I'll be right back."

They sat making small talk until Arleen reappeared about thirty minutes later. She'd accepted Lisa's challenge and transformed herself into an absolute beauty.

Again, all heads turned as she glided up to Dillon in a black and purple, figure-hugging cocktail dress and six-inch heels. He was amazed. "You look really gorgeous."

"She always did clean up nice," Lisa said snippily.

"Okay, boys, where are you taking us?" Arleen asked.

Carl chuckled. "I guess Applebee's is out of the question."

CHAPTER THIRTY-NINE

They had a lovely dinner at the local country club, after which Carl dropped them back at the bar, kissing Lisa chastely on the cheek as he said goodbye. Back at the apartment Dillon finally vented his frustration. "What the hell are you two up to?" he shouted.

Arleen suddenly got serious and replied, "I'm just trying to make the best of a bad situation without making Carl suspicious. You and he are friends, just like Lisa and I are supposed to be. It's only natural that the four of us would go out together."

"I guess so," Dillon said, calming down a little. "But what's with the outfits? You guys look like you're trying out for the Miss America pageant or something."

Arleen laughed. "We'll take that as a compliment. Now, down to serious business. I've got that key ready for you, and you still need to do your report."

"Do I have to?" Dillon complained.

"Yes, you do!" Arleen said sternly. "You and Lisa seem to have forgotten that the only thing keeping both of you out of prison is the success of this mission. Speaking of which, I'll be driving Lisa to the airport tomorrow morning. Her time here is done."

"What!" Lisa shouted. "You bitch, you just want Daniel all to yourself."

"Diedra's orders, not mine," Arleen said calmly. "Her exact words were, 'if she doesn't cooperate we'll put her ass back in prison and throw away the key.' That also means that you stay the hell away from here until the mission is over. Got it?"

"Got it," Lisa replied sullenly.

"Good," Arleen said. "Now, I'm not totally insensitive to your situation. Once Dillon's finished his report, you two can use my bed to sleep, or whatever. Just keep the noise down, and I guess I'll have to replace the sheets tomorrow."

"Thanks for that," Dillon said. "Where will you sleep?"

"I picked up an inflatable mattress today, it'll have to do," she replied.

"Thank you," Lisa said softly. "I'm sorry that I called you a bitch."

Arleen waved dismissively. "That's okay, I understand. Thank you for helping us get that key. Speaking of which." She went into the bedroom and returned with a pair of Dillon's shoes. "The key's hidden in the left heel, in case they search you. You twist it like so to open it."

Dillon practiced a few times. "They still search everyone, even Carl gets searched. That reminds me." He told Arleen about the mysterious truck that wasn't subjected to a search.

"You need to get in there and find out what's inside," she said. "After tomorrow everything should be calmer."

"Why is that?" Dillon asked.

"Do you know a guy by the name of Vincent Post?" she asked.

"Sure, nice guy around forty or so." He searched his incredible memory. "Used to be a firefighter in New York."

Arleen quickly gave him the details of what they'd uncovered before saying, "Burns is going to give his name to Director Wells at precisely noon tomorrow. You need to lay low and observe the fall-out, maybe get into the barn if you get the chance."

Dillon was surprised. "Can't believe I thought that pervert was a nice guy. I'll do my best on the barn, but it'll have to be late at night."

"That's fine, now quickly do that report and get to bed," Arleen said, giving him a wink.

———

About three hours later Dillon said in exasperation, "It's no use!"

"What's wrong, babes?" Lisa asked. "You've never had this problem before."

"Don't know, maybe the stress is just getting to me."

"Maybe," Lisa said, unconvinced. "Are you sure it's got nothing to do with her sleeping out there?"

"Of course not, let's just get some sleep," he muttered.

Outside the bedroom door Arleen turned away, a smile playing across her pretty face.

CHAPTER FORTY

Diedra and most of the team gathered in the war-room as Alec Burns made the all-important call to Deputy Director Wells. Burns had the phone on speaker and motioned for everyone to keep quiet. "Wells here," they heard.

"Good day Deputy Director, it's Agent Burns."

"Burns, about damn time I heard from you, I'm running out of patience. What do you have for me?"

"Good news, sir, I've discovered the identity of the FBI agent inside the AAM."

Roger Wells' attitude changed dramatically. "Excellent work Alec, I knew you could do it."

"It wasn't easy, sir," Burns said. "Had to sneak onto one of the computers after everyone had gone to bed."

"Good thinking," Wells said. "What's the name?"

"Vincent Post," Burns replied. "There's a whole file on his back-stop alias, supposedly used to be a New York City fireman. His real name is Quinton Small."

"Does Agent Baker know about this?" Wells asked.

"No, sir, you told me to be discreet."

"Good, I only sent her along as window dressing. She doesn't seem to have much talent. You on the other hand have a very bright future here at Homeland. I've had my eye on you for a while."

Amanda Baker pulled a face and mouthed the word, *asshole*, as Burns accepted the compliment. "Thank you, sir, I'm glad to hear that."

"Now, I need to count on your discretion, Alec. No matter what happens, no one can ever know about this phone call. Can I count on you?" Wells asked.

"Of course, Deputy Director."

"Good. Keep me updated on events on that side as they unfold. I need to know every little detail."

"Will do, sir, I'll call you as soon as anything happens."

"Again, good job, Agent Burns." Wells ended the call.

Alec Burns returned his phone to his pocket and turned to Diedra. "I'm afraid that you are probably correct, Agent Wolfe, he's definitely up to something."

"I'll say," Amanda Baker said. "Can't wait to see his fat ass in prison."

Diedra smiled at her. "Don't take what he said about you personally, I actually think that you have great potential. Agent Burns, we'll know pretty soon if Deputy Director Wells has something to hide. Agents Olson and Hicks are observing the compound as we speak."

———

Dillon glanced once again at his watch, noting that it was one twenty-five and almost lunchtime at the compound. Shortly before twelve he'd lain on a deck chair situated on his patio and pretended to read a book. This afforded him a clear view of Small's cabin, but so far nothing untoward had happened. *Maybe Diedra got it wrong,* he thought, *maybe Wells isn't the mole.*

One of his roommates stuck his head through the rear door. "You coming to lunch or what?"

Dillon closed the book. "Today's burger and fries day, wouldn't miss it for the world." He took his time as he meandered down to the dining hall, eventually entering and taking his assigned seat.

He surreptitiously observed the leadership group's table, where most of them were eating in stony silence. At the main table, the two co-founders were involved in an animated discussion, their heads close together. Sandra Woods eventually shook her head vigorously and sat back, barely picking at her food.

Something's definitely going on, Dillon mused. He didn't have to wait long to find out. Jerry Barnes strode to the podium and grabbed the mic. He usually waited until everyone had finished eating before giving his daily discourse on the evils of Islam. "Can I have your attention please?" Barnes said loudly. Surprised by the interruption, everyone immediately stopped eating and gave their leader their undivided attention,

"It appears that one of you is not who he says he is," Barnes said cryptically.

Good thing I knew about this or I would have shat myself, Dillon thought. He was watching Small, who had turned pale at Barnes' words. *If you weren't a pervert I might actually feel sorry for you.*

"We thought that we'd probably got rid of the FBI infiltrator, but it seems that we were wrong," Barnes continued. "Isn't that right, Mister Small? Or should I say Mister Vincent Post."

The man almost knocked his chair over as he jumped to his feet. "Wait, you've got it wrong!" he protested. "I'm not a fed."

"What is your real name?" Barnes barked.

"It is Vincent Post," the man stammered, "but it's not what you think."

"Enough!" Barnes shouted. "Bring him!"

Carl and one of the other leaders grabbed the hapless man and marched him onto the stage. "This is what a traitor looks like!" Barnes spat venomously. There were boos from the crowd, and one of the men actually hit the prisoner with a well-aimed throw of a hamburger bun.

Sandra Woods joined the small group on the stage, taking the mic from Barnes. "Our initial reaction was to treat this man as all traitors should be treated," she began. Before she could continue a chorus of shouts rang out from the crowd demanding his death, torture and even dismemberment. *What a bloodthirsty bunch,* Dillon thought. *Sure glad that's not me up there.*

Woods waited until the noise died down before continuing, "But eventually cooler heads prevailed." She glanced at Jerry Barnes. "Killing or harming a federal agent is the last thing we need right now. We haven't broken any laws. I say we let him go and report that to his superiors." There was muttering and whispering amongst the crowd, obviously unhappy that their bloodlust would remain unfulfilled.

Vincent Post was unceremoniously hauled off the stage and marched towards the rear door. "What about all my stuff?" he griped.

"I'm sure that the FBI can afford to buy you new stuff," Carl said sarcastically.

CHAPTER FORTY-ONE

"Well, there's our confirmation." Diedra hung up the phone. "Wells is definitely our mole."

"So he took the bait?" Amanda Baker asked.

"He did indeed." Diedra smiled at her. "Thanks to your clever idea, Olson just called to say that Small was frog-marched to the front gate and kicked out of the AAM compound."

Burns asked, "Now what?"

"Olson and Hicks ran to their vehicle, drove like crazy and grabbed Small while he was still in view of the front gate," Diedra replied. "Being picked up by a black SUV so quickly will leave them with little doubt that he was the FBI spy."

"Good thinking," Burns said. "What will happen to Small now?"

"We'll charge him with identity theft and hold him in custody until this operation is concluded. After that we'll release him," Diedra replied.

"What about his sex-offender status?" Baker asked.

"There's no evidence that he committed any further crimes once he became Vincent Post," Diedra answered. "We'll let him continue with the alias after putting the fear of God in him. I'll let him know that the FBI will be watching his every move in the future. We'll also give him a thorough interrogation about the AAM since he's been in the secure compound way longer than Dillon. Perhaps he has some information that may be of help to us."

"I still don't like the idea of someone like him running around scot-free," Baker said.

Diedra grimaced. "Believe me, after this brush with the law he'll stay on the straight and narrow. Besides, we've got much bigger fish to fry, including the deputy director of Homeland Security."

———

Dillon noticed an immediate relaxing of the atmosphere inside the AAM compound since the FBI spy had apparently been ousted. After lunch Jerry Barnes and Sandra Woods had given long speeches about loyalty to the organization, which they equated with being patriots of the United States. They also thanked all the members for their patience during the heightened security measures.

Carl went looking for Dillon and asked him to join him for a celebratory drink at the bar. "I feel much better knowing that the imposter has been caught," he said.

Yeah, you horny bastard, Dillon thought. *You just want to hang out with Lisa again, pity for you she's already left town.* He agreed, and they arrived at the bar a short while later.

Arleen seemed surprised to see them again so soon. "You guys are starting to look like a couple of alcoholics."

Dillon laughed. "If only that were true. Actually, it is the far more alluring and dangerous pursuit of female companionship that draws us here so regularly. Speaking of which, where is the lovely Lisa?"

"Sorry to say she received a call this morning informing her that her mother was ill in hospital," Arleen replied. "I drove her to the airport just before my shift started. She caught the first flight to the Atlanta hub and is probably already on her way to Iowa."

Carl tried not to show his disappointment but failed miserably. "I'm sorry that I never got to say goodbye."

"Me too," Dillon added, not sounding in the least bit sorry.

Arleen gave Carl a consoling smile. "Don't worry, I'm sure that she'll be back as soon as her mother recovers. She really seemed to like you a lot."

"You honestly think so?" Carl asked, perking up a bit.

"Of course, woman's intuition," Arleen said. "Believe me, you haven't seen the last of her."

Like hell! Dillon thought. *She's out of the picture, buddy.*

CHAPTER FORTY-TWO

Dillon had once again received permission from Carl to spend the night at Arleen's. Upset by Lisa's sudden departure, Carl had returned to the compound after a couple of beers.

Dillon and Arleen were seated on the small couch in her apartment watching re-runs of The Big Bang Theory. He'd just completed his report on what had transpired in the compound when poor old Quinton Small had been fingered as the FBI spy.

"You should have seen his face." Dillon chuckled. "You could tell that he was of two minds on whether to admit that he was actually a sexual predator or not. When he realized that they weren't going to harm him, I thought that he was actually going to cop to being an FBI agent."

Arleen smiled. "Far more honorable than being a sleazy pervert. Anyway, it all worked out for the best. It'll probably be far easier now to figure out what they're up to, now that their suspicions have be lowered."

Dillon agreed. "My first task is to find out what was on that truck. Let Diedra know that I'm going to try for some time late tomorrow night. She needs to have someone watching the compound in case I get caught. I've got a nasty feeling that I won't get off as lightly as our scapegoat did today."

Arleen took his hand. "I'll do that, just please be careful, I don't want anything to happen to you."

"Careful, Agent Cooper, or I might just get the wrong idea that you really care about me."

She blushed. "Actually I do. You remind me so much of your brother. You're not as bad a person as you think you are. Your brother would be really proud of what you're doing here."

"Thank you for that," Dillon said softly. "For what it's worth, I'm really starting to enjoy this secret agent stuff."

Arleen laughed. "Maybe you're also destined for a career in the FBI."

"Yeah right, like they'd ever hire someone with my record."

"Believe me, stranger things have happened. Come now, it's time for bed."

Dillon grabbed the clicker and turned the TV off. "You don't have to ask me twice."

"Careful, Mister, remember the no-hands rule," Arleen said with far less conviction than previously.

———

"Yes, sir, that's what I just heard," Burns said. "The FBI's undercover agent in the AAM compound got busted and expelled from their camp." The team was again gathered in the war-room as Burns made a call to Deputy Director Wells.

Wells' voice crackled over the speakerphone. "That is very unfortunate, especially since we finally knew his identity. I wanted you to get as much information as possible from him, allowing us to upstage those prima donnas at the FBI."

Yeah right, Burns thought, *I wasn't born yesterday.*

"What do you think happened?" Wells asked.

I know exactly what happened. Burns smiled. "With the heightened security measures, they possibly dug a little deeper into everyone's background and discovered his name change."

"You're probably right," Wells agreed. "What is the FBI going to do going forward?"

"According to the undercover agent, he hadn't seen any major breaches of the law," Burns replied. "Just a few illegal weapons that wouldn't really amount to much in court. They're just going to continue observing the compound and hope that something else comes up."

"Will the FBI try to insert another agent into the organization?" Wells asked.

"I doubt that they'll even try," Burns answered. "The AAM would have learnt their lesson from this. They'll run much deeper background checks on any new potential members, making it almost impossible to penetrate the group."

Wells appeared satisfied. "Understandable. Let me know immediately if anything comes up. I just want you to remember that I've got my eye on you for greater things."

Burns used his best ass-kissing tone. "Will do, and thank you, sir."

After he'd hung up the phone, Diedra said, "Good job, Agent Burns, I think he bought it."

Burns turned to her. "I sure hope so. What happens now?"

"My director has already approached the president for approval on surveillance and wire-taps on Director Wells," Diedra replied. "We should be hearing from him shortly."

CHAPTER FORTY-THREE

The following night Dillon went to bed early after a long day of kitchen duty. He fell asleep around eight-thirty, but not before he'd set his mental alarm clock for two the next morning.

His eyes popped open at exactly one fifty-nine a.m. according to his bedside clock-radio. He crept stealthily from bed, careful not to cause the wooden floorboards to creak. After donning the dark clothing and rubber-soled sneakers he'd laid out, he let himself out the front door.

The camp was quiet and peaceful as he wandered down in the direction of the large barn. Should anyone accost him, his premeditated excuse was that he was taking a late night stroll because he couldn't sleep. Fortunately a thick layer of cloud obscured the moon and stars, and once his eyes had adjusted to the darkness, he observed no movement whatsoever.

Reaching the front doors of the barn, he knelt down and pretended to tie his shoelace, glancing around to see if he was being observed. Satisfied, he rose and quickly inserted the key into the heavy padlock. It opened with a satisfying click and within seconds he was inside.

He retrieved a small flashlight from his jacket pocket and turned it on. It shone a narrow red beam that was not as easily discernible as a white light would have been. Moving carefully he made his way to the left side of the huge structure, where the large shape of a truck loomed.

Upon reaching it, he played the flashlight upon the rear doors, surprised to see that they were unlocked. He carefully opened the doors, wincing when one of them squealed slightly. He clambered onto the truck-bed and made his way forward, his flashlight dimly illuminating four large shapes ahead.

He shone the dim light on the shapes and took a deep breath of surprise. *What the hell?* he thought. He was staring at four large, innocent-looking upright water-heaters. He inspected them closely, even tapping the flashlight gently against all four of them. He was rewarded with a hollow ring that proclaimed their emptiness.

Why would they sneak these things in so late at night? There's no problem with any of the camp's water-heaters as far as I know, certainly not with four of them.

Disappointed with his findings he carefully closed the truck's doors, re-locked the padlock and made his way back to his cabin. Back in bed, he lay there trying to figure out what he'd seen. Eventually he gave up and thought, *maybe Diedra has the answer,* and went back to sleep.

———

Back at the FBI mansion, Diedra breathed a sigh of relief after getting a call from the agents observing the compound. Dillon's late-night excursion to check out the barn had gone off without a hitch.

"What do you think he found?" Amanda Baker asked. Burns had accompanied the rest of the heavily armed agents who'd been instructed to extract Dillon should he be compromised.

Diedra grinned. "I'm hoping something really juicy, like explosives or rocket-launchers or something. I'm getting a little tired of this cat-and-mouse game. We need to raid that compound sooner than later and finally put these assholes away. HQ is getting impatient, not to mention how much this operation is costing the federal government. Deputy Director Shaw was on my ass about that earlier tonight."

Agent Baker nodded. "On the positive side, at least we discovered that Director Wells is dirty."

"There is that, yes. All thanks to you."

CHAPTER FORTY-FOUR

It was several days before Dillon was able to get his not-so-exciting information to his handlers. He'd been on three straight nights of guard duty before being given Saturday night off.

"Water-heaters, that's it?" Arleen asked in disbelief. They were in her apartment, where Dillon was giving his report.

Dillon frowned. "My reaction exactly. Hardly incriminating evidence, is it?"

"Diedra is going to be so disappointed." Arleen sighed. "She was all gung-ho to raid the compound, even had the HRT team on high-alert."

"Sorry to be the bearer of such insignificant news."

"It's not your fault. I'm just glad you didn't get caught sneaking around the barn."

"Amen to that. I don't know if it'll be of any help, but I memorized the make and serial numbers of the water-heaters. I'll put it in my report."

"At least that's something."

"I'll give it a day or two before I check out the barn again. Hopefully I'll have something more interesting to report."

"I'll let Diedra know," Arleen said. "How are things at the camp?"

"Security's been relaxed somewhat and everyone seems way more laid-back, especially the leadership group. It was a brilliant idea of Diedra's to find a fall guy amongst the members."

"Actually the idea originated with that young Homeland Security agent, Amanda Baker."

"Well, kudos to her. What's going to happen to her boss, Wells?"

"The FBI have received permission to put him under surveillance. Wire-taps on his phones and everything."

"You guys should feed him some more juicy information to pass on to the AAM leaders. If you can tape that call, you'll have definitive evidence that he can't deny. Of course, he's probably using a burner phone."

"Doesn't matter, there are bugs in his office, home and even his car."

Dillon smiled. "You guys sure don't mess around. Okay, let me finish my report and then I'll take you out for dinner."

Without thinking Arleen said, "It's a date."

———

While Dillon was enjoying a relaxing late-night dinner with Arleen, a vehicle once again approached the guard station at the AAM compound. This one was a beat-up Ford panel-van, and just like its predecessor it was waved through without even a cursory examination. The two agents on surveillance duty noted the relevant details in their log-book.

CHAPTER FORTY-FIVE

"They're definitely up to something," Dillon remarked. "That's two mysterious late-night deliveries that didn't get searched in less than a week."

He was being driven back the following morning by Arleen, who'd just received a call from Diedra concerning the latest late-night arrival at the compound.

"Diedra appears to agree with you," Arleen said. "She wants you to investigate this secretive new arrival as soon as possible."

"That's going to be a problem." Dillon grimaced. "I'm back on guard-duty tonight, as well as tomorrow night. I probably won't be able to get back in there until Tuesday night."

"I'll let her know," Arleen said. "Same time?"

"Yes, around two in the morning seems to be about the best time. Just make sure that Diedra has the extraction team on standby."

"Of course, wouldn't want anything to happen to that ruggedly handsome face of yours."

Dillon smiled. "If I didn't know any better, I'd say that you were flirting with me, Agent Cooper." He'd noted a definite change in her attitude towards him since Lisa's departure. Last night's dinner had the distinct feeling of a real date, although maybe he'd just imagined it.

———

"That's a helluva lot of C-4," Carl said. He was in the barn helping to offload the contents of the panel-van.

Jerry Barnes smiled broadly. "Sure is. Going to make one hell of a bang, or should I say four bangs."

"What's the targets?" Carl asked curiously.

"You and the others will know soon enough," Barnes answered. "Now that the damned FBI spy is out of the picture, we can stop screwing around and get down to the real business at hand."

"Which is?" Carl asked.

"Why, ridding this wonderful country of every last Muslim son-of-a-bitch." Barnes cackled.

Carl noted the fanatical glint in his leader's eye and felt a little uncomfortable. Sometimes he got the distinct feeling that Jerry Barnes was completely and utterly insane. He knew for a fact that if it hadn't been for the other founder, Sandra Woods, Barnes would have drilled a neat bullet hole into Small's forehead as he stood on the stage.

The other five men present failed to notice anything amiss and continued to carry the wooden boxes containing the bricks of C-4 explosive into the sectioned-off armory area. Carl had been an explosives expert in the Navy SEALS and knew that just one quarter of the amount of C-4 present was enough to take out almost an entire city block.

The driver of the delivery vehicle stood and watched the proceedings with folded arms and an air of superiority. He was a nasty-looking character, and Carl wondered where he fit into the picture.

CHAPTER FORTY-SIX

"**D**ammit," Dillon cursed softly. Once again he was disappointed by what he found during his late night excursion. The panel-van was completely empty save for a pile of old army blankets.

He nudged the blankets with his foot as he shone the red-beamed flashlight on them. While doing so he noticed a sticky substance that adhered to one of the blankets. He quickly retrieved the Swiss Army knife from his pocket and cut off a small piece from the corner.

He checked out the rest of the barn's cavernous interior, noticing a pile of wooden boxes in the armory section that hadn't been there before. Curiously, the four water-heaters stood alongside the pile. *That's strange*, he thought, *why so much security just for plumbing equipment?*

He checked out the lock on the armory gate, but it was a modern, high-tech combination lock. *No way I'm getting in there without the code*, he thought.

He carefully locked the barn doors and stealthily made his way back to his cabin. He'd just entered the front door when a loud voice asked, "Where've you been?"

He almost jumped out of his skin and looked around wildly. One of his roommates popped his head around the corner leading to the kitchen. "Ben, are you insane?" Dillon asked. "You almost gave me a friggin' heart attack."

"Sorry." Ben shrugged. "Just getting myself a late-night snack. What you doing wandering around this time of night?"

"Couldn't sleep, so I went for a stroll," Dillon replied casually, his heart still thumping in his chest.

"It's all this damn guard-duty," Ben said. "Throws your whole internal clock off, that's why I'm suddenly hungry so late at night. Had the same problem when I was in the army."

The last thing Dillon wanted was a long chat, so he murmured a comment and headed for his bedroom. "Wait!" Ben said loudly. *What now?* Dillon thought. *The asshole's going to wake everyone.* "You want one?" Ben asked, shoving a sticky pb&j sandwich in his direction.

Trying his best to remain patient, Dillon muttered, "No thanks."

"Your loss," Dillon heard as he finally made it through his bedroom door. After undressing he carefully extracted the piece of blanket and placed it inside an empty pill bottle. He lifted a loose floor plank in a corner of the room and placed the sample in the gap beneath.

———

Milford Olson hung up the phone and turned to Diedra. "Okay, he's back safe in his cabin."

"Good thing, I just hope that he found something more interesting this time around."

"The water-heaters actually weren't a complete bust." Olson punched the keys furiously on his laptop's keyboard. "I managed to trace the purchase to a plumbing-supply warehouse in Jacksonville, Florida."

"So what?" Diedra asked sarcastically. "Last I checked, buying plumbing equipment wasn't illegal."

"It's not what he bought but who bought it that's interesting,"

Olson replied. "The dude paid cash and gave the name and address of a fictitious plumbing company in Florida. Fortunately, the warehouse captured his image on their security cameras and it's no one we know from the compound. I've been running facial-rec for the last few hours and finally got a hit from Defense Intelligence's database."

"And?" Diedra asked impatiently.

"And the dude is bad news," Olson said triumphantly. "His name is Peter Williams, former US Army demolitions expert. He received a dishonorable discharge seven years ago for striking a superior officer. Since then he's been in and out of prison on assault and misdemeanor battery charges, amongst other things."

"Sounds like he has quite the little temper. Do we know his current whereabouts?"

"That's what I'm busy with right now. I'm trying to clean up the surveillance photos from the other night. I'm not a hundred percent sure yet, but he could be the driver of the mysterious Ford panel-van."

Diedra grinned. "Now that's interesting, they've brought a demolitions expert into the compound. I'm really curious to find out what Dillon discovered last night."

CHAPTER FORTY-SEVEN

"That's all you've got?" Arleen asked later that evening. She held the pill bottle in her hand and inspected the small piece of cloth inside.

"Sorry, but they're not going to leave incriminating evidence just laying around," Dillon said defensively.

"No, I'm sorry, you obviously did your best. I'm just glad you didn't get caught while snooping around."

Dillon told her about Ben and his sandwich and she laughed. "It's not funny," he said. "I just about had a coronary."

"I'm sure." Arleen suddenly turned serious. "While you finish your report I'm going to drop off this sample at the mailbox. I'll pick us up something to eat on the way back. I'm not really in the mood to go out and eat tonight."

"Fine by me, grab some beers too. I see you're almost out."

"How about a movie? There's a video-rental store next to the post office."

"Sounds good, just no chick flicks please."

"What, you don't want me to see a grown man cry?" Arleen teased.

"Yeah right, like that'll happen. Oh, and don't forget the popcorn."

"Yes, sir," she said, letting herself out the front door.

Dillon concentrated on his report and was almost done by the time Arleen returned an hour or so later. She laid out a meatball sub for him as well as a fresh beer. He thanked her and peered at the plastic container in her hand. "What's that?" he asked.

"Salad. I'm putting on way too much weight what with all the pizza and beer."

"Yeah right." Dillon eyed her body appreciatively.

Arleen blushed a little. "I got an action movie for you and The Notebook for me."

"Sure sounds like a chick flick to me."

Arleen gave a mischievous smile. "One of the best. I can't believe you've never seen it."

"Like I said, not my thing. Anyway, I'm done here so we'll watch your silly little movie while we eat."

They moved over to the couch where Arleen curled up like a kitten next to him. She picked up the clicker and pushed play. "Ten bucks says you won't make it through this movie without at least one little tear."

"You're on, be the easiest money I ever made."

Once the movie finished Arleen giggled as Dillon forked over a crumpled bill. "Told you, you have to have ice in your veins not to shed a tear during that movie."

Dillon was embarrassed. "Probably just my allergies," he mumbled.

"Don't worry, many women find a man who can cry very sexy," Arleen said, leaving the innuendo out there.

"Does that mean that you think I'm sexy?" Dillon asked, very conscious of the heat emanating from her body so close to his, not to mention the intoxicating aroma of her perfume.

She turned her face to his and stared deep into his eyes. "Yes, I do. What you going to do about it?"

Without thinking he leaned forward and kissed her on the lips.

She responded hungrily and he became instantly aroused. He pulled back a little and gasped, "Do you think this is a good idea?"

Arleen moaned. "Probably not, but it's the only one I have right now."

He picked her up and carried her to the bedroom, laying her gently on the bed. "Undress me!" she commanded.

He turned on the bedside lamp and happily complied, marveling at the beauty of her body. Her taut stomach and small, pert breasts had him mesmerized, and he quickly ripped off his clothes before joining her on the bed.

CHAPTER FORTY-EIGHT

Dillon woke early to find Arleen snuggled up tight against him, her right arm across his chest. *What have I done?* was his first thought. *I've totally betrayed Lisa's trust in me.* Not that he hadn't thoroughly enjoyed making love to Arleen. She was a great lover, and her small, athletic body had given him much joy.

He felt her stirring and she eventually opened her eyes and gave him a seductive smile. "Hi, sexy."

"I'm so sorry," was his automatic response.

"Sorry, what do you mean sorry?" Her voice started rising. "It seemed to me that you really enjoyed yourself last night."

Dillon immediately became defensive. "I did, I really did. It just shouldn't have happened is all."

"Oh, is that all?" Arleen's face was flushed with anger. She sat upright in the bed, modestly covering herself with the sheet. "You've done nothing but flirt with me since the day we met."

Dillon was totally flustered by her angry response. "Sorry about that, it's just who I am. I really didn't expect things to go this far. I'm totally in love with Lisa, and I've never cheated on her before."

"Sorry, there's that word again!" Arleen shouted. "Well, let me tell you something, you are one SORRY son-of-a-bitch!" With that she wrapped the sheet around her and stormed from the room.

That's done it, Dillon thought. *What the hell was I thinking?*

An aloof Arleen returned to the room five minutes later. She was fully dressed and angrily pulling a brush through her short hair. "Get dressed and I'll drive you back to the compound," she said frostily.

"Don't you think we should talk about this?" Dillon asked carefully.

"It seems that you've already said everything that needs saying!" she retorted.

"Look, I really like you," Dillon began.....

"Save it, Mister!" Arleen interrupted. "From here on out, ours is just a professional relationship. Finish doing what needs to be done and then get the hell out of my life!"

Dillon was starting to lose his cool and he said nastily, "Fine, if that's the way you want it!" He rose angrily from the bed, still totally naked.

"And cover yourself up!" Arleen flung a towel at him. "I certainly don't need to see THAT ever again!"

"Believe me, you won't!" Dillon wrapped the towel around him and headed to the bathroom.

Needless to say, the drive out to the compound was made in stony silence. Dillon exited the car without any goodbye, slamming the door for good measure.

Carl walked forward to meet him as he stalked towards the boom gate. "Lovers' tiff?" he asked.

"Something like that," Dillon replied. He noticed the wand in Carl's hand and snuck a glance at his watch. *Oh shit!* he thought. *It's almost seven-fifteen.* "Can you just give me a minute?" Dillon asked the big man. Without waiting for a reply, he turned and watched as Arleen angrily spun the tires as she pulled off. Trying to distract Carl and buy some time, he asked, "What is it with women?"

"You've got me, buddy. I thought that Lisa and I were hitting it off, but then she left town without so much as a goodbye."

"That was different, her mother was ill. I think she was really into you."

"So maybe I should give her a call then?"

"What, she gave you her phone number?" Dillon asked in disbelief.

"Yes, what's so strange about that?"

"Nothing, of course, I'm just still upset that Arleen accused me of also having a thing for Lisa."

Carl laughed. "That's crazy, it's totally obvious to everyone that you're madly in love with Arleen." He moved closer to Dillon who once again glanced at his watch. *Seven-sixteen*, he noted, *hope to God it's accurate.*

Carl lifted the wand and Dillon raised his arms, holding his breath as he did so. There was no tell-tale beep, and Carl said, "You're good to go, buddy. I tell you what, just give it a couple of days and everything will be back to normal with Arleen."

Dillon looked skeptical. "I sure hope so, but I doubt it."

———

Arleen had just arrived back at her apartment when her burner phone rang. "What do you mean he's left already?" Diedra asked.

Arleen thought quickly. "He's on kitchen duty, so he had to be back early to prepare breakfast."

"I see. A little heads-up would have been nice."

"Sorry, I forgot," Arleen said contritely.

Diedra's voice became stern. "We can't afford any mistakes at this point. I have important information to give him."

"Once again, I apologize. What is it?"

"The guy who purchased and delivered the water-heaters is an Army demolitions expert. His name is Peter Williams, and I wanted to tell Dillon to try and get close to him. We really need to find out what the hell this so-called militia group is up to."

"I'm sure that Dillon will be back in a day or two," Arleen said without conviction. "I'll tell him then."

"I hope so, we're seriously running out of time." With that, Diedra ended the call.

Arleen was furious with herself and flung the phone onto the couch. *You're jeopardizing the mission with your little schoolgirl crush,* she admonished herself. *You're supposed to be a professional.* She knew in her heart that the anger she'd shown towards Dillon should have instead been directed at herself. *He's the one out of his depth, not you,* she thought. *Give the poor guy a break. Besides, who made the first move?*

CHAPTER FORTY-NINE

A t lunch Dillon immediately noticed the new guy seated at the leadership table. *Looks a lot like the driver from the other night*, he thought. *Wonder why they haven't introduced him?* He was still in a foul mood following the argument with Arleen and subsequent close call with Carl. *I really need to up my game and concentrate on this mission. No more distractions or I'm toast*, he concluded.

After the meal Burns once again took the podium. "As you all know, our mission statement is to rid our wonderful nation of all followers of the blood-thirsty religion known as Islam!" This was greeted by cheers and applause, which Burns acknowledged before continuing, "To this end, we have devised a plan that will drive fear into the hearts of every Muslim living in the United States. There will almost certainly be some collateral damage during these attacks on Islam, which I like to call reverse-jihad, but that unfortunately is the price to be paid during a war. And make no mistake, my loyal followers, we are at war with Islam. If anyone here feels that they don't have the stomach for such a war and its consequences, please feel free to leave right now and nobody will think any less of you." Burns gazed sternly at the audience, and when no one moved he continued, "I thank you all for your loyalty and sacrifice, but none more so than these four heroes." He indicated the four young people seated with Sandra Woods at the main table, motioning them onto the stage.

Once the four teenagers had assembled on either side of him, he continued, "As we all know, the biggest weapon that Muslims have at their disposal is the will of those that are prepared to give their lives to further the cause of Islam. Yes, I'm talking about suicide bombers." A murmur went up throughout the crowded hall and Burns waited for it to subside before continuing. "These four brave soldiers have agreed to make the ultimate sacrifice to avenge the loved ones they have lost during this war. Many of you have probably wondered who they are and why they weren't allowed to interact with the rest of you. They have been receiving intensive counseling from Miss Woods and myself and have agreed to spearhead the first battle to be fought against Islam on American soil."

Dillon was shocked. *You've got to be kidding. I guess by counseling, he actually means brainwashing and indoctrination.*

Burns indicated the young girl next to him. "This is Mary. She took her thirteen-year-old sister to a concert in Manchester, England. Mary was herself only seventeen years old at the time but ended up cradling her sister's shattered body in her arms after a suicide bomber detonated a massive explosive device." He turned to the girl. "Mary's life was forever changed on that night. She blames herself for her sister's death and has thought of nothing but retribution ever since. The tragedy caused her parents' marriage to fail, something she also feels responsible for."

So you're using her guilt to turn her into a weapon, Dillon thought. *What a total asshole.* He paid attention again as Burns resumed speaking. "I won't go into specific details at this point, but during one of the upcoming Muslim holidays these four dedicated soldiers will drive explosive-laden vans into mosques in four different cities and detonate the deadly cargo."

A hush fell over the congregation as they digested what Burns had just revealed. Even the toughest, most battle-hardened veterans seemed shocked by the revelation. "I know what you're thinking, not all Muslims are evil, especially the women and children. Well, I've got news for you, you're wrong." Burns motioned for the four teenagers to return to their table and pushed a button on a remote control. A large screen slid down from the ceiling and he called for someone to dim the lights. "What you are about to see are images from several Muslim countries on the day that the Twin Towers collapsed, killing thousands of innocent civilians including women and children." He pushed play and the screen was immediately illuminated with scenes of joyous celebration, each one captioned with the relative country. Thousands of people, including women and children, thronged city streets as they jubilantly rejoiced at the massive blow struck against the *Great Satan*. Many of the clips featured the burning of American flags along with effigies of Uncle Sam. A group of young girls were shown spitting upon the stars and stripes before the flags were doused with petrol and set alight.

The show continued for almost half an hour, and everyone was speechless and exhausted by the end of it. "I can tell by your expressions that most of you are shocked by what you've just seen," Woods said as she took the podium. "To be honest, you should be. It's one thing for Taliban or Al-Qaeda fighters to be celebrating, but to see the joyous rapture on the faces of so-called innocent civilians is truly unsettling to say the least. Little girls running around the street celebrating the deaths of thousands of people gives you a small glimpse into what the teachings of the Quran are all about. Also keep in mind the celebrations by Muslims in Turkey, Saudi Arabia and the Philippines, so-called allies of the United States."

Dillon was quiet as he made his way back to his cabin after the lecture ended. *If what I just saw was real, I don't know if these people really are crazy or not*, he thought. *Maybe their cause truly is just.*

CHAPTER FIFTY

D illon didn't make it back to the bar for several days, which he thought was probably for the best anyway. Arleen had just finished her shift and hesitantly approached him as he took a seat at the bar counter. "Are you still pissed at me?" she asked reticently.

"I'm over it, how about you? You were far angrier than I was."

"After much reflection I realized that I acted like a total bitch. I basically seduced you and then acted like a scorned schoolgirl when you felt guilty about betraying your girlfriend."

Dillon grinned at her. "I'll take that as an apology. I, in turn, apologize for acting like a complete jerk."

Arleen smiled. "Accepted. So, we're good?"

"Yes, we are." He leaned over and whispered, "Listen, I've got some really important information that I need to get to Diedra as soon as possible."

"Let's go upstairs right now then." She took his hand and led him to the door.

Once they were in the apartment she chuckled. "Everyone probably thinks we came up here for make-up sex. I don't know how, but our fight seems to be the talk of the town."

Dillon laughed. "Same at the compound; one of the guys actually had the cheek to ask me if he could take a shot at you."

"I don't know whether to be flattered or insulted. Now, what's this important info you have?"

He gave her a brief synopsis of the planned attacks that Barnes had mentioned were coming.

Arleen was excited. "You're right, this can't wait. We'll give it about thirty minutes before driving over to the mansion via the movie theater."

Dillon laughed. "Only thirty minutes. You want people to think I've got no staying power?"

She almost said that she knew better but decided to stay off the subject of sex. "We ID'd the truck driver from the other night; his name is Peter Williams and he's a demolitions expert," she said instead.

"Makes sense, he's probably the guy who's manufacturing the bombs for the attacks. I wondered why he wasn't introduced. Seems like a bit of an asshole anyway."

"Unfortunately, Diedra wants you to get close to the asshole and get as much info out of him as you can." Arleen gave Dillon a brief rundown of the man's criminal history and propensity for violence.

"That's just great. Not that I'm afraid of him or anything."

"Of course not," Arleen quickly agreed. "You want a beer before we leave?"

"Better not, I want a clear head when I give Diedra all the details."

"Coffee then?"

"Sounds good, but only if you're having."

They finished their coffee and forty minutes later exited the movie theater parking lot and headed for the edge of town. Arleen kept glancing in the mirrors to make sure they weren't being followed.

"Oh, I almost forgot," Dillon said and told her about the close call with Carl and his wand at the front gate.

"Damn, now I really feel bad. And I also would have been able to give you the information about the truck driver, if not for our little indiscretion."

"Don't beat yourself up, we were both to blame. I guess we've learned a good lesson from this."

"It's why agents in the field should never get involved. I'm really mad at myself for acting so unprofessionally."

"Diedra can never know about what happened. She'd probably throw my ass back in prison."

"Not to mention firing my ass as well. I really don't know what I was thinking."

"It can't be easy slinging drinks all day long when you're a highly qualified federal agent."

"That's no excuse. Look at you, risking your life in bank robberies and such, and you're just a civilian."

"I don't know, this is turning out to be quite an experience. My normal civilian life is going to be totally anticlimactic once this is over."

Arleen glanced at him. "Well, given this new information, that might be fairly soon."

CHAPTER FIFTY-ONE

Amanda Baker was shocked. "Teenage suicide bombers, are you kidding me?" She and the rest of the team were in the war-room, where Dillon had just finished giving his report. Thanks to his incredible memory, he'd managed to give both AAM leaders' speeches word for word.

Diedra addressed Dillon. "This is truly worrisome. We've just received analysis of that blanket sample we sent to the FBI TEDAC in Huntsville, Alabama."

Dillon knitted his brow. "What the hell is a TEDAC?"

Diedra gave him a wry smile. "Sorry, keep forgetting that you're not a real FBI agent. TEDAC stands for Terrorist Explosive Device Analytical Center. Our initial analysis identified the gooey substance as C-4 explosive, so we sent it to Huntsville. According to them, the C-4 originates from a batch that was 'jacked about a year ago."

Dillon was impressed. "How can they possibly know that?"

Olson answered the question. "Each batch of explosive has a unique chemical signature that can easily be traced."

"That's correct," Diedra said. "The bad news is that the amount stolen was roughly two hundred pounds, none of which has been used or recovered."

"Don't know a damn thing about explosives," Dillon said, "but that sounds like a lot."

"It sure as hell is!" Diedra confirmed. "If we take four targets at fifty pounds of C-4 each, that will pretty much flatten anything within a two-hundred-yard radius of the detonation point."

"Can't let that happen," Arleen said decisively. "When are we going in?"

Diedra grimaced. "Bad news on that score; attorney general's office won't give us a warrant until we have definitive proof that the explosives are actually on the property."

"You're shitting me?" Dillon said. "I saw the boxes stacked in the armory; what more do they want?"

"Unfortunately my director agrees with the AG, you need to eyeball the actual explosives," Diedra said. "Not only that, but you need to take photos as well."

Dillon just laughed. "Take photos with what? I'll never be able to smuggle a camera in there."

"Orders are orders," Diedra said decisively. "We'll make a plan."

"This is crazy, and I thought those guys were nuts," Dillon said. "Speaking of which, the footage they showed us of Muslims worldwide celebrating nine-eleven, was that real?"

Diedra nodded sadly. "It was."

"And just about everyone there has lost loved ones to Islamic suicide attacks," Dillon said. "I'm beginning to think that maybe they're not really the bad guys after all."

"Having second thoughts?" Diedra asked gravely. She quickly tapped the keyboard on her laptop and turned it to face Dillon. "That's the results of just five pounds of C-4. Imagine what ten times that will look like."

Dillon had been sickened by the graphic images on the screen. Barely discernible, bloody human bodies were laid out in a row, many of them missing limbs. "We start behaving like them, then we become them," Diedra said harshly. "You seriously want to be a part of that?"

Dillon was barely able to speak. "I guess not," he muttered.

Diedra gave him a searching look. "Well, you'd better be absolutely sure. I can't have anybody involved in this that isn't totally dedicated to bringing down these assholes. Using four young, traumatized civilians to deliver mass destruction and blow themselves up in the process. I don't know about you, but it sickens me."

Dillon pushed the laptop back towards the FBI Special-Agent-In-Charge. "Okay, I get the point."

"Just so we're all on the same page," Diedra said. "Now, I need ideas about getting the camera inside."

"Size and weight of the smallest one we have?" Olson asked.

"About the same as a normal-sized flash drive," Diedra answered.

"What about rectal insertion?" Olson asked.

"Whoa!" Dillon shouted. "I ain't shoving nothing up my ass!"

Arleen grinned. "Wouldn't work anyway, the scanner would still pick it up."

Dillon cast Arleen a thankful glance as Diedra concurred. "Any other suggestions?" she asked.

"What about the owl drone?" Arleen asked. "Could we attach it somehow?"

Olson jumped up and eagerly retrieved the lifelike drone from a side table. "Of course, the weight of the camera shouldn't have too much impact on its performance."

Diedra smiled. "There you go, problem solved."

"There's a wooden post on the west side of the barn," Dillon said. "Think you could land it there?"

"Are you kidding?" Olson replied. "I'm a pro at operating this baby, just tell me when."

Dillon hesitated. "Let's see, I'm on guard duty tomorrow night and laundry duty on Thursday, so let's say two o' clock Friday morning."

"Done," Olson said. "I'll leave the owl on the post until you come back out the barn. If you managed to get the photos just re-attach the camera and I'll fly it out. If not, just hide the camera until you get a chance at the photos."

Dillon nodded. "Sounds good. There's a loose floorboard in my bedroom where I can hide it. Problem is, the armory has a combination lock, so how do I get in?"

"Can you describe what the lock looks like?" Diedra asked.

Dillon gave her a funny look. "Really?"

"Sorry, forgot," Diedra said. She punched the keyboard on her laptop again before turning the screen towards him. "Any of them?"

Dillon studied the featured locks carefully before saying, "Nope, these are mostly round ones. We're looking for a square-shaped one."

Diedra once again hit the keyboard before turning the screen back to him. "Any of those?"

After careful consideration Dillon replied, "This one here. It's identical, just black, while the one I saw was blue."

"Great," Diedra said. "Agent Olson, get hold of someone in Quantico that can help us with this."

Olson picked up his cell phone. "Will do."

"Right, next on the agenda," Diedra said. "Agent Burns, tomorrow I want you to phone Deputy Director Wells and tell him that the FBI operation appears to be winding down, and that you and Agent Baker should be back in Washington soon."

"Okay," Burns said. "If he asks the reason?"

Diedra thought a minute before replying. "Tell him that the FBI budget can't support an operation that doesn't seem to be going anywhere. Tell him that we recently surveilled a truck and van entering the compound late at night, but the distance was too great to get an image of the driver."

"Good thinking," Burns said. "We need them complacent."

"Hopefully Wells will call the AAM with the news and we'll have him cold," Diedra said. "Anything else before Dillon and Arleen leave?"

"Just one thing," Dillon said.

"What is it?" Diedra asked.

"Can I go for a swim?"

"Can you… what?" Diedra spluttered.

Dillon grinned. "The pool looked so inviting the other night. It's damn hot and dusty out there. Just thought a relaxing swim would be nice is all."

"This isn't Club Med," Burns said severely.

Diedra glanced at her watch. "No, it's fine, they've got time. Agent Olson, please provide Dillon with a towel and bathing suit." After they'd left the room, Diedra turned to Burns. "He isn't like the rest of us." She sounded somewhat envious.

CHAPTER FIFTY-TWO

Homeland Security Deputy Director Roger Wells was a happy man as he drove home in his luxurious German-made sedan. He'd received a call earlier from Burns that the FBI operation in South Carolina was all but over. He'd waited patiently before giving the good news to Barnes. Although his office was swept daily for bugs, he felt more secure calling him from his car.

He used the vehicle's high-tech hands-free system to make the call on his burner phone. Barnes answered after a couple of rings. "What's up?" he asked.

"What's up is that it looks like you guys are free and clear."

"What do you mean?" Barnes said shortly.

Barnes' surliness didn't detract from Wells' mood. "My contact just informed me that the FBI operation is winding down now that their mole is gone."

"Nothing that I didn't expect," Barnes said gruffly.

"Is the mission still on track for August twenty-second?"

"Of course, I would have told you if anything had changed."

Wells laughed. "Just wanted to make sure that I'm out of the country when the shit hits the fan."

"Where you going?" Barnes asked.

"London, I'm attending a security symposium."

"Good idea, just make sure that none of your loved ones are in New York, DC, Atlanta or Miami on that date."

"Already done, my wife's coming with me to England and my daughter's spending the summer in Colorado with a classmate."

"Okay, let me know immediately if anything changes on that side." Barnes ended the call.

Rude bastard, Wells thought as he swung into his driveway. Still, he didn't mind; Barnes was just a means to an end. After the attacks on American soil he would probably take over the reins at Homeland Security. His job would be made even easier with the expected exodus of Muslims from America. He smiled at himself in the rearview mirror, oblivious to the fact that his entire conversation with the AAM leader had just been transmitted to the surveillance team on his tail.

———

Diedra was ecstatic. "Got you, you traitorous son-of-a-bitch!" She and her team were gathered around the war-room table listening to the recording of Wells' conversation with Jerry Barnes.

"More important, we have the date and target cities for the attacks," Olson said.

"True," Diedra said. "Someone tell me what's so special about the twenty-second of August."

Amanda Baker did a quick search on her laptop. "Got it."

"Tell us," Diedra ordered.

Agent Baker began reading, "Eid al-Adha, also called the 'Sacrifice Feast,' is the second of two Islamic holidays celebrated worldwide each year and considered the holier of the two. It honors the willingness of Abraham to sacrifice his son as an act of obedience to God's command. Before Abraham sacrificed his son, God provided a male goat to sacrifice instead. In commemoration of this, an animal is sacrificed and divided into three parts: one third of the share is given to the poor and needy; another third is given to relatives, friends and neighbors; and the remaining third is retained by the family. In the Islamic lunar calendar, Eid al-Adha falls on the tenth day of Dhu al-Hijjah. In the international or Gregorian calendar, the dates vary from year to year drifting approximately eleven days earlier each year. Eid al-Adha is the latter of the two Eid holidays, the former being Eid al-Fitr. The word 'Eid' appears once in Al-Ma'ida, the fifth sura of the Quran, with the meaning 'solemn festival.' Like Eid al-Fitr, Eid al-Adha begins with a prayer of two rakats followed by a sermon or khutbah. Eid al-Adha celebrations start after the descent of the Hujjaj, the pilgrims performing the Hajj from Mount Arafat, a hill east of Mecca. Eid sacrifice may take place until sunset on the thirteenth day of Dhu al-Hijjah. The days of Eid have been singled out in the Hadith as 'days of remembrance' and considered the holiest days in the Islamic Calendar." She finished by saying, "This year's Eid al-Adha is scheduled to take place on the twenty-second of August, ten days from now."

"Thank you, Agent Baker," Diedra said. "So basically, all the mosques across the United States will be filled to capacity on that day."

Baker's horrified voice conveyed what everyone was thinking. "The carnage from the four bombs will be indescribable."

Diedra grimaced. "Undoubtedly. Also, very clever of Wells to be out the country when that happens. The director of Homeland Security will probably be sacked, putting Wells in the top spot."

CHAPTER FIFTY-THREE

Dillon woke just before two a.m., dressed quickly in dark clothing and crept noiselessly from the cabin. He'd become highly proficient in his late-night quests, knowing which creaking floorboards to avoid. He certainly didn't want a repeat of the sandwich incident.

He arrived at the barn without incident and checked out the five-foot-high wooden post on the west side. There it was, the owl drone perched on top of the post, looking as realistic as ever. Its head even swiveled as he approached, the large eyes fixing on him menacingly.

He checked to make sure that he was alone before detaching the miniature camera. Once inside the relative safety of the barn, he moved quietly towards the armory gate. The combination lock was engaged and he flipped it over, shining the red flashlight on the back. Olson had given him detailed instructions on how to disable the lock, and he followed them carefully, hearing a satisfying click after a couple of minutes.

As he approached the stack of wooden boxes, he noted that the water-heaters had been moved and were nowhere to be seen. He removed the canvas sheet covering the boxes and opened up the closest one. Empty... He went through the rest and was dismayed to find that they were all as bare as the first.

Dillon scratched his head. *What the hell, where could they have moved the C-4 to?* He hastily inspected the rest of the armory but came up empty-handed. He hesitated a moment before opening a cabinet that housed a variety of pistols and selected a Glock, along with three full magazines. *Never know when it'll be useful to have.*

He carefully relocked the gate and did a quick inspection of the barn. As he shone the flashlight at the four beefed-up panel vans he noted that they now had writing on the sides. He investigated further, finding that the vans sported magnetic stick-on decals that advertised Dick's Rural Plumbing Services. The contact details on each were different, the first being Florida, while the rest advertised New York, Georgia and Virginia addresses and phone numbers.

He surmised that these were the vehicles to be used in the attacks and that the completed bombs were probably already inside. He tried desperately to get inside one of the vehicles, but all four were locked up tight. An inspection through the rear windows showed that each one contained one of the large water heaters, along with a bunch of tools, pipes and other plumbing equipment. Dillon gave an exasperated sigh. *Bet those water-heaters are actually the bombs. How the hell am I supposed to get photos of the explosives now?*

Frustrated, he locked the barn and returned to his cabin. He placed the Glock, spare magazines and camera in the hiding space under the floorboard before climbing into bed. Sleep didn't come easy as his thoughts alternated between gaining access to the bombs and how time was running out.

———

"Damn, no photos this time," Olson said softly. He was speaking to Diedra, who was standing twelve feet below where he balanced in a large tree overlooking the compound.

Diedra face showed her frustration. *Yeah, that would be too damned easy.* The pair were about one hundred and twenty yards from the west side of the compound, right at the edge of the owl-drone's range. Olson had a clear view of the barn and the wooden post upon which the owl currently perched. He'd just observed Dillon exiting the building and heading back to his cabin. Three more heavily armed agents were concealed just within the tree-line in case Diedra and Olson were spotted and needed backup. "Bring the drone back," she ordered.

With deft fingers Olson soon had the owl airborne, which he brought in for a soft landing next to Diedra. As Olson scrambled down the tree, she spoke into her mic and told the three agents to meet them back at the observation post on the hill.

Once the team had regrouped, they trekked down to where their SUV was parked. Diedra glanced at Olson. "What do you think went wrong?"

"Maybe he couldn't get the lock open."

"Doubt it, he practiced on three similar locks and never had any problems with them."

Olson shrugged. "Guess we'll just have to wait to find out. Hope it's damn soon though, times nearly up."

CHAPTER FIFTY-FOUR

They didn't have to wait long. Dillon entered the bar at five-thirty that afternoon. The second that they entered the apartment above, Arleen spun around. "What the hell happened? Diedra called and said you weren't able to get the photos."

Dillon appeared crestfallen. "All the wooden boxes were empty." He went on to describe what he'd seen in the four vans, which were now ostensibly part of a fleet of Dick's Rural Plumbing Services.

Arleen took a seat on the couch before commenting. "Very clever of them. It explains away the big tires, bull-bars and the water-heaters, in case they get stopped for any reason. I think you're right by the way, water-heaters would make a perfect bomb. Imagine a center core containing fifty pounds of C-4, surrounded by thousands of ball-bearings or nails."

"The killing power would be incredible. No one in any of the four mosques could survive that."

Arleen nodded while extracting the burner phone from her jeans pocket. "We need to get this information to Diedra ASAP."

While Arleen made the call Dillon began recording his report on the laptop, and within an hour he was done. "Diedra had some interesting news," Arleen told him once he'd finished. "We now know that the attacks will take place on the twenty-second, a week from tomorrow."

"Doesn't give us much time."

"She seems to think that they've narrowed down the four targets in New York, Washington, Atlanta and Miami."

"How?" Dillon asked.

"They checked out the largest mosques in each target city where a vehicle would easily have access to the front doors from the street."

"Good thinking. Let's just hope that it doesn't come down to evacuating them. Did you tell Diedra that I did take photos of the empty boxes as well as the water-heaters in the vans?"

"I did, she said it's easily explained and not enough proof. DOJ still won't issue a warrant."

"So now what?"

Arleen smiled. "Now I take you back over to the FBI base and you learn how to open a Dodge panel-van without a key."

"Where they going to get one on such short notice?"

"As I told you before, anything is possible with the FBI. The van should be there by the time we arrive."

———

Abdul Zadeh stared impatiently as Zuzer Mian's fingers flew across the computer's keyboard. Abdul was the Imam of the largest mosque in Newark, New Jersey, and had no knowledge of computers or any such devices that the infidels let rule their pathetic lives. Zuzer was an accountant and trusted member of Abdul's large congregation, to whom Abdul preached radical Islam and Sharia Law.

After a couple of minutes Zuzer looked up and smiled. "All done."

"You're certain that they won't be able to trace the source of the funds?" Abdul asked.

"Of course," Zuzer replied. He went on to describe such things as shell corporations and digital encryption until Abdul held up his hand.

"Enough!" he barked. "I have absolutely no idea what you're talking about." Abdul's concern was due to the fact that Zuzer had just deposited a fairly large sum of money in three different accounts, which financed the same number of Islamic terror cells currently active in the greater New York area.

Zuzer changed the subject. "Are you excited about Friday?"

"I don't get excited," Abdul said sternly. "But I do feel honored that Allah has blessed me so." He and many of the top Muslim clerics in the United States would be boarding a chartered 747 on Friday before winging their way to Mecca in Saudi Arabia for the annual Hajj or pilgrimage.

The Hajj was scheduled from Sunday the nineteenth of August until Friday the twenty-fourth of August. The chartering of a private aircraft had recently become necessary, as many of the aforementioned clerics' names appeared on the no-fly list. Abdul's name also appeared on the list, which only applied to regular commercial flights and not private charters.

Abdul gave Zuzer a grave look. "I apologize for not getting you on the flight." Along with the roughly three hundred clerics and elders were about forty randomly selected devout Muslims who were rewarded with a seat on the plane.

The accountant appeared downcast. "I'm sure that you tried your best."

"Perhaps next year," Abdul said.

"Perhaps, if Allah so wishes." Zuzer glanced at his watch. "I must leave now. Do you require my assistance in locking up?" The large mosque had many doors that required locking, along with several alarms that needed to be set.

"No need, I'm in no hurry," Abdul replied. "You go ahead."

After the accountant left, Abdul did his daily rounds closing and locking windows and doors and punching in codes on alarm keypads.

He finally exited through the rear door and crossed the narrow two-lane road that was as usual, devoid of traffic this late at night. Suddenly, he heard the revving of a high-powered engine and looked to his right in terror. In the light of the dim streetlamps a large SUV was barreling down on him at high speed, its headlights off. Abdul launched himself towards the far sidewalk but didn't quite make it. The heavy vehicle swerved to ensure that it connected him full-on. With a dull thud his limp body went flying through the air. The vehicle's headlights flicked on, and without slowing down it continued down the deserted street.

CHAPTER FIFTY-FIVE

Dillon was getting frustrated as he once again failed to pop the lock on the van. "Take your time, you're rushing it," Diedra commented.

"You need to feel the pressure before you jam it down," his instructor said patiently. The man once again fed the plastic strip into the driver's side window and within seconds the lock popped open.

The van was relocked and this time Dillon used all his patience. He fiddled with the plastic strip until he felt it jam up against the locking mechanism. He pushed down sharply and was rewarded with a satisfying click as the door unlocked. "Finally!" he shouted triumphantly.

Arleen chuckled. "About time."

Dillon gave her a look. "Yeah, I'd like to see you do it."

Arleen grabbed the strip, relocked the door and within ten seconds had it open again. She gave Dillon a cheeky grin. "They teach us many things during our training in Quantico."

"Well done," he said sheepishly.

Diedra interrupted. "Enough screwing around. Ten times in a row and I'll be satisfied."

While he continued with his attempts, Arleen turned to Diedra. "Where's he going to get hold of a plastic strip like that at the compound?"

Dillon overheard. "It's okay, I'm on kitchen duty tomorrow. There's plenty of plastic packaging laying around. I'll cut a piece when nobody's looking."

"Good," Diedra said. "Remember, if you get the photos out tomorrow night we'll be raiding the compound at exactly thirteen hundred hours on Thursday. That's one in the afternoon in civilian time."

"I know," Dillon said testily.

"When the raid starts you are to go directly to your cabin and wait in your bedroom," Diedra continued. "All the agents will know your location and you'll be secured as quickly as possible."

"Why not attack early in the morning while everyone's asleep?" Arleen asked.

Dillon chimed in, "Good question."

"I'll tell you why," Diedra answered patiently. "At one 'o clock everyone but the guards will be in the mess hall. Better to have them congregated in one place instead of spread out. Also, most of the guys are ex-military and would expect an attack to happen in the early morning."

"That's true," Dillon said. "They always double the number of guards just before sunrise. Now I understand why."

———

Back at the apartment there was an awkward moment between Dillon and Arleen when it came to bedtime. "I can sleep in the living room on the inflatable mattress if you like," he said.

"Don't be silly, the next two days are going to be hectic and you need to get a good night's sleep," Arleen countered. "We're two responsible adults, I'm sure that we can get through the night without doing anything stupid."

Dillon nodded amenably. "You're right, of course we can."

Seven hours later Arleen stirred. "So much for not doing

anything stupid." She was buck-naked and curled up in Dillon's arms.

He picked his words carefully. "It may have been stupid, but it sure as hell was fun."

"Mm," she murmured and nuzzled his neck. "What say we give it one last shot? This is probably the last time we'll ever be in bed together. After tomorrow it should all be over."

The feel of her delightfully soft and warm body already had him aroused, and he'd seemingly lost the ability for rational thought. He pulled her on top of him, marveling at how well their bodies fit together.

Afterwards as they lay breathless alongside each other, Arleen turned to him. "I really like you a lot." Dillon opened his mouth to speak, but she pressed a finger against his lips. "Let me finish. I know that you love Lisa and will never leave her for me, which is probably just as well. I just want you to take care for the next couple of days and don't do anything crazy. I would hate to have to ship you back to her in a body bag."

CHAPTER FIFTY-SIX

It was just after two in the morning as Dillon nervously rounded the barn. The Glock was nestled comfortably against the small of his back, while the plastic strip rode the inside of his pants leg. He breathed a soft sigh of relief as he saw the owl-drone perched on its regular spot. A few minutes later he was inside the barn, playing his flashlight on the driver's door of one of the vans.

He clamped the flashlight between his teeth and was about to insert the strip of plastic when he suddenly froze, a chill running down his spine. There it was again, a slight creaking noise. He quickly extinguished the light and crouched down beside the van, staring intently at the back of the barn from where the sound emanated. His patience was eventually rewarded as a dark shadow entered through the small and rarely used rear door.

Fully expecting the lights to come on and for the barn to be bathed in light, he scrambled as quietly as possible over to the west side, hiding behind the mini-tank. Strangely enough the intruder left the lights off and instead switched on a small flashlight.

Dillon strained his eyes but couldn't make out the person's face in the dull glow. However, from the person's bulk and the way he moved, Dillon had a sneaking suspicion that it might be Carl. *What the hell is he doing creeping around here so late at night?* Dillon mused. *Maybe someone saw me sneaking in the front door.*

Dillon tried to slow his breathing as he fumbled for the pistol tucked in his pants. *Dammit, should have left a round in the chamber,* he admonished himself, aware that cocking the pistol now would signal his presence. However, it soon became evident that Carl, or whoever, had other things on his mind besides searching for intruders. There was a slight jangling of keys and moments later the feeble light shone through the back of one of the plumbing vans.

Dillon watched as the figure moved from one van to the next, spending about five minutes inside each one. Eventually, his mission completed, the interloper extinguished his flashlight and exited through the rear door of the barn.

Dillon waited a few minutes to ensure that the coast was clear before sneaking back to where the vans were parked. *What the heck did I just see?* he wondered. *Surely, if that was Carl, he has every right to be inspecting the barn, so why all the secrecy?* He shrugged off the thought and quickly got down to the business at hand.

Dillon removed the plastic strip and inserted it in the driver's door of the first van. He was still trembling a little from the close call and the door failed to unlock on the first attempt. He took several deep breaths and, feeling a little calmer, tried again. This time he was successful and carefully opened the door. He crawled through the pass-through and inspected the water-heater. It was standing upright, secured by several straps.

At first glance there were no obvious signs that it had been tampered with. He used his trusty Swiss Army knife's screwdriver to remove the top plate. There was only just enough space for him to peer inside, and what he observed set his nerves on edge. The center of the heater contained a large, cylindrical cardboard tube, similar to what architects would use to transport blueprints. It was filled with a putty-like substance that he presumed was the C-4 explosive. Surrounding the tube were thousands of ball bearings of various sizes.

Dillon quickly snapped several photos with the miniature camera, praying that the flashes wouldn't be noticed. He replaced the cover and inspected the lower part of the water-heater. There was an inspection cover, which he quickly removed. Inside was a small complicated looking device with several multi-colored wires. He took a couple of photos, presuming that it was the detonator.

While replacing the cover he noticed a cable running from the bottom of the heater and along the floor of the van. He followed it to where it ended on the left side of the driver's seat. It was connected to a small box containing one large button, and he took a photo of it as well.

Before leaving the van, Dillon sat in the driver's seat. He carefully picked up the box and held it in his left hand. *This is what those youngsters are expected to do*, he thought grimly. *Smash the van through the front doors of a mosque, then calmly sit here and press this button, sending themselves and hundreds of other people into oblivion.* He shuddered at the thought and quickly replaced the box before exiting the van.

Dillon checked that the door was locked before randomly selecting the third van for a similar inspection. This time he had no problems, unlocking the vehicle in record time. The water-heater looked precisely the same as the previous one, but before replacing the top cover, he had a brainwave. He gingerly scooped up a little of the putty-like substance with his finger and smeared it on the camera's casing. *They can analyze that to make sure that it's the C-4*, he thought, proud of his ingenuity.

Dillon carefully inspected both vans to ensure that no trace of his intrusion was visible before leaving the barn. He re-locked the padlock, thankful that Carl, or whoever, had decided to use the rear entrance for their mission, whatever its purpose may have been.

The owl was still perched stoically on the wooden pole. He looked around carefully to see if he was alone before approaching it. He attached the camera firmly, did a quick about-face and headed stealthily back to his cabin. *Mission accomplished*, he thought as he climbed into bed.

CHAPTER FIFTY-SEVEN

"Son-of-a-bitch, he did it," Olson whispered down to Diedra. He was once again perched in the tree overlooking the west side of the compound.

"Thank God for that," Diedra whispered back. She'd just about had a heart attack earlier when Olson observed an unknown person entering the barn through the rear door.

Olson repeated his previous performance, bringing the drone in for a soft landing next to his boss. Diedra quickly detached the camera, feeling the sticky substance that adhered to the casing. She mentioned it to Olson once he'd returned to terra firma. He laughed softly. "That dude's not quite as inept as some people believe. I bet that it's a sample of the explosive from one of the bombs."

Diedra sniffed the camera. "I believe you're correct. Damn good thinking on his part."

Diedra recalled the team and upon their return to the mansion quickly inserted the miniature memory card into a specialized port on one of the computers. Olson had already handed off the camera to a technician for analysis of the foreign substance.

He and the two Homeland Security agents peered over Diedra's shoulders as she slowly scrolled through the photos. "This should definitely get us the warrant," she said, satisfaction evident in her tone. She turned to Olson and told him to get the FBI's Hostage Rescue Team, or HRT, to their location as soon as possible. As the ATF would be providing backup to the HRT, one of their agents made the call to give them a heads-up. Agents Burns and Baker would be the only Homeland Security agents in play, as Diedra didn't want to tip off their traitorous deputy director.

The technician returned a few minutes later waving the small camera. He gave a triumphant grin. "Definitely C-4."

"Awesome," Diedra said. "I'll make the call to DOJ for the warrant. The rest of you get some sleep, we have a long day ahead of us."

"It's almost four in the morning," Amanda Baker said. "Surely there won't be anyone awake at Justice right now?"

"Got somebody waiting over there," Diedra answered. "I had a gut-feeling that Dillon would be successful this time."

"He's certainly earned his pardon," Arleen chimed in. Her stint as a bar-lady had come to an abrupt end. She would lead the small team that was tasked to secure Dillon Hunt, aka Daniel Harper.

After everyone had left and she'd completed her call to the Justice Department, Diedra made one more call. FBI Deputy Director Walter Shaw answered the call within a couple of rings. "Don't you ever sleep?" she asked.

"Crime never sleeps," was his abrupt answer. "What's going on?"

Diedra quickly updated him on recent events before saying, "DOJ has authorized the raid and we go in at precisely thirteen-hundred hours, roughly nine hours from now."

"Excellent work, Agent Wolfe. I have a team watching Wells' home right now. I'll take care of him before he leaves for the office. Once he's there he might find out that something's afoot with the AAM and tip them off about the raid."

"Good thinking, sir, I'll keep you updated from this side as events unfold. Right now I'm going to try to get some shut-eye."

"Okay, good luck for the mission. And just remember, we don't want another Waco."

"Won't happen, sir," Diedra said confidently. "Waco was full of civilians; this time we only have one to worry about. If they want a full-on fire fight, we'll give it to them."

CHAPTER FIFTY-EIGHT

Despite his late-night excursion, Dillon woke feeling refreshed and ready for whatever the day would bring. While shaving he grinned at the image in the mirror. *Today I'll either be dead or truly earn my freedom.* Despite his apprehension he felt a jolt of adrenaline that reminded him of his mindset during the successful getaway from the bank robbery. He wondered what it would be like to return to normal civilian society after all he'd been through lately. *Maybe I'll take up skydiving, bungee-jumping or something equally exciting.* He'd done a few static-line and freefall parachute jumps during his abbreviated training in Quantico and had really enjoyed the rush.

A little later, while eating breakfast in the dining hall, Dillon observed the leadership group as unobtrusively as possible. There was only one other guy as large in stature as Carl. However, he didn't move with the agility that Carl somehow managed despite his considerable bulk. *I'm almost positive that it was Carl in the barn last night,* he ruminated. *I wonder what the hell he was doing in there.* Despite Carl's obvious infatuation with Lisa, Dillon still considered him to be a nice guy. He felt a pang of regret that Carl would either be dead or languishing in a federal prison by day's end.

Jerry Barnes mounted the stage as the breakfast session was

winding down and grabbed the mic. "Would the following people please remain behind." He read off a short list of eight names that included both Carl and Dillon.

This caught Dillon off-guard. *What now? Hope it's nothing that's going to screw up the raid.*

After everyone else had vacated the hall, Barnes and Sandra Woods invited Dillon, Carl and the other six to accompany them to their impressive-looking residence. It was the first time that Dillon had been inside, and he was astounded by the opulence of the place. They were led down to the basement, which was just as lavishly furnished as the upper floors.

The four teenagers were already seated at the far end of a long conference table, and Dillon wondered if this was where their indoctrination had taken place. Barnes appeared to be in an expansive mood. "Please be seated, gentlemen." He took his seat at the head of the table, while Sandra observed proceedings with pen and notepad in hand.

"I suppose that you are all wondering what you're doing here," Barnes said. "Let me begin by saying that you are all privileged to be included in the first strike against Islam on American soil. As I mentioned a while back, these four brave young people will sacrifice themselves when we target four of the largest mosques in the United States for destruction. However, they can't do it alone, so you'll be split into four teams of three." He read out the teams and asked that everyone reposition themselves so that teammates were seated together. Dillon's team consisted of himself, Carl and the British girl, Mary.

Once the reshuffling was complete, Barnes continued, "Each team will consist of a team leader, a driver and a heroic martyr." *You mean sacrificial lamb,* Dillon thought. "The drivers' jobs are to get the four vehicles to their destination cities without incident or detection." He proceeded to list the four cities, and Dillon's team ended up with Miami.

"Team leaders will play an important role in securing suitable accommodations in each city within close proximity to the actual target. I suggest a motel or something that has a secure parking lot,"

Barnes said, "but I'll leave the exact details up to the team leaders. They will also rent a vehicle in each of the cities that will be used to reconnoiter each of the target mosques." *Not to mention that we'll need it to escape since the vans will be vaporized,* Dillon thought. "Any questions so far?"

"When will all this take place?" Carl asked.

"I was just getting to that," Barnes replied. "The actual attacks will take place next Wednesday on the twenty-second at precisely seventeen-hundred hours. That's five in the afternoon for you non-military people." He smiled in turn at each of the teenagers. *The date and time you all get to die,* Dillon thought angrily. *What an asshole.*

Barnes continued, "The twenty-second is a very religious holiday for all Muslims, called Eid-al-Adha, so the mosques should be filled to capacity."

Barnes looked very pleased with himself, and it took all of Dillon's self-control not to jump up and punch him in the face. A glance at Carl seated alongside him made Dillon think that maybe the big man felt the same way.

Impervious to the animosity emanating from the two men, Barnes continued with his briefing. "All teams will leave here early on Sunday morning the nineteenth, which means you'll avoid Monday morning rush hour in all target cities if you drive straight through. It will give you two days to do recon of the targets, which have already been preselected. Team leaders have the locations and other details in their briefing packets, along with ten thousand dollars in cash. Remember to pay cash for everything; we don't want to leave a paper trail." Barnes nodded to Sandra, who stood and handed out large manila envelopes to Carl and the other three leaders.

"What about the car-rental?" Carl asked. "We'll need a credit card for that."

"There is a fake one in every packet specifically for that purpose," Sandra said, looking proud at her forethought. "It will pass cursory examination, but use cash to pay for the actual rental."

Barnes once again smiled at the four teenagers. "The rest is just boring detail, you guys are excused." He waited until the foursome had left the room. "Each of the vans has a detonation button that each of those brave youngsters will use to detonate the device. However, there remains the possibility that one or more of them may lose their nerve at the last moment. Each team leader will be issued with a remote detonation device in case that happens. You are to park your rental in a position that allows you to observe the front doors of your target. If the bomb doesn't detonate within ten seconds of the van entering the mosque, you are to detonate it yourselves."

Dillon fully expected Carl to object, but he just sat there with a slight smile on his face. A couple of the other team leaders appeared uncomfortable, and Barnes addressed them. "You don't have a problem with that, do you? If you do, tell me now and I'll get someone else to replace you."

"No, sir," they said, almost in unison. Dillon had the distinct feeling that they both knew the consequences for refusing.

Barnes nodded. "Good. The drivers are now excused, while the team leaders will remain behind for additional details."

———

Dillon followed the other three drivers up the stairs and shut the door loudly behind him. The main level appeared deserted, and as the four men exited the main door Dillon said, "Shit, left my sunglasses down there. I'll catch up with you guys."

He crept back to the basement door and opened it a little, thankful that there was no direct line of sight from the lower level. He listened intently and could just make out what Barnes was saying. "What I'm about to tell you doesn't leave this room!" he said sternly. After a few muffled acknowledgements the leader continued, "The mosque attacks are just a smoke-screen to throw off the feds; the main target will in fact be destroyed tomorrow."

Dillon was so shocked by this revelation that he lost his balance and almost fell through the partially open door. He quickly gathered himself and continued listening. "Tomorrow's attack will result in heightened security, making your missions all that more difficult to complete."

"I thought that you said they were just a smoke-screen?" Dillon heard Carl say. "You mean we're still going to proceed with them?"

"That's correct," Barnes replied. "But only if there's little or no chance of you getting caught. I'll leave it up to you team leaders to decide whether to proceed or abort the mission. It would be preferable to destroy at least one of the mosques, which would only serve to compound tomorrow's attack."

"What is tomorrow's target?" one of the other leaders asked.

Barnes just laughed. "None of you need to know that. All I can tell you is that the plan is already in motion and can't be stopped, no matter what."

"Are you expecting a lot of collateral damage?" Carl asked.

"Not at all," Barnes replied smugly. "With one decisive blow we're eliminating the most radical and dangerous Muslims in the entire country."

Shit, I've got to stop the raid somehow, was Dillon's first thought. He gently closed the door, turned, and was filled with dread.

The British girl, Mary, was watching him suspiciously from about ten feet away. "What are you doing?" she asked.

"Oh, nothing," he said quickly. "I was just waiting for them to finish so I could get my sunglasses." He walked past her towards the front door.

"Wait!" the girl said.

"What?"

"What about your sunglasses?"

Dillon tried to act nonchalant. "It sounds like they'll be a while, I'll pick them up later."

"I'll bring them to you when they finish," she said in her cute British accent. "Which cabin are you in?"

He told her and added, "Thanks, you're a doll," before escaping through the front exit.

CHAPTER FIFTY-NINE

F BI Deputy Director Walter Shaw strode confidently up the long driveway leading to Roger Wells' house. It was a large, elegant home, as befit his status as deputy director of Homeland Security. Shaw was accompanied by two mean-looking, beefy FBI agents. They'd patiently waited until Wells' wife and daughter had left in a new-model Lexus SUV, presumably to drop the girl off at her friend Clara's house on the other side of town.

The FBI surveillance team had been listening in on all of the Wells family's phone calls. They'd determined that the daughter was to spend the rest of the summer holidays with Clara and her parents at their cabin in Vail, Colorado. Roger Wells and his wife were scheduled to catch a British Airways flight to London the following day.

Wells suddenly opened the front door, and his face expressed surprise to find his FBI counterpart standing there, flanked by two large men. "Walter, what the hell are you doing here?" His voice reflected concern.

"Sorry, Roger, didn't mean to startle you," Shaw said pleasantly. "I was just about to ring the buzzer when you opened the door."

Wells quickly recovered his composure. "That's okay, what brings you to my humble home?"

Shaw smiled. "Got some breaking news for you on this AAM thing."

"Couldn't it have waited 'til I got to the office? I was just on my way there now."

"Absolutely not, I'll explain in a minute. Got a quiet place for us to talk?"

"Follow me." Wells turned and led them down a hall to a well-appointed, wood-paneled study. Shaw ordered the two agents to remain outside the room and closed the door. Wells nodded inquiringly. "What's with the muscle?"

Shaw shrugged dismissively. "Bodyguards, due to recent death threats. You know how it is in our business."

Wells took a seat behind an ornate wooden desk. "I sure do, got a few myself recently." He gestured for the FBI man to sit, and Shaw sank into a large club chair, facing Wells across the desk.

"So what's so important about the AAM that it couldn't wait?" Wells asked.

"Several things, actually," Shaw replied. "First off, we've just received reliable intel that they plan to bomb several mosques next Wednesday."

Wells feigned surprise. "You've got to be kidding. I thought they were just some half-assed militia group, painting graffiti on mosques and Muslim-owned businesses and such."

Shaw gave wry smile. "They seem to have rapidly graduated to the big time."

"You said there were several things, what else is there?"

"We have confirmation that the bombs are presently inside the AAM compound. Justice just issued a warrant and we're raiding the compound later today."

Wells looked shocked. "Who's we, and why wasn't I informed?"

Shaw remained calm. "To answer the first part of your question, ATF and the FBI will be taking point on this."

Wells became highly agitated. "I thought that Homeland was supposed to be in on this?"

"That brings me to the second part of your question," Shaw answered with relish. "You weren't informed because the AAM have a mole inside Homeland Security."

Wells' surprise was genuine. "What? You must be joking."

"Ah, Roger, if only I were."

"Do you know this so-called mole's identity?"

Shaw gave a wolfish grin. "Indeed we do, Roger." He produced a miniature recorder from his jacket pocket and pushed play. Wells sat ashen-faced as the recorded conversation between him and Jerry Barnes played at full volume. As it ended, Wells' right hand made a move for the top drawer of his desk.

Shaw produced his Glock 9mm pistol with lightning speed. "Don't even think about it!" He stood up and walked behind the desk, his pistol pointed steadily between Wells' eyes. He opened the drawer and removed a .38 Special revolver. "Now, your service piece and your ankle backup. Slowly, and by the barrel, place them both on the desk."

Wells complied before pleading with the FBI deputy director, "Walter, listen to me, what these guys are doing is the real deal. All we have to do is turn a blind eye, and they'll take care of the Muslim problem in America for us."

"So terrorism is okay as long as we're the ones doing it?"

"That's just the thing, we won't be the ones doing it."

"Shut up, you sick fuck! Now this can go one of three ways." Shaw produced an envelope. "In here is a warrant for your arrest for high treason and espionage. If you don't get the death penalty, you'll rot in prison until the day you die. Also, you'll lose your pension and all benefits, and your wife and daughter will have to live with the disgrace for the rest of their lives. Of course, we also have the option of handing you over to the CIA as an enemy combatant. You will probably spend the rest of your days in solitary at some obscure black-site."

Wells interrupted tearfully, "I'll take the third option. I'll testify against the AAM in exchange for immunity, or even a reduced sentence."

Shaw tried to control his anger. "Don't get ahead of yourself,

Roger; that option's not even on the table. Once we get those bombs, we won't need your crappy testimony."

Wells sniffled. "So what's the third option?"

Without a word, Shaw held up the .38 special and ejected all but one round. He placed the revolver on the desk and looked at Wells dispassionately.

Wells' face expressed disbelief. "What, you want me to kill myself?" he shouted.

Shaw nodded. "It's a win-win situation for everyone, except for you of course. We'll keep quiet about the charges and ensure that your wife and daughter are oblivious. They'll be well taken care of, and we avoid a nasty press-frenzy about another corrupt government official. Like I said, win-win."

Wells pleaded tearfully, "There must be another way."

"Sorry, Roger, time to step up for your family and be a man," Shaw said softly. He retrieved Wells' other firearms from the desk and left the room without so much as a backward glance.

The FBI deputy director was walking down the long hallway when, even though he was expecting it, he flinched at the sound of a single gunshot.

CHAPTER SIXTY

Diedra watched as the assault teams assembled before her. They were presently gathered in a large clearing near the observation post, out of sight of the compound. Forty-five members of the FBI's HRT would penetrate the compound, while forty ATF Agents formed a perimeter and provided backup. In addition, eight HRT snipers would be placed in positions overlooking the compound. As the person in charge, Diedra gave her final orders. "We go at exactly thirteen-hundred hours. That gives you just over thirty minutes to take up your positions. Remember the rules of engagement; only fire if you are fired upon."

As the men dispersed, Olson turned to Diedra. "What are the chances they'll put up a fight?"

"About fifty-fifty, I reckon. The guards are the only ones armed besides the leadership guys, and they only have side-arms. That's why I've ordered the snipers to keep everyone away from the barn where the automatic weapons are stored. If they manage to arm all fifty-odd members, we'll be in for a serious shit-storm."

Olson nodded grimly. "Amen to that." He would accompany Diedra as they approached the guard gate at the compound to serve the warrant. They would approach using an armored HRT vehicle similar to the ones used by SWAT. Besides them and the driver, Homeland Agents Burns and Baker and the senior ATF agent would be the vehicle's only other occupants.

Diedra glanced at her watch. "Let's get going, we don't want to be late for our own party."

———

Dillon quietly ate his lunch as he considered his options. *If the raid goes ahead we'll prevent the mosque attacks, but tomorrow's attack will in all likelihood still proceed. It appears as if Woods and Barnes are the only ones here with all the details.*

Before lunch he'd planned to stand in the open parking area, pretending to stretch and do some exercises. He'd wave his arms, hoping that the watching federal agents would notice. They'd realize that something wasn't right and postpone the raid.

He'd been walking past the barn to the parking lot when Carl had called to him from the entrance of the large structure. "Just the man I was looking for," he'd said. "Get in here, Dillon, I want you to go over your van and make sure everything's okay for Sunday's little excursion."

"Can't it wait?" Dillon had pleaded. "I was just about to get some exercise."

"Get in here now!" Carl had ordered in an irritated tone. "This is way more important."

"Sure thing, boss," he'd said, following the big man to the rear of the barn.

Carl had unlocked the door to the van that was destined for Miami, and the two men had checked the vehicle's oil, water, brake fluid and tire pressures. Next they'd ensured that all the lights were in proper working order. "Don't want to get pulled over for something as stupid as a broken taillight," Carl had said.

Finally they'd inspected the rear compartment where the water-heater bomb was situated. Carl had checked the straps that held it upright and ensured that the cable leading to the detonation button was hidden from sight. A comfortable seat had recently been installed in the rear section, and Dillon had asked about it.

"You'll drive and I'll ride shotgun," he'd answered. "Mary will sit in the back and if anyone asks, she's just an apprentice plumber. We'll be wearing dirty coveralls as if we're returning from an out-of-state job."

"You've thought of everything," Dillon had said, impressed with the foresight.

Carl had grinned. "You bet I have."

Dillon's reverie was broken by the guy next to him asking him to pass the salt. He complied and glanced at his watch; two minutes to one. He reached behind his back to confirm that his pistol was still neatly tucked away. *Better be ready to use it if necessary*, he thought.

CHAPTER SIXTY-ONE

Diedra held her breath as they approached the boom-gate. Adrenaline coursed through her veins and she wiped her gun hand to dry the sweat that had formed there. She yanked the heavy pistol from its holster on the front of her tactical vest as the vehicle came to an abrupt halt. She opened the door, jumped down and trained her gun on the approaching guard. He stared at her in astonishment as she shouted, "Federal agents, we have a warrant to search this property! Drop your weapon and kneel on the ground with your hands on your head!"

The man glanced back at the other guard before complying. The other guard wasn't quite as accommodating. He raised his weapon, pointing it menacingly in Diedra's direction.

"Drop it right now or you're a dead man!" Olson shouted at him. He and the other three occupants quickly fanned out on either side of Diedra, their weapons trained on the guard.

For a moment it appeared as if he would ignore the order and open fire. The closest FBI sniper had him in his crosshairs, carefully observing as the guard's trigger finger began to tighten. Just before the sniper fired, the hapless guard seemed to come to his senses, flinging his Uzi submachine-pistol to the ground.

The biggest downfall of the Israeli-made weapon was its propensity to fire when dropped, and that's exactly what happened. The finicky weapon discharged a six-round burst, narrowly missing the federal agents. His fellow guard wasn't quite as fortunate. One of the 9mm bullets hit the unfortunate fellow in the left butt cheek. He cried out in pain and pitched forward on his face.

"Hold your fire!" Diedra yelled into her tactical mic, worried that one of the snipers would take the blameless guard out. She needn't have worried; the highly-trained men had observed everything that had transpired.

Olson turned to Diedra. "So much for the element of surprise." The plan had been to quietly surround the dining hall and, using a bullhorn, order the occupants out with their hands raised.

Diedra grimaced. "Shit happens." She shouted into her mic, "Breach now, secure all prisoners! I need a medic immediately at my position!"

Two reinforced HRT vehicles roared past them, smashing the boom-gate as if it were a toothpick. They came to a halt just before the dividing fence and ten agents streamed from the back of each. They quickly searched and secured the southern section of the compound, finding it deserted.

Simultaneously the remaining HRT operatives, concealed just within the tree-line, rushed the compound fence. Using bolt-cutters, they quickly cut through the insubstantial obstacle.

Meanwhile, Olson and Agent Burns cuffed the two guards, loading the injured one into the back of an arriving ambulance.

"Guard the other prisoner!" Diedra shouted to Amanda Baker. "The rest of you, back in the vehicle!"

They quickly complied and Diedra ordered the driver to smash through the gate in the dividing fence. He gunned the powerful engine and the heavy armored vehicle crashed through at about thirty miles an hour. Diedra was yelling in her mic for the agents in the southern section to follow them when the driver mashed the brake pedal, bringing the vehicle to sliding stop. Diedra was thrown forward. "What the hell?" she shouted.

"We're taking heavy fire!" the driver yelled back. "We've got to retreat!" He threw the vehicle into reverse and backed through the gap at high speed. The bullet-proof windshield was scarred by multiple bullet strikes, and there were constant pinging sounds as other rounds ricocheted off the vehicle's armor.

"That wasn't supposed to happen!" Diedra shouted. "What the fuck's going on?" She ordered the driver to stop his vehicle in a sideways position about fifty yards back from the broken gate. She and the other occupants quickly took refuge behind it, while the other two vehicles' drivers parked nose to tail next to them. Several agents ran up and took cover behind them as well. "Keep your weapons trained on that gap!" Diedra yelled. "Anyone armed comes through, take them out!"

CHAPTER SIXTY-TWO

Dillon was just clearing his plate when all hell broke loose. The sound of an Uzi firing a short burst reverberated throughout the large hall. He'd fully expected to hear the sound of Diedra's voice over a bullhorn and wondered what the hell had happened.

He remained rooted to his seat with indecision, although most of the other militia members reacted with inbred military training and instinct. Jerry Barnes ran to the stage and tossed the podium and mic stand off it. He shouted at the six leaders and they quickly joined him. The seven men then lifted the lid off the stage.

Dillon was horrified as they reached in and come up holding a medley of assault rifles, mostly AK-47s and M-16s. They urgently began passing them out, shouting orders as they did so. He urged himself to move and joined the throng near the stage, cursing himself for not knowing about the secret weapons stash.

The last four men to receive weapons, Dillon included, were ordered to escort Jerry Barnes and Sandra Woods to their residence.

They exited through the smaller rear door and immediately two of the escorts went down to sniper fire. "Follow me!" Barnes shouted, crossing the open ground with remarkable speed and agility.

They took cover behind one of the cabins and Dillon asked, "Now what?"

"We leopard-crawl across that narrow gap until we reach our cabin," Barnes replied. "If you keep low enough the snipers can't get you."

Dillon waved his arm. "Be my guest, you go first."

Barnes flashed him a grin and set off, M-16 cradled in his arms. Once he reached cover, he stood and motioned for the others to follow. Dillon went next, hugging the ground and fully expecting to die in a hail of bullets. However, he made it and watched in fascination as the older Sandra Woods scrambled across with amazing dexterity. The other escort went last and wasn't quite as lucky. He raised his head too soon and immediately paid the price. A high-velocity round penetrated the back of his head, scattering blood, brains and bone splinters all over the ground.

Dillon started gagging and almost threw up. Barnes grabbed his arm. "No time for that crap, follow me." They entered reached the cabin without further incident and Barnes said, "Quickly, down to the basement, there's a way outta here."

As Barnes moved towards the basement door, Dillon spotted a black-clad HRT operative rounding the corner from the rear of the building. "FBI, drop your weapons!" he shouted, his gun trained on Jerry Barnes.

Barnes swore and dropped his rifle, and Dillon followed suit. Sandra Woods was unarmed and raised her arms in surrender. The FBI agent was momentarily distracted by the movement and Dillon reached behind his back, freeing the pistol that still rode there. Without hesitation he aimed and fired at the distracted agent.

The man cried out and dropped to the floor. Barnes turned to Dillon. "Good job, now let's get the hell out of here!"

The two men grabbed their assault rifles and hurried down the basement stairs with Woods right on their heels. As Barnes reached the conference table he produced a small remote and clicked the button. Dillon watched in amazement as the entire table tilted to the right, revealing a narrow stairway.

Barnes grinned at Dillon. "Always have a plan-B."

Barnes went first, followed by Woods, with Dillon bringing up the rear. Once they were all through the opening, Barnes clicked the remote again and the long conference table shifted back into place. He grabbed a conveniently placed flashlight and started down a narrow tunnel, bending his tall frame slightly. "This comes up about three hundred yards past the perimeter," Barnes said over his shoulder to Dillon.

———

The fire fight above ground was increasing in intensity. Diedra received multiple reports of heavy resistance, with several agents down. "What about Dillon?" she shouted into her mic. "Anybody have eyes on him?" All of the insertion teams had studied a photo of Dillon before the op.

"Thought I saw him heading towards the large cabin at the back," one of the snipers replied. "I had a clean shot, but didn't take it 'cause I wasn't sure whether it was him or not."

"I want a full team to that location immediately!" Diedra shouted. "Let me know once he's safe." She and the rest of the agents in the southern section had their hands full trying to contain a mounting threat as several well-armed militiamen tried to breach their position.

"What the hell?" Diedra heard someone shout in her earpiece.

"What is it?" she asked.

"Looks like a fucking tank!" the voice came back. "Just broke through the side wall of the barn and now headed towards the east fence!"

"Get out of its way!" Diedra yelled. "Is it firing?"

"Thank God, no," came the reply. "It just crashed through the perimeter and is hauling ass through the forest, dragging a big section of fence with it."

Diedra swore. "I want the ATF guys on it immediately, could be Barnes and Woods. They get away and this whole mission is a bust!"

CHAPTER SIXTY-THREE

Carl Boyd let out a loud "Whoop!" as he steered the mini-tank between the larger trees and flattened the smaller ones. As a seasoned special-forces operative, the first thing he'd done years ago upon his arrival at the compound was figure out multiple escape scenarios.

Using the tank to break out had remained the only viable alternative, and one that had almost been shut down. He'd taken heavy sniper fire as he'd crept towards the small rear door of the barn, with similar results at the larger front door. Never one to give up, he'd taken refuge on the east side of the large structure and carefully inspected the log wall. He finally found a spot that seemed slightly weakened by rot and termites.

With his back to the wall he'd kicked backwards with his heavy-duty army boots until he'd created a gap large enough to crawl through. After clearing the barn he'd unlocked the armory enclosure, grabbing several weapons along with the key to the mini-tank. Once he'd had the heavily-armored vehicle running he'd crashed through the weakened section of wall and torn through the camp at high speed, trying desperately to avoid running anyone down.

He kept one eye on the GPS as he weaved the surprisingly

nimble vehicle around larger obstacles. Part of his escape-route planning had involved stashing an old but reliable 4X4 SUV in a deserted wooden building near a major road. Over the years he'd periodically checked on the vehicle to ensure that it still ran smoothly.

He reached the abandoned shack without incident and brought the tank to a stop amongst a thick clump of trees. He figured that the feds would already have dispatched helicopters to search for it.

Once inside he pulled the dusty cover off the battered-looking Chevy Tahoe and opened the rear door. He removed a small water-proof bag from under the spare tire and checked its contents. Inside were passable driver's license and passport forgeries under the name John Smith. There was also two thousand dollars in small bills and a well-oiled 9mm pistol with several spare magazines. He racked the slide on the pistol to chamber a round, engaged the safety and tucked it into his belt.

A few minutes later he was driving south on Route 49, keeping well under the posted speed limit. As he passed the turnoff to the AAM compound he encountered several law-enforcement vehicles speeding in the opposite direction, lights flashing and sirens blaring. He also observed two helicopters heading in the general direction of his recently discarded getaway ride.

After about ten minutes he left the tar-road, turning right onto an almost indiscernible dirt track. He eventually arrived at a deserted, overgrown farmstead which featured an old wooden barn out back. He parked the Tahoe in front of the barn, unlocked the thick clasp padlock and rolled the heavy wooden door to the side. It moved smoothly on well-oiled tracks, belying the building's decrepit condition.

He climbed back in the still-running Chevy and pulled it into the structure, coming to a stop alongside the two vehicles that had been used in the recent robbery in Montgomery. He briefly contem-plated using the powerful Jeep for the rest of his long journey to the Mexican border but thought better of it. *Don't know if the feds' inside man saw it and gave them its description*, he thought. *Better safe than sorry.*

Carl went to the back left corner of the barn that contained a rusting piece of farm equipment. He muscled the old plough to one side and lifted the wooden floorboards upon which it had recently rested. He reached down and hauled up several canvas postal bags. They contained most of the proceeds of the robberies that he and the other AAM members had carried out in the past. *Should be well over ten million dollars in here*, he mused. *More than enough to retire on.*

Twenty minutes later he pulled back onto Route 49, traveling south again until he reached a large freeway interchange. He turned west on the I-20 towards Texas. Once he reached the Lone Star State he'd head south again to Corpus Christi. He now had plenty of cash to charter a large fishing boat from the coastal Texas city. When they were out at sea he would bribe the skipper to drop him off somewhere on the Mexican coast. By now they'd have his photo at all border posts, so entering Mexico by car was out of the question.

Once inside Mexico he planned to use his contacts there to launder the cash and deposit the proceeds into his Cayman Islands account. He would live on one of the lesser known Caribbean islands, sipping frozen drinks on the beautiful beaches and basking in the sun. He had a sudden thought and dialed his cell. *Just got one more person to call before I ditch this phone.*

CHAPTER SIXTY-FOUR

Dillon was sweating profusely as he and the two AAM leaders surfaced from the escape tunnel. They were in a heavily wooded area of the forest, far enough from the compound to escape detection but close enough to hear heavy gunfire. "Sounds like the rest of the guys are putting up one hell of a fight," he commented to Barnes.

Barnes shrugged indifferently. "Just doing their job." He started down a barely discernible track. Sandra Woods followed with Dillon bringing up the rear.

They scrambled through the forest for roughly fifteen minutes, the sounds of the fire-fight gradually receding in the distance. Barnes came to an abrupt halt as the dirt track suddenly widened considerably. "Gets a little easier from here on out," he said as he entered a thick clump of bushes. Dillon followed and watched as Barnes pulled camouflaged canvas covers off a couple of quad-bikes. "You know how to ride one of these?" he asked Dillon.

Dillon nodded. "Of course."

"Good, Sandra will ride with me and you'll follow. If I suddenly duck into the bushes, you do the same. They'll be searching for us from the air before long."

"Where exactly are we going?" Dillon asked.

"Not too far, you'll see when we get there," Barnes replied before starting one of the quads.

They sped down the track for about twenty minutes or so, taking refuge on two occasions when a helicopter passed overhead. Barnes finally brought his bike to a halt and he and Sandra dismounted. They pushed the quad deep into the brush and covered it with one of the camo tarps. Dillon followed suit before looking around. "We're in the middle of nowhere, now what?"

"The middle of nowhere is the last place they'll come looking for us."

Sandra Woods looked at Barnes with concern. "Do you really think we should show him? How do we know he can be trusted?"

"He pretty much proved that by shooting that federal agent and saving our asses," Barnes replied. "Besides, Williams didn't make it out, so Dillon will have to take his place."

Dillon was pissed that they were speaking about him as if he weren't even present. "Show me what? And who the hell is Williams?"

"Peter Williams was the guy who manufactured the bombs and sat with us in recent days," Barnes replied.

"Yeah, I saw him. Mean-looking dude," Dillon said.

Barnes laughed. "Ugly as sin too. However, he was necessary for our mission. Come, follow me and prepare to be amazed." He walked to the edge of a large clearing, reached down and lifted a steel trapdoor. It was painted the same color as the surrounding dirt, making it almost invisible to the naked eye.

After Barnes had disappeared from sight, Woods motioned for Dillon to follow him. He clambered down a fifteen-foot steel ladder, ending up in a large underground bunker.

"So, what do you think?" Barnes asked.

"What is this place?"

"Welcome to the real nerve center of the AAM."

Woods joined them. "The compound was really a distraction to keep the feds away from this place."

Dillon carefully studied his surroundings. The space was large, roughly eight hundred square feet, he estimated. There was a comfortable-looking sitting area with a couple of couches facing a flat-screen TV. One corner held four bunk beds while another featured a small kitchenette and dining area. There were three doors leading from the main area, and Dillon asked Barnes where they led.

"The first one leads to the communal bathroom. The second is our bedroom." Barnes leered at Sandra.

She pointedly ignored the look. "We have our own en suite bathroom."

"It's amazing. I've only seen stuff like this on TV. What was that show?"

"Doomsday Preppers," Barnes replied. "It's where I got the idea from."

"And the third door?" Dillon asked.

Barnes opened the door and Dillon followed him inside. Besides a variety of technical-looking electronic equipment, the large room also held three occupants. One of them was a girl sitting cross-legged on yet another bunkbed. She was tapping away at a laptop keyboard and looked up in surprise as the door opened.

Dillon recognized her immediately. "I wondered what happened to you!" he exclaimed.

CHAPTER SIXTY-FIVE

"Give me the latest sit-rep!" Diedra shouted above the gunfire at Olson. She and the others were still taking cover behind the three HRT vehicles, preventing any of the militiamen from escaping through the gap in the fence.

"Two friendlies down, one confirmed KIA!" he shouted back. "Nine hostiles down, five dead, four badly wounded and twelve in custody."

"The snipers are doing a good job, tell them to continue taking out anyone with a weapon. We need to end this confrontation as quickly as possible."

"Will do!"

"What about Dillon and the two primary targets?"

"Nothing so far, Dillon's tracker pinged at one fifteen. He was inside the large cabin."

"I want that place searched right now, we need to find him ASAP!"

Olson nodded. "Roger that!"

Arleen was working desperately to find and secure Dillon. She quickly worked her way to the leaders' cabin after hearing that he'd been tracked there a short while ago. She reached it without incident and hooked up with a five-man HRT team that was about to breach the front door. "Use extreme caution," she advised. "We have a friendly inside."

"We've already been notified," the leader said brusquely. He sent two of his men to the rear of the cabin, and once they were in position, the rest of them entered cautiously through the front door.

They were busy clearing the adjoining rooms when one of the men shouted, "Friendly down!"

Fearing that it might be Dillon, Arleen rushed over. She was somewhat relieved to find that it was a black-clad HRT guy. "How is he?" she asked.

The injured man struggled to a sitting position before gasping, "I'm okay, just a little bruised. I took a round to my vest."

Arleen noted the round embedded in the upper right corner of the Kevlar vest. "Lucky, an inch or two higher and you'd probably be dead."

He stood shakily. "Good to know, but that's not all, the guy who shot me was your so-called friendly."

Arleen paled considerably. "What? That's not possible. How sure are you?"

"One hundred percent," the injured man replied confidently. "He was with the two AAM leaders."

CHAPTER SIXTY-SIX

"Good to see you too." Alicia grinned at Dillon. The young hacker had vanished shortly after the Montgomery bank robbery.

"Alicia is my niece," Barnes interjected. "She came to live me after my brother was murdered on the USS Cole."

"My mother died when I was still a baby," Alicia said in a pained voice. "Uncle Jason took care of me after those Al-Qaeda bastards killed my dad. He even paid for me to study computer science at MIT."

Dillon acted confused. "Who's Uncle Jason?"

"My real name is Jason Price," Barnes said. "For obvious reasons I decided on a name-change. As did Sandra, whose real name is Kaitlyn Forbes."

Dillon turned to the older woman. "I like Kaitlyn better, it suits you."

"Whatever." She looked angrily at Barnes. "That's way more information than he needs to know."

"It's time for you to start trusting Dillon!" Barnes said harshly. "Not only did he take out that cop in Alabama, but he also just saved our asses from being arrested. He's done more than enough to prove his loyalty, don't you think?"

"I suppose he has," she answered penitently, turning to Dillon. "I apologize, it's just that we've been hounded by the feds since we founded the AAM. You're new to our group while everyone else in this room has been with us since the beginning."

"I completely understand." Dillon smiled. "I would have reacted the same in your position."

"Good, so we're all friends then?" Barnes asked sarcastically, glancing at his watch. "We're wasting time; we need to get Dillon to the airport in under thirty hours."

"Airport, what airport?" Dillon asked.

"Stewart International Airport in Newburgh," Sandra answered.

"Where the hell is that?" Dillon asked.

"Sixty miles north of New York City," Barnes replied. "We'll explain everything on the drive up."

———

"What the hell was he thinking?" FBI Deputy Director Shaw thundered. "Has he gone rogue?"

Diedra had her phone on speaker and answered confidently, "We don't think so, sir." She glanced at Arleen and Agent Olson, who both nodded their acquiescence. They were gathered in the room where Dillon had shot the HRT agent. The fire-fight was finally over and the remaining AAM members had capitulated.

"What makes you so sure?" Shaw asked.

"I personally observed his firearm training," Diedra replied. "He was deadly accurate with a pistol at short range. I even told him to always go for a head-shot if his target was wearing a vest. If he'd wanted to kill the HRT agent, he would have. He hit his vest in an area that would cause the least damage."

"I'm going to trust you on this one," Shaw grudgingly conceded. "Just know, it's your head on the chopping-block if you're wrong."

"I'll take full responsibility, sir," Diedra agreed.

"You bet your ass you will." Shaw abruptly hung up.

Diedra turned to her two colleagues. "We'd better be right about this, otherwise we'll all be looking for mall-cop jobs."

"I trust Dillon's judgement," Arleen said emphatically.

"Me too," Olson agreed. "I have to admit that I wasn't crazy about him in the beginning, but he quickly proved me wrong."

"Okay, so why would he help the two people we were after escape?" Diedra asked.

"The only thing that comes to mind is that he needs more information from them," Arleen said.

"Information about what?" Olson asked.

Diedra jumped in. "Another attack maybe."

"It's the only thing that makes sense," Arleen agreed.

"So what's our plan?" Olson asked.

"We follow his trail via his tracker," Arleen answered. "We'll still be two hours behind him, but maybe we can figure out where he's headed."

CHAPTER SIXTY-SEVEN

Dillon was pleased with himself. He was currently seated in the back of a car speeding northward, with Barnes at the wheel and Sandra riding shotgun. He'd managed to delay their departure from the bunker long enough to ensure that his tracker would ping at its location.

"All right, time to let you in on what's really going on," Barnes eventually said. "We've known for a while that several federal agencies have been tracking our activities. We came up with the mosque attacks as a smoke-screen to disguise our actual primary target."

"Which is?" Dillon asked.

"For the last five years, the top Muslim clerics in the United States have chartered a large aircraft to fly them to the annual Hajj at Mecca. The reason being, many of those same Imams appear on the no-fly list, which of course only applies to commercial flights."

"Let me guess, you're going to take down that plane with the entire Muslim leadership aboard?" Dillon tried to keep the horror from his voice.

"Damn right we are!" Sandra interposed. "Those sons-of-bitches need to feel what it's like to be on the other side of a bomb for a change."

"Damn straight!" Barnes grinned. "There'll be a few token Muslims aboard that couldn't ordinarily afford the trip, but most are Imams of the biggest Muslim mosques in America."

"Impressive." Dillon tried to put as much conviction as possible into his voice.

"Indeed it is," Barnes agreed. "That's where you come in. Our bomb-maker, Peter Williams, was supposed to plant the bomb on the plane. Now you'll have to do his job."

"But I know virtually nothing about explosives," Dillon protested.

"Doesn't matter," Barnes said. "You'll have help. We'll explain the exact details once we reach our destination."

———

"There's nothing there," Olson said. Back at the war-room, he and Diedra were watching real-time footage shot from a chopper. It was hovering over the area where Dillon's tracker had pinged twenty minutes earlier.

"Have them switch to geo-thermal imaging," Arleen said as she entered the room.

"Good idea." Diedra gave the necessary instructions to the FBI flight-crew.

A few seconds later faint thermal images appeared on Olson's laptop. "Well, I'll be damned," he exclaimed. "Three warm bodies in what appears to be an underground bunker."

"I want a ground team at that location ASAP," Diedra instructed. "They are to use extreme caution. Dillon may be one of the occupants."

While Milford Olson gave the necessary instructions, Arleen pleaded with Diedra to let her be on the breach team. "Sorry, you appear to have more than just a vested interest in rescuing Dillon," Diedra said gently. "Is there something you want to tell me?"

Arleen stayed silent as she contemplated the question. Finally she blurted, "All right, we slept together a couple of times, okay! Is that what you wanted to hear?"

Diedra's face showed no surprise. "You weren't fooling anyone, Agent Cooper. I knew that the second I saw you two together."

"How come you didn't pull me?" Arleen asked in surprise.

Diedra patted her gently on the shoulder. "Are you kidding? It just made your roles more believable."

"But it's totally against regulations," Arleen said.

"Screw the regs, whatever it takes to get the job done. What are your true feelings towards Dillon?"

Arleen hesitated briefly. "I think that I may be in love with him."

Diedra laughed. "Now that's what I've been waiting to hear. Get your ass over to that bunker right now and save your man. I'll clear it with the team leader."

CHAPTER SIXTY-EIGHT

Dillon woke to the sound of a slamming car door. "Where are we?" he asked sleepily.

"At a cheap motel on the outskirts of Newburgh, about five miles from the airport," Barnes replied.

Night had fallen and the two men waited in the car while Sandra entered the motel lobby and registered for a room. She paid cash and used a fake driver's license, knowing that her previous two identities had probably been compromised.

Once they were settled in the room Dillon asked, "Now what?"

Barnes glanced at his watch. "It's late, try to get as much sleep as possible. You've got a long day ahead and you'll need to be alert and at the top of your game."

"I slept plenty in the car, why don't we go over the plans for the bomb instead?"

"I guess that now is as good a time as ever." Sandra was busy setting up her laptop on a small table. "Come and stand behind me."

Dillon quickly complied and was joined by Barnes. "That's our target aircraft," he said as a picture appeared on the screen. "It's a Boeing 747-400 operated by a French charter company. The

Muslim leadership have used the same company and aircraft the last four years for the trip to Mecca in Saudi Arabia."

Dillon leaned in closer for a better look. "That's one big-ass plane. It'll take quite a large bomb to bring it down."

"Not necessarily," Barnes said. "It's all about the placement."

Dillon looked at him. "Which is where?"

"In the nose-cone where the radars are situated. Once the bomb detonates it'll cause a sizeable hole in the nose. The plane will be at an altitude of over thirty thousand feet leading to explosive decompression."

Sandra chimed in, "Standard operating procedure for the pilots is a high-speed dive to a level of about sixteen thousand feet."

Barnes' face took on a dreamy expression. "Which will eventually cause the aircraft to disintegrate into thousands of pieces."

Dillon ignored the fanatical look in his eyes. "You guys seem to have put a lot of thought into this."

Sandra turned and smiled. "We've been plotting this for over two years, so trust me, every contingency has been planned for."

"I believe you. So how do I get the bomb on to the plane?" Dillon asked.

"I told you that you'd have plenty of help," Barnes answered. "That includes the airport's chief baggage handler as well as the plane's flight engineer."

"You're kidding!" Dillon exclaimed. "Won't the flight engineer be killed as well? Is he another suicide-bomber?"

"Not at all, in fact he's being paid handsomely for his assistance," Barnes answered smugly.

"Also helps that his brother was killed by one of the ISIS attacks in Paris," Sandra interjected. "The baggage guy is also a long-standing member of our organization. He will ensure that the bomb gets onto the plane undetected."

"Stewart International Airport mainly handles smaller charter flights and security is not nearly as strict as, say, JFK or LaGuardia," Barnes said. "They only have basic x-ray machines, no bomb-sniffing equipment or such."

"Speaking of x-ray machines, that's how we'll get the explosives aboard," Sandra said. "A portable x-ray machine destined for a clinic in the Middle East will be loaded into the forward cargo bay in a lead-lined wooden crate. The crate has a false bottom that allows us eight inches of space for the bomb. The lead lining will negate the airport's x-ray screening, and even if security opens the top of the crate for inspection they won't notice anything suspicious."

"Very clever," Dillon said. "Though I still don't see where I come in."

"The planting of the bomb is a two-man job, and the flight engineer will require your assistance," Barnes said. "That's why you'll be loaded into the cargo hold in a coffin."

"A what!" Dillon said incredulously.

"Relax, it's all set up." Barnes laughed. "We ensured through a little hit and run accident that one of the passengers would be making the trip in, shall we say, less than alive condition. It's happened before and they're even using the same funeral home. All we need to do is replace the recently departed Imam with you."

Sandra appeared to be enjoying herself. "The x-ray screen will only show your skeleton, not whether you're alive or not."

"It requires a special key to open the coffin, so you'll be safe from detection," Barnes added. "When the flight engineer and baggage handler do their final inspection of the cargo hold they'll unlock the coffin. The baggage guy will also hand over a gun to the engineer, not that it should be necessary."

"Why don't the two of them just plant the bomb then?" Dillon asked.

"Not enough time," Barnes replied. "There's panels to be removed and retrieving the bomb from the crate will also take a while."

"So how do the flight engineer and I get off the plane before it takes off?" Dillon asked.

Sandra laughed loudly. "You don't!"

"What!" Dillon turned to Barnes. "I thought you said this wasn't a suicide mission?"

"Relax, it's not. The two of you will plant and arm the bomb while the plane's in flight, then parachute out just before it explodes."

CHAPTER SIXTY-NINE

"What do we have?" Arleen asked the assembled men.

The team leader stepped forward. "We've discovered the trap-door leading to the bunker." He walked her over to where the well-concealed entrance was located.

"Thick steel and really solid," Arleen observed. "Is it locked?"

"Haven't touched it yet, didn't want to set off any alarms. Doesn't matter anyway, we're going to breach using explosives." He looked at his watch and motioned one of his men forward. "Set the charges, we go in ten minutes."

Arleen used the time to don her protective gear and check her weapon. Due to the narrow confines of the bunker, only side-arms would be used during the assault.

Once fully prepared she re-joined the team-leader. "My men go first with you bringing up the rear," he told her.

"Have you informed all your men that one of the occupants may be a friendly?"

"Of course, they've all studied his photo. Now take cover, we're about to blow the lid on this pot."

Arleen found a large tree and knelt behind it, covering her ears. A short while later a large blast shattered the stillness of the peaceful setting. She peeked around the tree-trunk and observed as several men rushed forward and dropped multiple flash-bang grenades down into the bunker below. Once the muffled explosions ceased, they swarmed down into the depths of the Earth.

Arleen quickly followed and was halfway down the steel ladder when multiple gunshots rang out. She cursed and dropped the rest of the way, landing awkwardly but managing to roll onto her side. She swiftly brought her weapon up and tried to find a target through the swirling dust. There were several shapes moving around the confined space, but she held her fire as she was unable to identify them.

Suddenly the team leader's voice rang out, "Clear, all threats neutralized! Holster your weapons!"

Arleen rushed towards him. "Is Dillon alright?"

"Who?" he asked impatiently.

"The friendly!"

"Oh! No, he's not here."

"Are you sure?" she persisted.

"Check for yourself." He indicated a doorway. "The only three occupants were in there. Two males put up a fight and were killed. One female was captured unharmed."

She rushed through the door and quickly examined the two bodies, relieved that neither one was Dillon.

She turned to the surprisingly young girl and barked, "Where is he?"

"Where's who?" she asked petulantly.

Arleen got right in the girl's face. "Dillon, you stupid bitch! What have you guys done with him?"

The girl suddenly laughed. "You're kidding, Dillon is one of you? Man, I never saw that coming."

"Where is he?" Arleen shouted again.

"No idea," the girl answered calmly. "You'd best be very worried, though; he's in very dangerous company."

CHAPTER SEVENTY

"You've gotta be shitting me!" Dillon stared at Barnes as if he were insane, which was probably true anyway. "Jumping out of a fast-moving jet-liner from over thirty thousand feet is pure madness!"

"Calm down and stop being such a pussy," Barnes said. "According to your résumé you've done quite a few jumps. Also the flight engineer will fake a scenario where the pilots have to reduce speed, and you'll both have portable oxygen tanks."

Dillon was only slightly mollified. "I take it we'll end up in the ocean, then what?"

"A boat will be waiting to pick you up. The flight engineer will have its exact GPS co-ordinates so you won't be in the water for more than a few minutes."

"The boat will take you both to a small island in the Caribbean. You'll stay in a safe house until we need you again," Sandra added.

"Sounds like you've thought of everything," Dillon grudgingly conceded.

"As I said earlier, every eventuality has been contemplated." She smirked.

Except the fact that you have a traitor in your midst. Dillon smiled inwardly. "Sure seems like it," he said.

There was a sudden knock at the door and Barnes stood. "Time to meet the other team members." He opened the door and three men quickly entered.

One was tall and well-built while the other two were average in just about every way. The tall one glanced at Dillon and turned to Barnes. "What happened to Peter?"

"Didn't make it," Barnes said offhandedly. "Dillon here will be taking his place."

Dillon stepped forward and extended his hand, which the man ignored. "Are you sure he can be trusted?"

"Dillon's proven himself on several occasions," Sandra said. "Now stop being rude and introduce everybody."

"Yes, ma'am," he said contritely. He shook Dillon's still-proffered hand firmly. "I'm Jack Silva and this here is Pierre LaMont, the flight engineer."

The Frenchman stepped forward and shook Dillon's hand somewhat weakly. "Pleased to meet you," he said in heavily accented English.

"Last, but not least, we have Miles Davis. He's the chief baggage handler at Stewart International," Silva said. "And before you ask, no relation to the famous musician, although his father was a huge fan and happened to have the same last name."

Miles stayed where he was and gave a small wave. Dillon thought that he and the Frenchman looked more like school teachers than international terrorists.

"Enough of the pleasantries," Barnes said brusquely. "I don't know if y'all heard, but our base was raided by the feds. It's only thanks to Dillon here that we managed to escape."

"Shit!" Miles exclaimed. "Now what?"

Barnes gave him a harsh look. "We go ahead as planned, that's what. This operation hasn't been compromised in any way."

"Except that every cop in the country will be looking for you three," Silva said.

Barnes turned to him. "Doesn't matter, Sandra and I will

remain here and wait for confirmation that the plane's gone down. Then we'll go underground for a while at our West Coast safe house."

"And him?" Silva pointed at Dillon.

"May as well go with you now and wait for the funeral home's hearse. Maybe he can catch a few hours' nap in the coffin." Barnes laughed.

"Pierre needs to be back at his hotel before the rest of the flight crew wake up, and I have to be at the airport in just over an hour," Miles said.

"If there's no more problems or questions you can all go right now, it's almost dawn anyway," Barnes said.

No one said anything, and Dillon sneaked a peek at his watch, almost five o' clock. *Damn, don't think we've been here long enough for my tracker to ping, and I won't be able to stall for fifteen minutes.* "Alright if I hit the restroom first?" he asked innocently.

"Make it quick," Silva said. "We need to get going.

CHAPTER SEVENTY-ONE

"Where is he now?" Diedra asked.

"Not far from his last location," Olson answered. He'd been tracking Dillon's northward journey by the two-hourly pings. The previous one had indicated him traveling north on the I-87 just before the junction with the I-84 in Orange County, New York.

"I want to know what's at that exact location ASAP," Diedra said.

"I'm on Google Earth right now," Olson said. "I'll have it for you in a minute."

Diedra turned to Arleen. "Ask the pilots how long before we're overhead his position." The three of them were currently on an FBI HS-125 business jet flying northwards at maximum speed. Also on board were Alec Burns and Amanda Baker, the two Homeland Security agents.

As Arleen made her way towards the cockpit, Olson exclaimed, "Got it!"

Diedra looked over his shoulder at the screen. "Looks like some sort of motel."

"It is indeed," Olson confirmed. "Just outside the town of Newburgh, NY. Looks like they've finally stopped for a while."

Arleen returned. "We'll be overhead his position in about fifty minutes."

"Good news," Olson said, "there's a big airport just outside Newburgh. Stewart International to be exact."

"Instruct the pilots to land there as quickly as possible," Diedra told Arleen. She turned to Olson. "I want local law enforcement to surround that motel immediately. Oh, and tell them to stay the hell out of sight."

"I've got a better idea," Baker said. "There's a Homeland Security office at Stewart International, let's use them instead."

Diedra turned to her. "Good idea, contact them immediately. They may need the help of the local cops as well, but Homeland will be in charge until we arrive."

Baker pulled out her cell. "On it!"

————

"How do you know for sure that the hearse will come this way?" Dillon asked Silva. They were sitting in a black SUV drinking coffee in the parking lot of the Stewart Citgo, having already dropped off the other two co-conspirators.

"It's pretty much the only route to take coming from New York on the I-87N. They'll have to take the R-207 west, which is that road there." Silva pointed to his right. "Then they'll turn north onto Breunig Road, which is the road directly in front of us. We'll follow them and when it's clear force them off the road and into the trees."

Dillon looked around the comfortable interior of the Range Rover. "May ruin your nice ride."

Silva chuckled. "Don't care, it's stolen. Picked it up late last night in New York City."

"I take it you were responsible for the man in the coffin's demise as well?"

"Indeed I was, and it was only a pleasure to take out such a scumbag. His mosque was funding several terror cells in the New York area."

Dillon was surprised. "You know that for sure?"

"Homeland had been tracking him for a while now, there's no doubt whatsoever."

"And you know that how?"

Silva laughed. "You'll be amazed how many high-ranking federal employees are secretly members of the AAM."

"Speaking of which, did you hear that the deputy director of Homeland Security committed suicide?" Dillon asked.

"Yeah, a big loss for us. Believe me, he was either forced to do it or taken out."

Dillon feigned shock. "He was AAM as well?"

"Yeah, Jerry and Sandra are still trying to figure out how he got burned. They're really pissed."

Dillon changed the subject. "Don't you feel bad that innocent people are going to die when the plane goes down?"

"War always has its blameless casualties." Silva glanced at him. "Collateral damage, we called it in the army. I reckon that at least half of the three hundred-odd people on that plane could be considered enemies of the United States."

"That many?" Dillon gasped.

"Don't fool yourself into thinking that only radical Muslims are the dangerous ones," Silva said grimly. "Imagine the bible, or in their case the Quran, commands all believers to commit brutal acts against non-believers in the name of God. Islam is the most violent mainstream religion on the planet and needs to be outlawed in the US if we're ever to live in peace and safety."

Silva's voice had remained calm and rational as he spoke, unlike Jerry Barnes' fanatical rantings. It got Dillon to thinking that maybe his beloved country would be better off if the plane went down.

CHAPTER SEVENTY-TWO

Diedra looked around as she disembarked at Stewart International Airport. It was just before eight on a Friday morning and the airport was coming to life. Several business jets dotted the tarmac, dwarfed by a colossal Boeing 747 parked at the far end of the apron. She gave it a cursory glance before turning to the man who strode up to greet her. "I'm Dan Brooks with Homeland," he said.

She held out her hand. "Diedra Wolfe, FBI-SAC. What's the latest?"

Brooks nodded at the other four as they exited the plane. "I'll catch you guys up as we drive." He indicated a black Chevy Suburban parked behind him.

As the vehicle departed the airport Brooks turned around from his shotgun position. "So far not much to report. I've got five agents on the ground and they're coordinating with the local sheriff's department. The motel is currently surrounded."

"All out of sight I hope," Diedra said earnestly.

"We know what we're doing," Brooks replied brusquely.

"I'm sure that you do, but one of my guys' life is on the line here."

"Understood. We checked out two vehicles that left the motel earlier, but they weren't connected to the suspects in any way."

Diedra leaned forward. "Has anyone spoken to the motel receptionist yet?"

"We followed the nightshift guy and pulled him over once he was clear of the motel," Brooks replied. "He confirmed from the photo of Sandra Woods that she'd booked a room, but he didn't see who she'd been with."

"Room number?"

"211 on the second floor," Brooks replied. "Here we go," he said as they pulled into the parking lot of a strip mall. "The motel is just visible through those trees on the north side."

Diedra and the rest of the team followed Brooks to where two of his agents and a sheriff's deputy were observing the back of the motel building. "Any movement yet?" he asked.

"Nothing so far," one of the men replied. "Thermal imaging has confirmed that there are presently two people inside room 211."

Diedra sounded surprised. "Only two!"

"Yes, ma'am," he replied. "There's only been two since we arrived here and no one's left the room, I'll stake my career on that."

She glanced at her watch and turned to her team. "Dillon's tracker will ping in just over an hour; we don't make any moves until we confirm that he's still inside."

Olson was studying the tablet in his hand. "Roger that. From this close we'll be able to narrow his location down to within a couple of feet."

———

Dillon's mind was working overtime as he contemplated his alternatives. On the one hand, his loyalty to Diedra and the rest of her team compelled him to ensure that the downing of the aircraft never happened.

However, he wasn't completely convinced that ridding America of both confirmed and potential enemies was such a bad thing. If he went ahead with the devious plot, his life would change forever. Everyone would assume that he'd been unable to prevent the bombing and had perished in the plane crash. He'd covertly contact Lisa, who would inherit his upcoming bequest. She would eventually join him in the Caribbean, where they'd live out the rest of their lives in peace and luxury.

His reverie was broken by Brooks. "Got it."

Dillon looked over at his companion who was studying the screen of a small tablet. "Got what?"

"Put a tracker on the hearse last night. It just turned onto the R207, should pass us in about ten minutes," he replied.

Dillon felt the weight of the pistol on his left hip that Brooks had given him earlier, wondering if now was the time to pull it and shoot his partner in the head. Brooks was obviously highly trained, and Dillon wouldn't even chance trying to overpower him.

Brooks glanced at him. "You okay?"

"Yeah, just a little nervous," Dillon replied.

Brooks smiled confidently. "Don't be, won't be more than two of them and they'll be unarmed. We got this."

"We going to kill them?" Dillon asked.

"Only if they put up a fight, which I severely doubt. We'll just gag and restrain them otherwise."

"Good, the fewer innocent lives lost the better."

CHAPTER SEVENTY-THREE

"There it is," Brooks said, cranking the engine of the SUV. He pulled out of the gas-station parking lot and fell in behind a black Cadillac hearse as it turned onto Breunig Road.

Dillon observed several cars approaching from the front. "What if we don't get a clear gap?"

"We will, it's a long road."

Sure enough, once the cars passed, the other side of the road remained free of traffic as far as the eye could see. "Here we go, hold tight." Brooks mashed the accelerator and the powerful SUV surged past the hearse on the left side. Once he was slightly in front of the slower-moving vehicle he swung the wheel over, forcing the driver of the hearse up onto the grass verge on its right side. It came to a dusty halt just short of a stand of trees, the big SUV right behind it.

Dillon and Brooks rapidly exited their vehicle, brandishing their weapons at the two terrified occupants of the hearse. "Out, out!" Brooks shouted. As they quickly complied, he turned to Dillon. "Get them into the trees and cover them." He jumped into the still-idling hearse and pulled it out of sight deeper in the tree-line.

Dillon motioned for the two men to follow their vehicle and ordered them to kneel once they were out of sight of the road. He watched as Brooks jumped out of the hearse and into the SUV, pulling it really deep into the woods.

One of the men pleaded with Dillon, "Please don't kill us! We don't have much money, but take what we have."

Brooks approached. "Just obey our orders and you'll be fine." He produced a roll of duct-tape and threw it at Dillon. "Gag them and tape their ankles and wrists."

Dillon caught the tape and had to holster his weapon while he complied with Brooks' orders. He watched from the corner of his eye as Brooks opened the rear doors of the hearse. *Do I try and take him now?* he wondered. Brooks still held his pistol in his hand, and Dillon decided that he'd wait for a better opportunity to present itself.

Brooks came back to Dillon and pointed at the hearse. "The coffin's in there; get the body out and into the back of the Range Rover."

Dillon looked at him. "What about these two?"

Brooks produced two syringes. "They're also going into the SUV, where I'll put them into a deep sleep." He led the two men away as Dillon headed over to the hearse. Brooks had used the special key to unlock the coffin and it stood open, its occupant looking serene with his hands folded across his chest. Dillon wasn't necessarily squeamish, but the thought of handling the corpse filled him with dread.

"What's the matter?" Brooks' voice said from behind him. "Never carried a dead man before?"

Dillon turned. "Actually, can't say that I have."

"I've carried plenty in my time," Brooks said wistfully. "Here, I'll help you, grab his shoulders and I'll get his feet."

They carried the surprisingly light corpse and deposited it in the rear luggage compartment of the SUV. Dillon noticed that the other two men were laid out on the two rows of passenger seats and appeared to be dead.

Brooks caught his look. "They're just knocked out. You can check if you want."

Dillon caught the threatening tone. "No need, I believe you. Now what?"

"Now we get you comfortable in the coffin. Hope you're not claustrophobic."

Dillon hadn't even thought of occupying the dead man's coffin until then, assuming that things wouldn't actually get that far. "I'm not, but probably will be after this stunt."

Brooks laughed. "Don't worry, you'll hardly notice it," he said cryptically.

"What about the Range Rover?"

"Nobody will find it here until it's too late. The drug that I gave the two guys will only wear off tomorrow morning some time. Now stop delaying, let's get you into that coffin."

———

Olson looked up from his tablet and turned to Diedra. "He's definitely inside room 211; what's the plan?"

"That means that either Jerry Barnes or Sandra Woods is with him," she answered. "I'd really like to get both of them, but if another attack is looming we need that info. Advise the Homeland and sheriff's guys of an imminent breach. We'll give them thirty minutes to prepare and get into position. Hopefully our missing target will reappear before then."

"Do you think that's wise?" Arleen asked. "Dillon probably has the situation under control. We might blow his attempt to uncover the potential target."

Diedra stared stonily at her. "I understand your concern for Dillon's safety, but we don't know the full situation in there. For all we know he's been compromised and is deceased. The geo-thermal would only show two people, and his tracker would still ping either way."

Arleen's hand flew to her mouth. "I'm sure he's fine," she said half-heartedly.

Diedra felt bad about her insensitivity and patted the distressed agent on the shoulder. "I'm sure that he is, but we desperately need whatever info he can give us. We'll do everything we can to ensure he survives the assault."

CHAPTER SEVENTY-FOUR

Silva laughed. "Perfect fit."

Dillon was unenthusiastically lying in the coffin in the rear of the hearse. "So glad to hear."

"Hand me your gun," Silva said.

"What?" Dillon asked.

Silva gave him a look. "Can't exactly have a corpse showing up on the x-ray strapping heat, can we?"

Silva's pistol still dangled in his right hand, so Dillon reluctantly handed over his gun. "I guess not."

"I'll keep the coffin lid slightly open until I'm ready to hand it over to Davis; don't want you to run out of air and die on us."

"Speaking of which, how long will it take to get the coffin on the plane?" Dillon asked.

"Davis will expedite the procedure. Shouldn't be more than an hour or so."

"Are you sure I'll have enough air to last that long?"

"Not normally, but I'm going to give you a shot that will knock you out and slow your pulse-rate and breathing way down. Don't want you moving about while they x-ray the coffin either."

Dillon tried to remain calm. He'd formulated a plan to knock on the coffin lid during inspection and warn airport security of the impending attack. "When do I get the shot?" he asked casually.

Silva grinned as he deftly produced a syringe and jabbed it into Dillon's neck. "No time like the present," was the last thing Dillon heard before darkness descended.

————

"Something's not right." Barnes turned from his kneeling position at the motel room's window and looked with concern at Sandra Woods.

"What do you mean?"

"It's too quite out there," he replied. "At this time of day there should be people all over the place, but it's as dead as a morgue."

"You're just being paranoid," Woods said derisively.

"What if the motel clerk recognized you when you checked in?"

Woods laughed scornfully. "After pulling an all-nighter he's probably fast asleep in his bed."

"There! I just saw a guy dressed in black take cover behind the office building, I swear he was carrying a rifle or shotgun."

Woods suddenly changed her attitude and joined her companion at the window. "Are you sure?"

Barnes racked the slide on his pistol. "Of course I'm sure, I didn't survive two tours in Iraq by being inattentive."

Woods looked down at the man beside her as she contemplated her options. Although she and Barnes had found comfort from their losses in each other's arms and had eventually become lovers, she certainly didn't love him. That was reserved exclusively for her dead husband, whose murder she was determined to avenge no matter the cost. However, she couldn't be sure that Barnes wouldn't give up their plan in exchange for a plea deal. She hesitated fractionally before drawing her own weapon and firing a shot into the back of his head. As his body slumped to the floor she opened the front door and stepped resignedly onto the walkway outside.

CHAPTER SEVENTY-FIVE

D an Brooks was with his squad at the bottom of the western stairwell when he heard the unmistakable sound of a gunshot. Through his earpiece he heard Diedra shout, "Shots fired, breach now!" Without hesitation he led the team up the stairs at full pace onto the second-floor hallway. A woman that he quickly identified as Sandra Woods was standing outside room 211; held in her right hand was a pistol clearly in view.

The agent next to Brooks shouted urgently, "Drop the weapon now!"

Woods turned her head, and Brooks noticed a small smile play across her face as she lifted the gun and pointed it straight at them. He and the man next to him fired almost simultaneously, both bullets hitting her center-mass. Woods dropped like a rag-doll as Brooks ran forward and kicked the pistol from her hand. He motioned the rest of the team through the open doorway as he bent and felt the inert woman's pulse. He heard someone shout, "Hostile down!" Then more shouts of, "Clear!"

Woods' white blouse had turned crimson, but Brooks detected a weak pulse. "I need a medic immediately!" he shouted into his mouthpiece.

One of his squad members came out of the room. "Barnes is dead, single GSW to the head, no sign of the friendly."

Brooks looked at him incredulously. "What? How is that possible?"

The man shrugged. "Beats me."

Just then Woods coughed and opened her eyes. Pink blood was bubbling from her mouth and Brooks realized that one of the rounds had pierced a lung. "Where's that damned medic!" he shouted. He spun and asked Woods loudly, "Where is Dillon Hunt?"

Woods tried to speak, but all she emitted was a gurgling sound. Brooks bent and put his ear closer to her mouth and through all the burbling and wheezing managed to make out two distinct words, "Fuck you."

He moved back as the medical team arrived and watched as they desperately tried to stem the severe bleeding. As they worked on Woods her eyes began to glaze over and Brooks knew instinctively that she was beyond help. Any chance of finding out about Dillon's whereabouts or the upcoming attack was dying with her, and he knew that Diedra was going to be furious.

———

Silva pulled the hearse over onto the gravel near the entrance to the airport and waited for a couple of cars to pass. Once it was clear he climbed out and opened the rear doors. Earlier he'd propped the coffin lid open with a jacket that he'd found behind the driver's seat. He lifted the lid and quickly checked that Dillon was still alive and well before closing it and locking it with the special key. He dropped the key into his pocket while thinking that he'd better not forget to give it to Davis.

Back on the road he drove for a while before taking the turnoff that was marked 'freight only.' As he pulled into the parking lot he noticed Davis waving at him from the loading dock of a large building. He came to a stop, climbed out and greeted the chief baggage-handler.

"How'd it go?" Davis asked.

Silva grinned. "No problems, a cake-walk."

The two men lifted the coffin onto a trolley that Davis had organized in advance, knowing that time was critical. "How much time left?" he asked Silva.

Silva glanced at his watch. "About fifty minutes, give or take."

Davis nodded. "Shouldn't even need half that. I'll personally take the coffin through security and onto the plane."

Silva handed over the key as well as Dillon's pistol. "How're you going to get these through?"

"No problem, the coffin's going through x-rays, not me. I'll use a side door for ramp personnel only. No checks for us 'cause we're coming in and out all day."

"Not the greatest security," Silva noted.

"This ain't exactly LAX."

"Suits us." Silva shook Davis' hand. "Don't forget to give the gun to LaMont when you guys do the baggage check. Well, I'm out of here, good luck." Davis nodded and began wheeling the trolley through the freight doors.

So far so good, Silva thought as he guided the hearse back the way he'd come.

CHAPTER SEVENTY-SIX

Diedra was inside room 211 trying desperately to understand the situation. "So Woods and Barnes are dead and there's no sign of Dillon?"

Brooks nodded. "Correct. Both of them are only recently deceased, so it was their heat-signatures that we've been observing all this time."

Diedra turned to Olson. "How the hell did Dillon's tracker ping in the room if he's not here?"

"Just give me a minute or two to figure it out," he replied.

Arleen exited the small bathroom. "No need, I found this on top of the medicine cabinet." She held up a tooth.

Diedra fumed. "What the hell, why would he remove the implant?"

"Maybe he has gone rogue?" Brooks offered.

"Bullshit!" Arleen retorted. "He left it here knowing that it would lead us to Barnes and Woods. He obviously figured that he'll be able to stop the impending attack by himself."

Olson jumped into the fray. "Look, at this point we don't even know for sure that there is another attack planned; it's just something we've surmised. The forensic team that ran the bunker reckon that the girl managed to wipe all the computers, communications and everything else. We've got absolutely nothing to go on."

Diedra grimaced. "What about the girl herself?"

"Apparently she's quite a tough cookie. She hasn't said a word besides asking for an attorney," Olson replied.

"Screw that, can't we treat her as an enemy combatant or a threat to national security?" Diedra said harshly.

Arleen was horrified. "You mean water-boarding and torture to make her talk?"

"Won't work, Justice will never go for it without proof," Olson said. "All we've got on her so far is participation in the bank robbery in Montgomery, and we'll need Dillon's testimony to convict her."

Diedra was beside herself. "Like you said, we've got nothing!"

"One interesting fact did emerge from the compound itself," Olson said.

"What's that?" Diedra asked.

"The detonators on the four bombs had been tampered with," Olson replied. "There was no way that any of them would have exploded."

Arleen said triumphantly. "I told you Dillon isn't a traitor."

"Oh, I doubt that it was him," Olson said. "Apparently it would take an expert to alter the detonators in such a fashion."

———

Miles Davis clambered up the portable stairs to the forward baggage compartment door, the flight engineer right behind him. It was their collective duty to ensure that all items in the freight compartments were correctly stowed and secured. Once inside, Davis produced the key, unlocked the coffin and lifted the lid.

LaMont knelt and felt Dillon's pulse. "Still alive."

Davis handed him a vial of smelling salts. "Wake him up."

A few seconds later Dillon coughed, spluttered and sat bolt upright. He shook his head to clear the cobwebs. "Am I on the plane?"

Davis' face swam into view. "Damn right, everything's going according to plan."

"Hurry, we can't spend too much time in here without raising suspicion," LaMont said.

Davis helped a wobbly Dillon out the coffin and led him towards a large wooden crate, LaMont following behind. "This is the crate containing the explosives," Davis explained.

LaMont examined the container. "How do we access them?"

Davis stepped over to a cabinet containing various tools and strapping equipment and selected a crowbar. He used it to pry off the bottom plank of the crate. "It's in there. The detonator is in a separate canvas bag."

LaMont nodded. "And the stuff I asked for?"

Davis indicated a smaller crate standing alongside the one containing the bomb. "In this one. It also contains your parachutes, life vests and oxygen canisters."

LaMont grabbed the crowbar and began working on the lid. "Didn't raise any suspicions?" he asked.

"Not at all, it's addressed to a parachuting club in Riyadh," Davis replied. "Now forget that crate, we've got to get going. Dillon will have plenty of time once you're in the air to retrieve its contents."

LaMont laid down the crowbar and turned to Davis. "Aren't you forgetting something?"

The baggage handler grinned, reached into his coverall pocket and handed over a pistol. "Never know if you might have a use for this."

LaMont said seriously, "If the pilots suspect that something is amiss, I'll definitely need it."

Dillon had been following the proceedings with as much clarity as his befuddled brain would allow. He wasn't too happy to observe that the flight engineer was now armed and he wasn't.

CHAPTER SEVENTY-SEVEN

Diedra and her team were seated in Brooks' office at the airport. She glanced at her watch, surprised to see that it was almost three in the afternoon. "We need to figure out what the potential target could be."

"Given our proximity to New York City, it would probably be somewhere there," Olson said.

"There are many large Islamic mosques in New York, not to mention New Jersey," Brooks offered.

Arleen shook her head. "Has to be something else. We've already foiled their plan to blow up four mosques." She briefly gave him a rundown on the AAM's suicide-bomber plans.

Brooks tapped at his computer keyboard. "The only major upcoming events on the Islamic calendar are next Wednesday, which is Eid-al-Adha, and September eleventh, which is the Islamic New Year."

Diedra shook her head. "Too far away," she said emphatically. "It has to be something happening this weekend. All of you, reach out to your contacts and find out what it can be."

———

Silva dumped the hearse in the woods alongside the stolen Range Rover. After a quick inspection to ensure that its occupants were still asleep, he set off through the trees in the direction of the nearby Homewood Suites hotel. He'd stashed another stolen vehicle in the hotel's parking lot, a nondescript silver Toyota that was now sporting fake California plates. His plan was to go back to the motel and join his two leaders, where they'd wait for news of a missing charter jet over the Atlantic Ocean. Once they had confirmation of the mission's success, he'd drive the three of them cross-country to a remote safe house deep in the Sierra Nevada Mountains, where they'd plan their next strike against Islam.

His mind was preoccupied with the mission as he turned the Toyota onto the street where the motel was situated. At first he failed to notice the commotion ahead, but as he drew closer he suddenly noticed a small crowd gathered in front of the motel entrance. He cursed and pulled the car to the curb, contemplating whether to turn and run or find out what had happened.

Curiosity finally got the better of him and he strolled over and joined the throng of onlookers. The entire motel property was cordoned off with yellow crime-scene tape and was a hive of activity. Local cops were keeping the crowd at bay while federal agents and crime-scene technicians swarmed all over the place.

Silva turned to an older gentleman next to him. "What happened here?"

The old man looked up at him and grimaced. "Some sort of shoot-out between the cops and two suspects."

Silva appeared shocked. "Oh, wow! Anybody dead?"

"No cops, fortunately, but both suspects were apparently killed. Seems like it was a man and woman that were staying in a room on the second floor of the motel."

"Know what they were wanted for?" Silva asked casually.

The old man shook his head. "No idea, the cops are being really tight-lipped about what happened." He gestured towards a small group of reporters. "Won't even give them any info either."

"Thanks anyway, I'd better get going," Silva said. As he walked back to the car he fished out his cell phone and made a call. When Davis answered he asked urgently, "Did the plane take off?"

"An hour ago, right on schedule," Davis replied.

"Thank God for that."

"What's wrong?"

"Barnes and Woods are dead, killed in a shootout with the cops."

"Shit!" Davis said. "I'd better get the hell outta here."

"No kidding. Park your car at the far end of the Homewood Suites hotel parking lot. I'll pick you up in about fifteen minutes."

"I'll be there." Davis ended the call.

CHAPTER SEVENTY-EIGHT

The plane had been in the air for almost an hour and Dillon had plenty of time to contemplate his predicament as he unpacked the contents of the second crate. He was still struggling with the dilemma of whether to help take down the plane or not. On the one hand, he was sure that it would be a huge blow to the terrorist organizations that had infiltrated his country. However, he wasn't a murderer and the thought of killing even one innocent person was reprehensible to him. In the end, it was the thought of his dead brother that helped him make up his mind. He was absolutely sure that Michael wouldn't hesitate to do the right thing. Dillon would honor his brother's memory by completing the mission that he'd begun.

With that issue resolved, he now had to figure out a way to prevent LaMont from successfully planting and detonating the bomb. He'd retrieved it earlier from the first crate, and now he inspected the device. It was almost the same size and shape as a Frisbee, with the plastic explosive molded onto one side of a metal plate. He decided not mess with it and inspected the detonator instead. It looked like some sort of timing mechanism with several wires attached to a pen-like device. He realized that there was no way of disabling it without LaMont noticing. He was fully aware that the flight engineer was armed and wouldn't hesitate to shoot him at the first sign of treachery. He figured that he'd play it by ear when LaMont arrived and wait for an opportunity to take him by surprise. He placed the heavy crowbar in an easily accessible position and settled down to wait.

———

Up on the flight deck of the wide-bodied aircraft, Pierre LaMont was preparing for the upcoming task. He was seated at his control panel, behind and to the right of the pilots. They were both French, and he'd flown with them many times. The captain was a bit of an asshole who tended to look down his nose at the rest of the flight-crew, so LaMont had no compunction at being the cause of his demise. However, the first officer was an alright guy who had always treated him well, and LaMont felt a twinge of regret that he had to die. He glanced towards the two pilots to ensure that they were both occupied and got to work.

First, he pulled the circuit-breakers controlling both the satellite and VHF radios, effectively disabling them. The aircraft had just passed out of radar range and the co-pilot had recently contacted air-traffic control. They weren't scheduled to check in for another hour or so, which should give him more than enough time.

Next he pulled the circuit-breaker that controlled the locking mechanism for the forward cargo door. This would enable him to open the door while the plane was still in flight. The next circuit-breaker to go was the one controlling the TCAS. The Traffic Collision Avoidance System radar was located in the nose and would have to be removed to make space for the bomb.

Finally, he replaced the bulb for the light that indicated that the rear cargo door was locked and secure. It was a defective bulb that he'd held onto for just this purpose. Sure enough, after a minute or two a red warning light began to flicker.

Satisfied that he was fully prepared, he spoke into his mic and informed the captain about the flickering warning light. "Probably just a faulty globe," the captain said gruffly. "Try replacing it."

"Already tried that, doesn't seem to help," LaMont said respectfully.

"I certainly don't want to turn around for a minor fault," the captain said impatiently. "What do you suggest?"

"I agree that turning around at this point may be premature," LaMont said. "However, it's not something we can just ignore. Why don't I go down to the cargo bay and make a visual inspection of the door?"

The captain perked up a bit. "Excellent idea, Pierre. Call me on the intercom once you're down there."

LaMont smiled as he unlatched his seatbelt. "Will do, Captain."

CHAPTER SEVENTY-NINE

Diedra was highly agitated. "This is ridiculous, we're still no closer to figuring out the damn target." They were still crowded inside Brooks' small office, whose desk was cluttered with empty coffee containers. All their contacts had the same thing to say. Besides the two upcoming celebrations and the annual pilgrimage to Mecca, no events were planned for the tri-state area. "I need to go outside for some fresh air," Diedra said. "Be back in a bit."

"Mind if I join you?" Brooks asked. "I could do with a cigarette."

Diedra glanced at him. "Only if I can bum one from you; looks like I picked the wrong time to quit smoking."

They headed down to a small grassy area next to the building and lit up. Diedra took a deep drag and instantly felt the nicotine doing its job as she began to relax. She looked through the chain-link fence at the airport apron where their jet was still parked. Something seemed different, but she couldn't put her finger on it at first. Then it hit her and she turned to Brooks. "What happened to that big-ass 747 that was here earlier?"

"Took off a couple of hours ago," he replied.

"Where was it going?"

Brooks extracted his cell. "Don't know, I'll call the tower and ask."

Diedra ignored Brooks as he made the call, concentrating on the relaxing effect of her cigarette. She heard a sharp intake of breath and swiveled to look at him, noticing how pale his face had become.

"What is it?"

"It's a charter flight headed for Mecca, full of the top Muslim leaders in America."

Diedra felt the blood drain from her face. "Son of a bitch, the target was right under our noses all along!" She flicked her cigarette away and flew towards the building entrance with Brooks right behind her.

The rest of the team looked up in astonishment as the two agents crashed into the room. Diedra gasped breathlessly. "The 747 is the target. It's carrying America's top Muslim clerics to Mecca for the Hajj!"

Olson was the first to respond. "How the hell did we miss that?"

"We all just assumed that the attack would be on American soil," Arleen offered.

"Well, we all screwed up big-time," Diedra said. "If that plane goes down, the shit's really going to hit the fan." She turned to Brooks. "Get me into that control tower immediately."

As the two of them were leaving Olson asked, "What do you want us to do?"

"Round up every person that had access to that plane. Run in-depth background checks and start interrogations immediately," Diedra replied.

———

Silva was relieved to see Davis waiting alongside his car in the hotel parking lot. He was concerned that the feds may have figured out what was going on. He pulled up alongside the worried-looking baggage handler. "Jump in," he ordered.

As they pulled away Davis asked, "What the hell went wrong?"

"Beats me, someone at the motel must have recognized them.

Their photos have been plastered all over the news since yesterday afternoon."

Davis nodded. "Yeah, I saw that this morning. What now?"

"We get the hell out of town as fast as possible and head for that safe-house in California."

"Can we stop by my place so I can pick up some things?"

Silva looked at him incredulously. "Have you lost your mind! They could be there right now looking for you. We need to put as much distance between the airport and ourselves before that plane goes down."

Looking suitably chastised, Davis asked, "What about clothes and stuff once we get there?"

"There's plenty of cash stashed at the cabin," Silva replied. "We'll just have to buy everything new and start over. The two of us are pretty much the only AAM members left. We'll just have to rebuild Jerry and Sandra's legacy from the ground up."

CHAPTER EIGHTY

Diedra and Brooks were speaking to James McCabe, the ATC supervisor. "What do you mean they're not on radar?" she asked in surprise.

"They passed from radar range about an hour ago. There's about a four-hour window on trans-Atlantic flights without radar coverage," McCabe explained patiently.

Brooks stepped in. "Call them on the radio and order the pilots to return immediately."

McCabe shrugged. "Already tried that, but they're not answering their satellite or VHF radios."

"Dammit, how can that be?" Diedra fumed.

"Someone must have disabled the comms," McCabe suggested. "The chances of both radios malfunctioning at the same time are extremely remote."

Diedra looked at Brooks. "I want your office to run a check on the entire aircrew immediately." As the Homeland agent left, she turned back to McCabe. "Any chance that the plane's already gone down?"

"It's possible," he replied. "However, they're still over a major shipping lane, and we haven't received any news of a plane crash."

"Coordinate with the Coast Guard to monitor all marine communications," Diedra ordered as she pulled her cell phone out and dialed her boss.

"What's the latest?" Walter Shaw asked without preamble.

"Bad news, sir," Diedra replied. She gave him a quick rundown of the evolving crisis.

Shaw was less than impressed. "Dammit, Agent Wolfe, you realize that we're both finished if that plane goes down. The president will have both our heads."

"I realize that, sir. Our only hope is that Dillon made it onto the plane and will be able to prevent it from crashing."

"Great, so both our futures are in the hands of a common criminal. Is there nothing else we can do?"

Diedra drew a deep breath. "Can you contact SECNAV and have her scramble a couple of fighters to track the plane?"

"What, you want me to ask my ex-wife for a favor?" Shaw snorted. "We're not even on speaking terms."

"I know that it's a lot to ask, sir. Going through the Chairman of the Joint-Chiefs will just take too long. Tell her that it's a matter of national security."

Shaw sighed. "Okay, I'll do it. Text me the flight details. After all I've been through with the divorce, the last thing I needed is to owe the damn woman."

———

"What's up?" the pretty hostess asked as LaMont entered the forward galley.

He smiled at her. "Nothing serious, I just need to go down into the cargo hold to check on something."

"Oh, we're just about to start food service. Will you be long?"

"I'll be quite a while, have to go all the way back to the rear baggage area," Lamont replied.

"Do you want us to delay the food?"

"No need, I'll contact you on the intercom when I'm ready to come back up."

"You could leave the hatch open," she offered.

"Against regs. Besides, don't want one of you lovely ladies falling through and hurting yourself."

"You're such a considerate gentleman," she said flirtatiously.

LaMont unlatched and lifted the hatch before descending down the steep ladder into the bowels of the giant aircraft.

The hostess closed the hatch, which locked automatically with a loud click. *Such a nice guy,* she thought, *wouldn't mind a bit of action with him on our layover in Riyadh.*

CHAPTER EIGHTY-ONE

Dillon was resting against one of the parachute packs when he heard someone approaching. He jumped swiftly to his feet and grabbed the crowbar. LaMont came into view and eyed the heavy metal implement. "Relax, it's only me." He was holding a pistol in his right hand, which Dillon looked at quizzically. LaMont gave a wry smile. "Don't take it personally, but I don't know you well enough to trust you completely."

Dillon looked him and shrugged. "Can't say I blame you."

LaMont grabbed the explosive device and detonator and pointed to a bag containing a cordless drill and several other tools. "Bring those and follow me, we have to move quickly."

LaMont led Dillon to the extreme front of the large cargo hold where a metal ladder led up to an inspection hatch. LaMont pointed at the metal door that was secured by several large bolts. "Get up there and use the drill to remove the bolts. The correct-sized bit is already attached."

While Dillon busied himself with retrieving the drill and climbing the ladder, the flight-engineer walked over to an intercom phone and lifted the receiver. Before dialing the flight-deck he said to Dillon, "Don't start the drill until I'm done here, or they'll wonder what the hell that noise is."

The captain answered curtly, "What's the situation, LaMont?"

"Just arrived at the rear cargo door, captain. It seems secure, although there's an odd vibration when I put my hand on it."

"That doesn't sound good."

"No, it doesn't," LaMont agreed.

"What do you suggest?" the concerned pilot asked.

"I recommend that you reduce our speed while I inspect the door further."

"Roger, will do. Keep me informed and for God's sake be careful. I don't want to have to explain how I lost a crew member at over thirty thousand feet."

LaMont replaced the receiver and nodded at Dillon. "Okay, you can start."

While Dillon deftly removed the bolts, LaMont went to work on the bomb. He carefully inserted the detonator and set the timer to twelve minutes. That would give the two of them ten minutes to prepare for their exit by donning their life vests, parachutes and oxygen masks. The opening of the cargo door would result in explosive decompression, although it would initially be limited to the cargo hold. The device would explode roughly two minutes after their departure while the huge aircraft was still in a high-speed dive to a safe lower altitude. The sudden appearance of a gaping hole in the nose would subsequently ensure the plane's complete destruction.

———

"He's got to be our guy." Diedra was emphatic. She was still in the control tower and was on a call from Arleen, informing her that Miles Davis, the chief baggage handler, had disappeared. Arleen had also just confirmed that he had performed the final cargo inspection on the 747.

"Agreed. Also, there's no surveillance footage of Dillon

anywhere near the plane, or the entire airport for that matter," Arleen added.

"He had to get on that plane somehow; we need to find out how," Diedra instructed. "In addition, I want an immediate BOLO out on Davis' car as well as a search of his residence."

Before hanging up Arleen said, "I'll get right on it. boss."

CHAPTER EIGHTY-TWO

Major Luke Edwards guided his F-18 navy fighter eastwards at full throttle. He and his wingman, Lieutenant Martinez, had been on a routine training flight off the New Jersey coast when the high-priority mission had come through.

They had the target aircraft's last known position as well as its speed and altitude, which Edwards had fed into his computer. They were closing in fast on the 'bogey's' estimated position when the major got a ping on his attack radar. "Target's transponder just showed up on my radar," he informed mission-control on the carrier USS Gerald R. Ford, stationed in Norfolk, Virginia.

However, it was the woman FBI agent, Diedra Wolfe, who was the first to reply. The tower at Stewart International Airport was monitoring on the same frequency, and he'd been instructed to follow her orders. "Great job," she said. "Time to intercept?"

"The target is at flight level three-three-zero on a heading of one-four-zero, airspeed is just under four hundred knots," Edwards replied. "We should have a visual in less than fifteen minutes."

Diedra noticed the perplexed expression on McCabe's face. "What's the problem?"

"The plane's heading and altitude are normal, but its speed is way too slow," he answered. "Something's not right."

———

Arleen and Agent Olson inspected the Buick sedan parked on the far side of the Homewood Suites lot. They were accompanied by two local cops who'd discovered the vehicle fifteen minutes earlier. "We normally stop by here during our break," one of the cops explained. "It's quiet and we can eat our lunch in peace."

"We'd just received the BOLO and the description was fresh in our minds," the other said.

Olson thanked the cops for their vigilance. "We need to get inside and search the vehicle," he added.

"What about a warrant?" one cop asked.

"Screw that!" Arleen said. "This is a matter of national security."

The police cruiser was parked alongside, and one of the cops opened the trunk and retrieved a strip of plastic. Within seconds he'd popped the lock on the Buick.

Arleen smiled at him as he held the door open. "Nice work." She donned a pair of gloves and thoroughly inspected the interior, while Olson checked the trunk. After a few minutes they concluded that there was nothing incriminating inside the vehicle.

Arleen turned to the senior cop. "I need you to contact your chief and get more personnel out here ASAP. They should search the surrounding forest; Davis could be hiding in there somewhere." To the other cop she said, "Go inside and ask the hotel manager if they have surveillance footage of the parking lot. If he had another vehicle stashed here, I need to know."

CHAPTER EIGHTY-THREE

Dillon was feeling frustrated since he'd had no opportunity to overpower the vigilant Frenchman. Lamont was presently up inside the inspection hatch working on removing the radar. After a while Dillon heard a muffled shout. "Get ready, here it comes!"

He climbed halfway up the ladder and grabbed hold of the complicated-looking device as it emerged through the hatch. "Be careful, it's heavy," LaMont warned.

"No kidding!" Dillon retorted as struggled with the cumbersome object, straining not to fall backwards off the near-vertical ladder. "I can see why this was a two-man job," he said after he'd lowered himself gingerly to the floor.

LaMont ignored him. "Just one more to go. The next one isn't quite as heavy."

Dillon was relieved that the Frenchman was correct and soon had the second contraption positioned alongside the first. LaMont's head popped through the hatch. "Now pass me the bomb and be damned careful. It has an anti-tamper mechanism that'll cause it to explode if any of the wires get snagged."

Dillon grimaced. *Great, I won't even be able to disarm it once it's set.*

He cautiously climbed the ladder and reluctantly handed the explosive device to LaMont.

———

"Inside a coffin?" Diedra asked in disbelief.

Arleen was on the other side of the line. "Looks like it." She and Olson were standing between the ditched vehicles as paramedics worked on reviving the two funeral-home employees. "The corpse was removed and the coffin is missing."

"I'll find out from my end if there's a coffin on the 747's cargo manifest."

"Also put out a BOLO for all late-model silver Toyotas," Arleen added. "Unfortunately the surveillance camera at the hotel was too far away to pick up the tags."

"There must be thousands of vehicles in the tri-state area matching that description," Diedra moaned.

"Davis' photo is already out there. If he's not in the car, the stops should be quick."

Diedra acquiesced. "I'll alert all law-enforcement agencies immediately."

CHAPTER EIGHTY-FOUR

"What's taking so long?" Dillon shouted up at the flight engineer.

"Patience, I'm tracking our recovery boat's position on my GPS," came the muffled reply. "I can only arm the device once we're ten minutes from its location."

A few minutes later LaMont's legs appeared through the hatch and he began to descend the ladder. *It's now or never.* Dillon decided. Moving quickly he climbed the first few rungs of the ladder, grabbed the unsuspecting Frenchman's legs, and gave a mighty tug.

LaMont yelped as he felt his body being pulled downward and unconsciously grasped for a handhold. He managed to stop his fall by grabbing the rim of the hatch entrance with both hands. He instinctively kicked out and by pure chance caught his assailant full in the face with his right shoe. Dillon was stunned by the blow and fell backwards onto the metal deck. He shook his head, trying to clear his vision. The first thing that swam into focus was the barrel of LaMont's gun pointed directly at his aching face.

The Frenchman had a triumphant look. "I was right about you all along; you just never seemed very enthusiastic about the prospect of killing so many of the enemy."

Dillon was still flat on his back, LaMont towering above him. "Think about what you're doing," Dillon pleaded. "What about all your innocent fellow crew-members?"

"Unfortunate, of course, but the blow to these murdering scum is well worth it."

While Dillon was speaking and distracting the Frenchman, he felt around him for something to use as a weapon. "You're no better than those murdering scum if you let this go ahead." His hand brushed the handle of a large screwdriver, one of the tools LaMont had used to loosen the first radar device.

"Fuck you, traitor!" LaMont leaned down and spat in Dillon's face.

It was the chance that Dillon had been waiting for. With snake-like speed, he brought the screwdriver up and plunged it deep into LaMont's right eye.

The Frenchman gave a high-pitched scream and collapsed on top of Dillon. With a mighty heave, he flung the heavy weight off him and staggered to his feet. Incredibly LaMont was still alive. He rolled over and aiming with his good eye brought his pistol up. "Time to die, asshole," he wheezed.

Dillon didn't hesitate. He stomped down with his right foot and drove the protruding screwdriver deep into LaMont's brain, killing him instantly.

————

Davis peered over at Silva. "Watch your speed, we don't want to be pulled over." His words were barely cold when a siren sounded behind them.

Silva glanced in his rear-view mirror and saw the flashing lights of a police cruiser directly behind them. "Damn, how did they get onto us so quickly?"

Davis looked stricken. "Now what?"

Silva was adamant. "We make a run for it."

"No, pull over. I don't want to die," Davis said anxiously.

"We helped to kill over three hundred people," Silva said cruelly.

"You're going to die either way." He floored the accelerator pedal and the Toyota leapt forward.

The powerful cop car had no problem keeping up with them, and within minutes it was joined by two more. They were on a narrow two-lane surface road and Silva swerved back and forth, not allowing any of their pursuers to come alongside. "Please!" Davis implored. "We can make a plea deal; we don't need to die!"

Silva looked at him scornfully. "Shut up! Be a man and take the consequences of your actions!" He looked forward, cursed and tried the slow the car as they entered a sharp right-hand turn. The Toyota was going way too fast, and it drifted into the left-hand lane, directly in front of an oncoming cement truck.

CHAPTER EIGHTY-FIVE

Diedra exhaled in relief as the transmission from Major Edwards came through her head-set. "I have a visual on the target, awaiting instructions."

"Hang back and observe for now," she said, elated that the 747 was still in the air. "Does everything appear normal?"

"No problems that I can detect," Edwards responded. "Airspeed does appear way too low though."

"Yes, we know about that. Stay far enough back that you can't be observed. We're not entirely certain at this point what the situation is, although it's safe to assume that there is at least one terrorist aboard."

"Roger that. Will contact you immediately if anything changes."

Diedra turned to McCabe. "Any suggestions?"

"They're still not answering their radios," the ATC supervisor replied. "How much faith do you have in your guy, Dillon is it?"

"He'll get the job done," Diedra replied emphatically.

McCabe nodded. "Best to just monitor for the time being then."

———

Dillon bounded up the ladder and through the hatch. He was horrified to see that the timer on the bomb now read just under eight minutes. He grabbed the device and tried to pry it off, but it wouldn't budge. *Think, how is it attached to the metal cone?* It didn't appear to be glued on. Then he noticed a large battery on the device that he'd missed earlier. *That's it, electromagnetic.* He felt around the metal rim before locating a small switch. He held his breath as he tripped the switch, hoping that it wasn't connected to the bomb. Sure enough, the device popped free and he swiftly but carefully descended the stairs.

He paused momentarily as he passed the intercom phone, glancing at the digital readout on the timer as he did. *Five minutes, no time to contact the pilots. I've got to get this thing off the plane.*

Upon reaching the forward cargo door, he gently laid the bomb down. He quickly put on the life vest before examining the parachute. It was different to the ones he'd trained on, and it took him a while to figure out the harness. Once he was reasonably certain that it was on properly, he grabbed the portable oxygen tank and slipped it into a pouch on the left side of the harness. He twisted the valve, closed the pouch and donned the mask.

The digital readout was down to two minutes and twenty seconds as he held the bomb to his chest and leaned his back against the cargo door. He took a deep breath, felt behind him, and twisted the lever.

Suddenly all hell broke loose. There was an ungodly shrieking sound as Dillon was swiftly plucked from the aircraft. His head smashed into the metal doorframe with a force that dislodged his oxygen mask and rendered him unconscious. The force of the wind pulled the bomb from his grasp and his limp body spiraled down to the uninviting grey water of the Atlantic far below him.

———

Diedra's blood froze as Edwards' calm voice came through her headset. "We appear to have a situation up here."

She tried desperately to match his composure. "What's happening?"

"One of the 747's cargo doors has opened and been ripped off. There's all sorts of objects being sucked out, including what appears to be two bodies."

"You mean two people?"

"From the looks of things, both appear to be lifeless."

"And the plane?"

"Currently in a controlled high-speed dive. Normal procedure for a situation like this."

"Try to contact them," Diedra ordered.

After what seemed like an eternity, Edwards' voice returned. "No joy, they're not answering."

"Okay, follow the plane down. Once it levels out, you need to get out in front and lead them to the closest airport."

"Roger, ma'am, that would be Goose Bay in Newfoundland. I'll send out a mayday and handle all radio transmissions on their behalf."

"Good luck, major. Keep me up to date."

"Son of a bitch!" Edwards suddenly exclaimed.

"What now?"

"An explosion just above sea level," the major answered. "Not only that; I have a deployed parachute canopy as well."

"Contact the Coast Guard ASAP and give them the exact co-ordinates," Diedra ordered.

"No need, a large motor yacht just released a high-speed tender that's rushing to the parachutist's aid."

Diedra thought quickly. *Must be part of the escape plan.* "Don't interfere with the rescue in any way. Are there any Navy vessels in the area?"

After a few seconds Edwards replied, "A few ships eighty nautical miles north of here. They're testing a new top-secret, anti-submarine drone."

"Helicopters?"

"Sure, one of the ships is a destroyer."

"Have your wingman shadow the motor yacht from high altitude. I'll get clearance from SECNAV for an armed insertion. Hopefully the person that they rescued is my guy."

EPILOGUE

Dillon Hunt, aka Daniel Harper, stood nervously before Vanessa Harper's door before reaching out and pressing the buzzer. It was three weeks since the US Navy had rescued him from the motor yacht, and he still sported a bandage around his head. He'd been suffering from a near-lethal combination of hypothermia, oxygen deprivation and swelling in his brain as a result of a severe concussion. He'd eventually regained consciousness, but the doctors at the naval hospital had induced a medical coma as they battled to save his life.

Suddenly, the door opened and he was confronted by his sister-in-law. Vanessa Harper was cradling an infant, whom she nearly dropped as she took in his appearance. "My God, you look exactly like him," she stammered.

"Sorry, I know that I should have called first," Daniel said.

"No, that's okay, come on in and say hi to your niece." Vanessa led the way into the living room, speaking over her shoulder. "Diedra explained to me how you took Mike's place and nearly got yourself killed. She said you'd be coming by once you'd recovered."

Dillon handed an envelope awkwardly to Vanessa. "Had some unfinished business to take care of."

She held the pretty infant out to Daniel. "Do you mind holding her? Her name's Cassandre."

Daniel tentatively accepted the baby, who immediately gave him a cute smile. His heart skipped a beat. "She's absolutely adorable."

Vanessa ripped open the envelope and gasped. "What's this? A check for three million dollars in my name."

"It's Michael's share of our trust fund; I want you to have it."

"No, it's too much. Michael had a life policy, and I receive his pension on top of that. We'll be just fine."

"Sorry, but it's non-negotiable," Daniel said resolutely. "I know that Mikey would have done the same thing if the situation were reversed."

Vanessa smiled. "You're nothing like the person I expected."

"You mean a habitual criminal with nothing but his own interests at heart?"

"Something like that."

"I guess that the last few months have changed my outlook on life."

"Nearly dying will do that," Vanessa quipped. "By the way, how was it parachuting from a jet airliner miles up in the air?"

"Don't recall." Daniel grinned. "I was oblivious to the entire event. Thank God my chute had a ground-proximity opening device, or I wouldn't be here right now."

Vanessa reached out for her daughter. "Well, we're glad that you are. Where to now, back to Vegas?"

"Nah, I'll be sticking around here for a while. I start full-time training as an FBI agent in Quantico in a few days. Hope you don't mind if pop in now and again?"

She walked him to the door and kissed his cheek. "You're always welcome. By the way, Mike would be really proud of who you've become."

"Thank you, I hope so."

Vanessa glanced at the vehicle parked out front. "Who's the girl in the car?"

"My girlfriend," Daniel replied. "She thought that it would be better if I introduced myself to you alone, considering what we've both been through."

"Very thoughtful of her."

"She's like that."

"Be sure to bring her in next time you visit. I'd like to meet her."

"Will do," Daniel called over his shoulder as he walked towards the car. He opened the driver's side door and climbed in.

"How was it?" the woman in the front passenger seat asked.

Daniel smiled, leaned over and kissed FBI Special Agent Arleen Cooper. "Easier than I thought," he said.

———

Carl Boyd was relaxing in the cockpit of his recently acquired eighty-foot sailing yacht as he contemplated the latest news. The yacht was currently berthed in a small marina on the tiny Caribbean island of Antigua.

He was still chuckling at the recent revelation by his newly arrived sailing companion that Dillon Hunt had indeed been an FBI operative who'd thwarted a disastrous aircraft bombing. He himself had disabled the detonators on the four vans inside the AAM compound.

He'd joined the militia group with the intention of taking on various radical and militant Islamic organizations. To his disgust he'd discovered that the faction would be targeting innocent civilians, no better than the terror groups themselves.

His reverie was disturbed as a beautiful woman exited the rear hatch, a frosty margarita held in each hand. Lisa Cox kissed him as she handed him one. "This sure beats the hell outta Vegas," she said.

Dear reader,

We hope you enjoyed reading *Imposter*. Please take a moment to leave a review, even if it's a short one. Your opinion is important to us.

Discover more books by Ray Floyd at https://www.nextchapter.pub/authors/ray-floyd

Want to know when one of our books is free or discounted? Join the newsletter at http://eepurl.com/bqqB3H

Best regards,

Ray Floyd and the Next Chapter Team

You might also like:
Poetic Justice by Ray Floyd

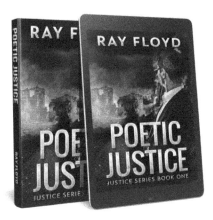

To read the first chapter for free, please head to:
https://www.nextchapter.pub/books/poetic-justice

ABOUT THE AUTHOR

Ray Floyd was born and raised in South Africa. He studied at the University of Natal (Durban) where he minored in Language & Communication. He is a veteran of the Angolan bush-war and is well-versed in Modern Warfare Weapons & Tactics.

Floyd moved to Las Vegas NV in 1992 but didn't pursue a writing career until 2016. *IMPOSTER* is his third novel and follows on the heels of *POETIC JUSTICE* & *BROKEN JUSTICE*.

Ray Floyd is married with two children and his interests include sailing, flying, swimming and reading. Given his aversion to cold weather he divides his time between his homes in Las Vegas and South Africa.

Lightning Source UK Ltd.
Milton Keynes UK
UKHW011848050321
379874UK00010B/949/J

9 781034 520962